Red Branch

G. B. HUMMER

Red Branch

SINCLAIR-STEVENSON

First published in Great Britain in 1993
by Sinclair-Stevenson
an imprint of Reed Consumer Books Ltd
Michelin House, 81 Fulham Road, London SW3 6RB
and Auckland, Melbourne, Singapore and Toronto

This paperback edition published 1994

A CIP catalogue record for this book
is available at the British Library
ISBN 1 85619 408 6

Typeset by CentraCet, Cambridge
Printed and bound in Great Britain
by Cox & Wyman Ltd, Reading, Berks

To Pammylove for onlie begetting
while summer spent itself,
and to Terry and Barbara for nudging Fate,
who knows who he is.

Foreword

The book that follows is a work of fiction. The town of Red
Branch does not exist. No person in the book is real. It is
not a disguised social history of a period of time and the
people who lived through that period. There are names and
locations that are taken from my experience, used in this
work of fiction for the flavor that they carry in my memory,
which has made them useful to my theme. That's all. Even
the persona of the storyteller is fictional. Find me and I am
not there.

Primitive people believed that every object had its identity, which was locked in a riddle to which there was no
answer because the creator of the object did not know the
answer himself. I believe that primitive people were on the
whole pretty intelligent, with some reservations, as you will
see.

1

The West Coast of the United States used to be a long way from anywhere. The train took four days to cross the country, and it was another eight days to cross the Atlantic Ocean by ship, unless you took one of the expensive, faster ones and cut down the trip by a day or two. Everything happened in New York hours before the news percolated out to the west, and Washington then as now communicated a remoteness that made it seem like a backwater town rather than the capital of the country. Opera on Saturday "direct from New York's famous Metropolitan Opera House", or a Sunday concert by the "world famous NBC Symphony Orchestra conducted by Arturo Toscanini" had to be enjoyed in mid-afternoon or not at all. The two of them made up the major part of a cultural heritage that had little of a directly human dimension to it. Culture was the radio, which was brown walnut veneer with a small bronze label letting listeners know that what they were hearing was Majestic. And politics, when shrunk to the dimensions of the radio, was not something to be believed in, even when it was history in the making as the announcers insisted. When Father Coghlan held his rallies in Chicago to denounce Jews and praise Hitler, the voice which was meant for the anonymous black of night where faces could be obscured in a natural way came hammering out of the radio on a hot, bright afternoon and seemed doubly insane.

A direct broadcast on the radio from Europe was unlikely because things didn't seem to happen over there at a time when Red Branch was awake. In 1939, when Hitler himself was heard in a re-broadcast from New York, the manic, melodramatic ranting that poured out onto shaded porches and sunlit lawns seemed somehow exactly right for that strange, faraway, outside world that lay somewhere to the east. It was hard to be alarmed. There didn't really seem much point in being alarmed, it was all so far away. The movies were just as bad. A cloud of dust with Africans running through it, one of them occasionally falling like a cowboy's horse, was Abyssinians fleeing from the bombs of Mussolini, a voice said. A shrieking, black bird falling suicidally until obscured by a gray cloud was a dive bomber working on an inert Spanish town, but you would never know it if you weren't told. The sense of people being victimized was real, Red Branch people could put themselves in the shoes of others and feel that life was unfair. What they found hard to believe was the insistence, couched in flat, worried, doom-laden voices, that any of this mattered to them. Mrs Hofer, in the Sunlite Bakery, had cousins in Germany, and everyone accepted that it very much mattered to her, though it was not clear why. The Jews were only being threatened, after all. The truth was that those columns of tanks in the March of Time films, angular slabs of gray with a soldier looking out of what seemed to be a large bean can with its top not cleanly off, were sometimes amusing and otherwise routinely dull. The kids at the Saturday matinée always said "Oof!" when one of these armored tractors nosed into a ditch and struggled up out of it with dirt streaming from its tracks. They had all done the same thing on someone's father's Allis Chalmers, hitching a ride to see what it was like to be a grown-up farmer. If that was war it wasn't much to be warned about.

Therefore by 1940 there was no shame attached to the

4

growing, grateful conviction that war was a good thing. The correlation between war in Europe and prosperity in America wasn't something that needed inquiring into, since like sunshine it was just there. It was enough that everything that could be grown could be sold. The government irrigation schemes that recently helped the farmers produce an unsaleable surplus every year now looked like the ticket to prosperity. The taming of the rivers that came as a result of the dams in the mountains to the east was symbolic, to those who looked for symbols, of the new assurance. In a land of plenty there was, finally, the beginning of plenty of money. The floats on Pioneer Day were no longer mounted on trailers and pulled by horses, celebrating the desperation and courage of the people who came to the valley in 1875 and, in an act of self belief that amounted to madness, founded the town of Red Branch; now the floats were on the flat beds of long haul trucks, celebrating a land of wheat and cotton and wine and every kind of fruit, even and especially celebrating the buyers lined up at the silos and gins and packing stations waiting to pay good money, eastern money, for the abundance that had escaped the pioneers. It would be an insane, thoroughly bad person who objected to the satisfaction that prosperity was beginning to bring.

It was, however, only a short step from that unacceptable criticism to the observation that Red Branch people were on a road that led to the kind of smugness that, put crudely, wore the face of selfishness. Harvey Pearson told the story of a latter day Okie family who came into his drugstore soda fountain. (They could come in there now, three or four years after the Dust Bowl spewed them west, since latter day Okies were cleaner people with a little bit of spending money who were trying to impress the locals so that they could find a job with some sort of a house attached to it.) The man ordered himself a chocolate soda and sat down to enjoy it, while his wife and two or three or four children – the family grew as the tale's currency spread – stood behind and watched. He tasted it, ate some of the ice cream with the spoon provided, then mixed it all up, soda and ice cream and chocolate syrup, and drank it off to the last drop. Wiping his mouth carefully on a paper napkin from the dispenser on the marble counter, he pronounced his verdict: "Lickin' good, Ma, buy you some." The story went into the repertoire of several raconteurs without anyone seeing the relevance, or the warning. Red Branch people had tasted prosperity, liked it, and recommended it to others, at their own expense and in their own time.

This had not always been the case. On the east side of the canal, where it crossed under Greenfield Avenue, a small, single storey, attractive building stood well back in a pond of lawn with graceful cypress trees on the side toward the canal and a line of rose bushes on the other. It was a small auditorium called the Business and Professional Women's Club. There was about the building something so feminine that it undercut the purpose of the enterprise, and the image of the successful business woman was supplanted by that of the kind, gray ladies who used it as a meeting room and lecture hall. The name, as well as its existence, spoke of a time that was still coming, as it had been when it was founded and built by donation. A class of business and professional women, aside from nurses, school teachers, librarians and the army of assistants that prop up the male professionals, had yet to surface. Next to it was the sprawling, mission style Jefferson Grammar School, its stucco painted a shade of off white that managed never to look clean. Not quite severe but definitely sober in style, it looked discomfitingly like its brown Franciscan models in which the lotus eating Indians were reconstituted into good Spanish Christians, their innocence replaced with guilt. Built in a large rectangle, its play area in a courtyard at its center, it seemed to resonate like some great machine going wrong, the sounds of shouting children coming from its bowels mismatched to its appearance. Beyond the school was the town's Carnegie library, a large but warm looking building in brown brick, crammed with windows from basement up, like the beacon of light Andrew Carnegie must have intended. Through the windows could be seen the librarian and her staff, smiling as if knowing a secret, moving at a stately pace, never speaking in that sanctuary of silence, where the rules of communication changed once the front door eased closed behind you. Facing the school was the graceless, solid, granite Courthouse, surrounded by hundreds of square yards of undecorated, unshaded lawn. It was the sort of building that gulped people into its interior, where offices hid their workers behind massive, intimidating counters and huge oak desks, and the citizen was triumphantly reduced to a cypher or a stage extra with the minimum of bureaucratic effort. The galleried courtroom smelled of the disinfectant used to clean the spittoons and was boiling hot winter and summer, distilling justice out of the sweat of the guilty and innocent alike.

Behind the library was a small botanical garden, with specimen trees and flowering shrubs mainly from Australasia. Almost unused, it was kept in immaculate condition, loved at least by its keepers. Across from the library was the Garfield Memorial Park, shaded and cooled by massive trees, mainly sycamores. Peacocks that kept their tail fans a primly folded secret dragged across the lawns shrieking. A band shell stood deep in the recesses of shade, with behind it a small labyrinth of paths that marked what was left of a still decaying zoo. If you found the path that led straight ahead it would reveal the First Presbyterian Church across Park Street. A diagonal would bring you out on the corner of Park and First streets with the War Memorial Hall on one side and the County Jail on the other. The Memorial Hall was a large, square building, its white portico the only break in what looked like a solid block of umber stucco with a tendency to veer toward shoeshine tan. The windows, meant to be large and imposing, somehow failed to break the solidity of the mass. Even when the dancing class was practicing the waltz to the tune of *Mexicali Rose*, because that was the record on the jukebox that could be played

7

without putting in a nickel, the figures struggling with each other and the music passed across the windows almost unnoticed. The jail, in disturbing contrast, was a gothic fantasy of red brick and gray granite, each detail taken into a pattern of medieval decoration that tried its best to disguise the real business of the establishment. It was entered through an arched doorway recessed behind clusters of stone columns that restricted the number of people who could approach the door at one time. Lead guttering edged an overhanging roof, wide enough to hold crossbowmen or sheriff's deputies. Tracery of steel in a fleur de lys pattern was spun over the windows, making bars redundant. Above the main entrance, as if oil was kept permanently on the boil in case visitors proved to be troublesome, was a small balcony that on close inspection could be seen to make a good guard post. The turrets at the corners of the building had arrow slits reproduced in perfect authenticity, as in some sort of miniaturized castle, and which were just wide enough to take a single barrel shotgun. It was a small, interesting building that pretended to be mocking its purpose, while doing in fact nothing of the sort. If you added to these buildings the small hospital a few hundred yards west of the BPW Club, Red Branch could be seen to be a town with a visible spine of civic pride and decorum. The spine was however showing its age, and nothing new had been added to it for many years. The town had been once a place of dreams that come from pride and ambition, which is not always or necessarily a recipe for vainglory. There once had been a reason to do things for Red Branch, because the town had been created from nothing and the good people knew what kind of town they wanted to create. At some time and in some way that had not been recorded, the reason had been lost. In conversation people would say that nothing had been the same since the Depression. Mr Marshall, the ancient permanent resident of the Mariposa Hotel, called "Old Man Marshall" behind his back because of his frequent and disbelieved boast that he could recall the events of the

8

Spanish–American War, once remarked that he had been to an operatic concert in the Memorial Hall the year it was built. No one believed him because, as they said, you'd never get an audience for an opera singer in Red Branch. However, Old Man Marshall also said he had given the library his stereopticon slides of Teddy Roosevelt and his Rough Riders in Cuba during the Spanish–American War. No one had believed him about that either, since the slides had never been seen, yet after he was dead the assistant librarian found them in three boxes stacked under the banned books and other things that were kept stored just in case tastes changed. An operatic concert, like the BPW Club, said something, not about the old Red Branch but about the new one, which made people uncomfortable. If you wanted to see a concert these days, you could go to Placid City. They had one there every once in a while.

No, you couldn't say the good people of Red Branch were smug. You couldn't even say they were blinkered, because that implies someone else put blind spots beside their eyes. It was more that, in a way, they were young in the ways of a new and different world. Life had formerly been hard, with dreams to relieve the harshness. Now dreams were no longer necessary, since it was obvious that money could buy the kind of dreams Red Branch had. Who would be fool enough to prefer a concert to a chocolate ice cream soda if he had been deprived of both? The few who might have been willing to identify themselves as just those fools said nothing. The town was unanimous in its pursuit of its destiny.

Barrel House Blues

The geography of Red Branch is as obvious and undramatic
as a freshman surveyor with a compass could make it. The
original grid of roads, slapped down on the flat floor of the
valley, is still there for all to see, mocking the grand design
of whichever founding father thought the town was an
incipient city. Greenfield Avenue, four times the width of
any other residential street, reaches west like a pointer
toward a great civic monument, which turns out to be Mrs
Rossi's Italian Grocery Store. To the left of her store is the
small, green oasis of the Atwater mansion, and to the right
a road winds out to the Italia Colonia Winery. This is the
whimper end of the avenue that begins with the bang of a
park, a library, a grammar school and a courthouse. West of
these, beyond a narrow irrigation canal, the avenue is lined
with substantial houses in various styles until about the two
thirds mark, at which point it looks as though the money ran
out. From there to Mrs Rossi's only one more house, lonely
among its humbler neighbors and vacant lots, is suited to the
Greenfield Avenue style. In it lives Mrs Cloda Poole,
although only the delivery boys see much of her since she
threw Ray out and Cass Dellon left town. Across from her
is a one-car garage surrounded by the ruins of several rows
of bulgy concrete columns which grape vines have taken

10

over. That is where Cass Dellon lived before he broke up Cloda's marriage.

Cass came to Red Branch as a young man not yet twenty years old, with no English and no past. Who he was and where he came from were his secret. He appeared late one afternoon on the avenue, in his humility walking out in the street instead of on the sidewalk, going west. He walked to the Italia Colonia Winery and used sign language to get a job cleaning out the vats. When pay day came, Laura Ferg had to put a name in the books beside the entry for his pay, and the best she could do with his French name was Cass Dellon. It was probably the only genuine act of creativity Laura ever performed, being a born accountant.

Cass didn't leave Red Branch for another twenty years. During that time he acquired a working vocabulary of about five words of English for every year spent in the town. However, he didn't need language for the way he lived. When he started with the winery, he lived in a bunkhouse that had been left empty a few years before when they converted from horsepower to trucks. As soon as he had the money he bought a vacant lot near the end of Greenfield Avenue, across from what was an empty house at the time. Then he saved some more money and bought a garage that Nettie Atwater was threatening to use for firewood. He borrowed a winery truck and moved the garage to the lot, giving him a one-car garage in the middle of a burned patch of dry weeds. Of course it was "Dellon's Folly" from the moment the first person laid eyes on it.

The nice thing about being labeled a fool is that nobody questions your behavior. The law will even bend for you in order to accommodate the fool in you. Cass scavenged at building sites and bought throwouts from the hardware store until he had improved his garage enough that he could move into it to live. His new house didn't meet anybody's idea of building by-laws, but no one complained; if the poor fool wanted to live there, let him. He then began to go back regularly to the places where he had got materials before,

11

keeping track of the level of the nails in the nail barrels. When the level got low, he would offer to transfer the nails to a quart size tin can, if he could have the barrel. The workmen laughed to his face about his collection of nail barrels; he couldn't find the words to explain why he wanted them, and the joke faded and died while his collection grew. The second spring that he was in his little house he bought sand, cement and reinforcing rods for next to nothing when Yates Building Contractors went broke. He took the bottoms out of some of his barrels and piled them on top of each other, stuck the rods down the stack of them and filled them with concrete, and when it was dry he knocked the barrel staves loose to reveal a column. They were odd looking columns but you could tell what they were meant to be. People liked the idea and began to take barrels to him in order to get a plan of the place drawn in the dust for them. It was going to have two long grape arbors made of columns, at right angles to each other. Where the arbors crossed, where his house was now, he would build a new house better than the old one he had left wherever it was he had come from.

The arbors lengthened and the vines flourished as the years went by. A few columns collapsed, so that it acquired a nice, ramshackle appearance, and the lot began to be littered with bits and pieces that could come in handy someday when work on the house began. It became, in short, a funny looking eyesore that people were fond of, a feature of the west end of the avenue.

Then many years later another building project caught the town's attention. Ray and Cloda Poole had sold their tiny little truck stop cafe out on Cloverleaf Boulevard and bought a decent sized beer joint on the highway. The previous owner was a Mexican who had to sell it for whatever he could get because it had been closed by the police; they couldn't ignore any longer that the customers were migrant workers who went there to meet imported girls with a mercenary view of the romantic side of life. The place was a

12

throwback to the old brothels up in the gold mining towns, the bar being a central building surrounded by little cubicles attached to it on three sides, like a hen with chicks. Ray made a hero of himself with the town's moral defenders when he tore down the cubicles. Then he started constructing a large globe of bent wooden laths around the bar building. When that was finished he covered it with rough stucco painted orange and had what looked like a big stem built on the top of it. The sign announcing The Giant Orange appeared before the second coat was dry on the green stem, and he was in business selling fresh squeezed orange juice whipped up with ice slush. Where there had been cubicles, big awning flaps opened up on three sides, with a separate high speed juicer on each of the three counters. Ray and Cloda might just as well have been squeezing money as oranges the way the cash rolled in. Red Branch had its first drive-in; the kids loved it, the old people liked the orange juice, the uniforms on the girls were spotlessly clean and very tight, and everybody was happy. Ray went shopping for a house that was up to his new status, and he bought the old place opposite Cass on Greenfield Avenue. In no time at all it was renovated, painted, reroofed, furnished and very impressive. Cloda retired from business life and became a housewife, while Ray promoted the prettiest of the girls to be his assistant manager.

Red Branch is no different from any other small town in western America when it comes to class distinctions: It is a classless society with rigid class barriers. Some of those barriers can be clambered over with help from a generous application of money. But first you have to find someone to take your money. Cloda started in a quiet way to entertain the good ladies of the town, then Ray started going to town meetings and talking about civic betterment, and then they began to invite the town's acknowledged bluebloods to their house. At this precise point the trouble started. From Ray's front porch, as he escorted his guests to their cars after an evening of elevated conversation, he looked across the gulf of the avenue to Cass's dilapidated dream house. There is no one so uppity as the newly up. Ray was up so high in his own estimation that he no longer breathed the same air as Cass Dellon. He decided that Dellon's Folly had to go. It didn't take many inquiries among his new friends to verify that what building there was couldn't be justified by any stretch of the legal imagination, if there is such a thing. Ray took steps to have the building inspector look into it. In order to get Cass into court, he put Cloda's name on an official complaint.

The day came for the court hearing. Cloda's complaint would be heard first, then an inspector's report was going to be read, and finally the lawyers would be left to get going on the steps needed to force Cass to demolish his folly. At the hearing, Cloda said yes, she was the one complaining, and from then on Ray did the talking. He said that the neighborhood was coming up, and Cass's collection of junk and columns shouldn't be allowed to stand in the way of progress. He announced that he planned to put a big garage behind his house for his two cars, and he had bought the lot next door in order to plant a few trees and a big lawn for entertaining. He pointed out that both places were zoned for a property value that exceeded any you could think of for a house built with nail barrels. He got a good laugh with that one.

It was late in the day when Cass got his chance to speak. The judge said that everyone knew he couldn't speak very well, so he should keep his remarks short. In other words the judge's mind was made up, and Ray had it in the bag.

Cass looked over at Ray with the hurt look of a whipped pup. "I got barrels, and he say I am wrong," he said. "He got orange, and that all right. Why goddam right?" He said the last as a quiet query, with no anger.

Possibly that is why everyone heard it so clearly and took so much notice of it. While the judge was telling off Cass about his language, everyone else in the room was absorbing

14

the fact that his question was a bombshell in the shape of a large, stucco orange built without by-law approval.

Ray paled six shades below his suntan, and Cloda asked, "What's wrong, honey?" in what seemed in the silent courtroom like a very loud voice.

The reporter from the *Red Branch Herald* giggled and leaned forward, waiting for Ray's reaction so that he could quote him on the front page. He got every word of it when Ray said, "That's different. With The Giant Orange there's a lot of money involved, and a lot of important people too."

Of all the people in the courtroom, only Cass was innocent of knowing what Ray's boast implied. "I hope you didn't mean that the way it sounded," the judge said.

What Ray had meant was that he had done the town's dirty work for it, getting the Mexican and his whorehouse out of the way. His act of civic betterment had been backed by a whole gallery of officials whose piratical condemnation order got the bar rock-bottom cheap for Ray in the first place, and who then couldn't focus beyond the ends of their noses when an obviously flimsy, unsanitary firetrap took its place. If some of them turned out to be silent partners when this commercial solution to a moral problem turned out to be a success, well, what of it?

Ray crossed his arms over his chest and waited for his influential friends to come to his defense. He too had his innocence, being serenely unaware that corruption was only okay as long as no one lifted up the rock that hid it. Having waited a decent interval, and having heard no voice raised on his side, Ray glanced around the room to find his friends busy looking at their fingernails, tying shoelaces, stretching collars, doing everything except responding to Ray's comment with anything that resembled support. They were similarly busy right through the next eight months. Dellon's Folly was forgotten as Ray fought condemnation orders as long as he could, then lost the case on fire regulations, industrial safety, and all the other ammunition the lawyers had got together by then. The *Herald* eventually stopped

15

hinting that more graft and corruption was about to be uncovered, and The Giant Orange quietly closed. The day that it did, Ray left town with his pretty, flashy assistant manager to open a chain of drive-ins down south called The Giant Peach.

Cloda was stricken. She languished loudly on her porch, telling callers what a snake in the grass Ray was. She got hold of an old torch song that had a line in it about being alone on the street of dreams. Tino Rossi came and moved her spinet piano out onto the porch for her, and she played and sang this song, and wept buckets, and mopped her face with her handkerchief, and then lay back on her sofa like a large zoo animal that had lost patience with the paying customers.

Cass observed this, until one day he went across to Cloda and tried to find the words to say how sorry he was that it had worked out this way.

"You and me, Mrs Poole, ain't got no need to hurt like this. You and me, just alike, didn't do nothing. You and me together, Mrs Poole."

That was all Cloda needed. In her mind she and Cass became two of the great romantics, harshly dealt with by the world, trapped in their dreams, separated only by Greenfield Avenue. She moved toward him, to wrap him in her arms and her forgiving soul. Cass quickly put the avenue safely between them and never was seen to cross it again.

Cloda had an explanation for her friends: "We're lovers of the spirit, kept apart by language. We're both alone on Greenfield Avenue, that's our street of dreams." When she wasn't singing her song, she sat at her front window or out on her porch with a handkerchief in her hand, ready to wave it seductively whenever she caught sight of Cass.

People at the winery said Cass seemed to lose all the English he had known, and anyone could see that Dellon's Folly was declining into a ruin. He hung on for another year, spending practically all his time at the winery. Some broken

16

lines of funny looking columns and a pile of nail barrels lost in a jungle of grape vines were the substance of what remained of his dream when he left the town one winter morning after telling Mrs Rossi he was going to try to find his old home.

2

With regard to their victory back in 1936 in the war with the Okies, the good people of Red Branch had some difficulties at first in getting the mythology straight. Reconstructing exactly how it had happened wasn't simple. It was generally accepted that Mort Thomas, the police chief, had short-stopped a telephone call meant for a deputy who was off duty. In fact there were no deputies regularly on duty in Red Branch; it was that kind of town. The legend says that Mort took a message from someone in some town well to the south of Placid City, saying that the Okies in the government camp there had suddenly formed up a convoy and were headed north for the cotton fields. The camp had emptied, meaning that there were maybe three hundred old cars and trucks making the move. He was calling, he said, because looking at the map, Red Branch was the easiest place to stop them, assuming you were going to stop them, which was against the law because they weren't doing anything illegal except possibly slowing up traffic on the main highway. He didn't give his name and hung up.

Mort probably grunted a few times, since he always grunted at any news that posed him a problem that had to be thought through. Then he went out, leaving the office open as he always did, in case there was any need of the jail, which he shared with the county sheriff, while he was gone. He drove to the main highway and left his car across from the Greyhound Bus Depot. From this point there are witnesses to the events, because he then crossed the light traffic on foot to speak to the manager, Harold Stoll. Mort told him he'd got hold of this rumor that there were Okie cars on the move and they might interfere with the buses coming up from the south. Harold got on the phone to depot managers down south and struck lucky with the man in Cloverleaf.

The Cloverleaf manager picked up the phone fairly breathless already, and when Harold asked if he'd seen any Okie cars go past, the man almost screamed into the mouthpiece. "Seen any, Harold? You crazy or something? Seen any? We ain't seen anything else for the last hour! We got bastard Okie cars stretching from someplace else to the fig ranch south of Placid City."

"Where are they going?" Harold asked.

"No place," was the answer. "One of 'em's broken down and the whole string of 'em are stopped while they pack their goods and kids in with other people. Then they'll shove the wreck off the road, I expect, and leave the highway people to come along and haul away their garbage."

"Where do you think they're going? As far as us?" Mort said afterwards that Harold's voice wasn't exactly steady when he asked that question.

"They ain't saying," was the answer. "If I was you, I'd lay me in a stock of axe handles. They're hungry, and you got cotton that needs picking."

Mort grunted a few times at the news, walked through a glass door that led off from the lobby of the depot, then down a short corridor to the barber shop next door. There was a stranger in the chair being shaved by Mike, the senior barber of the firm of Mike and Gene. The Chief of Police outranked a stranger any day, and Mike said, "You," with a bob of the head, "take over here" to Gene.

Gene got down from the unused shoeshine stand where

19

he had been sitting reading the paper. "Who you telling to take over for you? I'm a partner, not a lousy employee, you don't talk to me like that. What's the matter, I'm not good enough to shave the police chief, is that it? Whatta you say, Mort, I'm not good enough?"

"What do you want to talk like that for in front of customers?" Mike answered, still scraping his razor across the stranger's face. As always, when their arguments started they both went white in the face and their hands shook. The stranger's eyes went wide, and he pressed his neck back against the headrest as far as he could get it from the cutthroat razor. "By Jesus," Mike swore, "if the bank would give me the loan I'd buy you out tomorrow, you don't know nothing about running a good business, none of you wops do!"

"What's Greeks know about anything?" Gene retorted. "Except how to give a partner ulcers." He clutched his stomach. "You're killing me, and you like it!"

Normally Mort would sit back and enjoy the show, but he felt pressed for time. "It's important, I'll have to wait," he said.

The atmosphere changed instantly. Gene went to the front door and turned the sign around so that it read Closed, then turned the bolt home in the connecting door to the bus depot. He got back up on the shoeshine stand but left the paper on a table near the patent combination ashtray and spittoon, from where he stared out the window and pulled his lips back against his teeth, impatient to find out what business Mort had that required an empty shop. Mike whisked through the rest of the shave, gave the stranger a vigorous rub with the Mennen's Menthol After Shave Lotion, took his money and saw him to the door. As he turned from the door, Mort was already climbing into Mike's chair, and Gene came down from his perch and pulled a wire backed chair close to the barber chair. "Put me some steam towels on," Mort said, "nice and hot."

Mike got two lukewarm white towels from the steamer

20

and laid them on Mort's face, and Mort tugged the top one down so that his eyes were covered. "You never know who's going to hear what you say when you've got these things on, do you," he said. Gene pulled his chair up closer.

"Feel kind of nervous," Mort said; "need to do some thinking." He paused and grunted for a few moments. "Got a call from down south, and Harold here" – he pushed a finger in the direction of the bus depot – "he heard the same thing. A whole highway of Okie cars is coming up this way. Don't know where they're headed. Say they want to pick cotton."

Gene said, "Lee Roy Stagg was in yesterday, said he was looking for pickers." He waited for the important information.

Mort said from underneath his towels, "Would he like a couple of thousand of 'em, and their kids?"

"Jeee-sus!" Mike and Gene said it almost together.

"Maybe Stagg oughta be warned," Mort said. "Maybe he'd take it as a timely warning if he knew there was three four hundred cars headed here, and God knows how many more yet to hit the road." After a pause he said, "It's nothing to do with me, you understand."

Mike looked at Gene, and Gene looked at Mike. "Sure, sure, we understand," Gene said as he unlocked the depot door and went to use the pay telephone. He walked as fast as a man can when he is fishing out the right change from his pocket at the same time. Harold Stoll had been restocking the candy trays, from where he could keep an eye on the door to the barber shop, and now he dropped the Mr Goodbar box half full and followed Gene to the phone, dragged along in his wake by the importance of the moment.

"What's Stagg's number?" Gene asked. Harold picked up the phone book to look for it as if bidden by a higher power.

Back in the barber shop, Mort said from under his muffling towels, "I'll have a shave." Mike turned the sign to Open and the conversation about the Okie caravan had never happened.

3

In that time of year which is late summer or early fall
depending on the time of day, darkness comes early and
deepens profoundly, like a warning of the black nights to
come. These are busy, exhausting days in an agricultural
town, with worry about crops and prices added to the hard
work of the harvest. The town goes to bed early, and even
the migrant workers give the town's only claim to night life,
the Rex Hotel, a wide berth until the weekend. That night
was different. In ones and twos the cars and small trucks had
been coming into town from all directions, but mainly from
the wide flatlands of the west side of the valley. By nine
o'clock the few stragglers burned the darkness with their
headlights, showing the playground of the Jefferson Grammar School packed with cars, and a row of trucks pulled up
beside the canal in Divisidero Road.

A tall man directed each new arrival to a parking place
with the words, "Put your car over there and cut your lights.
What did you bring?"

The answer varied. Some said an axe handle or the whole
axe, some said a baseball bat, a few said a shotgun; some
said they hadn't got anything to bring and apologized like a
Boy Scout turning up for a campfire without any
marshmallows.

22

"I'm sure sorry, Mr Stagg, I looked everywhere." Stagg and everyone who heard it knew that this meant the wife or mother of the emptyhanded man had vetoed any sort of weapon and had probably threatened unnamed consequences if he so much as went, then gave in on the going but not on the arming. How else was she sure to find out what went on?

Stagg had an answer, however. "We've got every axe handle the hardware store could find, and all the hardwood bats from the high school gym. Which do you want?" At any hesitation, he added, "Hurry up, we got to get moving."

Shortly after ten, a car came fast from Greenfield Avenue and swayed its way to a halt beside Stagg. The driver had been in the cigar store, long closed to anyone else, where he had got the news by telephone as the Okie convoy moved within range.

"They crossed the Placid River Bridge a quarter of an hour ago, travelin' very, very slow. I put them at Telegraph Road in about an hour. That's the leaders. There's more cars now than they was this morning, and more comin' onto the tail all the time. No doubt about it, they're makin' a move to swamp us this time." The words were spoken in a lilting Tennessee drawl, soothing, reassuring, utterly belying the content of his message. The speaker didn't get out and pulled back into his car seat in the shadows, revealing to everybody that he was Sheriff Herb Atwater and not officially involved, and wasn't even there. "They'll pick the cotton, and they'll cut the grapes, and then they'll sit and they'll wait for the welfare to get 'em through the winter," he gently intoned.

Stagg raised his voice enough to be heard by a circle of his supporters. "Not on my taxes, they won't!" His backers muttered their agreement.

To the occupant of the car he said, "You're not hearing this, but listen. Some of you boys get set up to block Telegraph Road. Let 'em go by, let 'em keep coming. Stay out of sight, but if anyone tries to turn your way then you

23

block the road. There's no roads going west until you get to Greenfield Avenue. That means they'd have to get to the middle of town in order to turn west, so we're stopping them in the eucalyptus trees a mile short of town. We'll stay on the west side of the trees, and make them turn around between the highway and the railroad tracks. Some of 'em might get stuck in the loose dirt. We'll push them out, as long as they head back south. When they've all made their turn, we'll follow them to the Placid and see they get across the county line. They can go back down south to the government camps."

The voice from the car said, "You got a vineyard behind you on the west side. The ground's so powdery they couldn't get a car through. A few might make it on foot."

Stagg answered, "I'm not inviting 'em, but I could use some pickers. A few get through, well, let 'em. But no two, three thousand, no sir."

"More than that, now," the voice replied.

The idea of an overwhelming plague of Okies settled it. Stagg didn't have to urge the move to the line of trucks. The men climbed in, and soon the trucks moved down Greenfield Avenue, turned south at the highway and drove to the long avenue of giant trees that usually welcomed travellers across the flat, featureless valley to the town of Red Branch. There would be no welcome tonight. The trucks let most of the men off along the way, then drove on beyond the trees and turned east at Telegraph Road, where the drivers parked behind a small stand of cottonwood trees.

It was these men at Telegraph Road who first saw the convoy when a glow began to light the sky from the south almost three-quarters of an hour later. It moved very slowly, growing toward them without losing any brightness behind. The men were struck, in spite of themselves, with the audacity of what they intended to do. It was one thing to stop a few cars, and quite another to stop an army. They were silent except for one man's outburst, "God almighty! It's Sherman marching through Georgia!" The first car that

24

passed them was travelling about twenty miles an hour, and laboring. Piled high on it was every piece of a migrant worker's claim to home comforts and furnishings. A rough wood cage had been built to fit the top of the car and then tied into place. Into this, as though it was a large box, had been stacked bedding, clothing, kitchen utensils, cardboard boxes, work shoes and tools tied into gunny sacks. From the wood slats flapped towels and an old Montgomery Ward catalog, left handy for use as toilet paper. Everything inside the cage was held down by two or three thin mattresses, and roped to the top of the pile, so they wouldn't fall off, were two boys sound asleep. Inside, the people were packed so tightly the doors had been turned back on their leather strap hinges and tied to the body of the car, so that arms and legs could project outside. No more than fifteen feet behind came the second, very similar to the first, then tight to its tail came the third, and so on. The cars were merely wreckage propelled by desperation, the occupants worn and faded and tired. In numbers it may have been an army, but it was a defeated army in retreat. The watching men, hidden behind the bushes growing along an irrigation ditch, took the measure of their miserable enemy and stepped into the open, quiet and calm as they had been ordered to be, but confident and bold now. The cars kept moving, the faces of the people who were awake set straight ahead, the eyes refusing to see the men.

Up the highway Stagg and his men, numbering some fifty, had never taken cover. When the lead car of the convoy got to about a hundred yards of them and picked them up in its headlights, it began to slow. Stagg got out a flashlight and waved it across his body as a warning. Once the car was definitely slowing, he moved toward it, followed by about a dozen of the men. The engine was making so much noise he had to move up to the shoulder of the driver to deliver his message. He shone the flashlight into the eyes of the young man driving and said, "This is as far as you go. Pull left, then turn right and turn around. You're going back where you came from."

"There's work here somewhere," the driver said, "pickin' cotton."

A woman's voice said, "The government man said so."

Stagg snorted. "Look at you. How many are there? You'd eat us up like the plagues of Egypt."

The woman spoke again. "Plenty of work. The government man said so."

"Turn around," Stagg ordered. He let his flashlight wander to the axe handles held by the men behind and around him.

Stagg hadn't seen a group of Okie men get out of some of the following cars and move silently up behind the lead car. Now they came out of the darkness at him. He backed away, into the headlights, as three men jumped him and beat him to the ground in a quick whirl of punches. Stagg's farmers shouted and went into battle. They lashed out with their weapons, thudding the wood into whoever came at them out of the dark. A baseball bat flew wild and went through the windshield of the car, and the dark was filled then with screams of women and the crying of children.

"Get 'em out of the way," the lead driver shouted. "I'll drive ahead. Come on! Keep going!"

One of the farmers, one who had an axe, broke off from the fighting and chopped into the tires of the second car, which lurched to its side perilously as two tires deflated with a sound like an exhaling frog. Then he drove the axe into the gas tank at the back of the car. The driver of the car behind, seeing the one in front of him immobilized and the gasoline gushing onto the road, tried to reverse his car, pushing into the radiator of the one behind him. Another farmer, carrying a shotgun, ran to the second car and shouted at the people, "Get out! Everybody! This car's a bonfire." They tumbled out, young and old, women and children, crying and terrified. He fired the shotgun into the air and, even in the noise of battle, it was a sound that shook

26

the earth. Everything except the wheezing car engines fell silent.

Stagg broke into the silence, appearing beside the pool of gasoline, lighting a match. "Turn those cars around!" he ordered. For an answer, more silhouettes moved along the line of cars, coming for him and his farmers.

"You asked for it," he shouted. From the car itself he pulled a piece of wrapping paper, lighted it quickly and threw it into the gasoline slick at his feet. He ran up the road past the lead car and disappeared into the darkness. When the fire caught and the car turned into a ragged square of orange and white flame, not a farmer could be seen. The first car, cut off by the blaze behind it from the rest of the caravan, lurched off to the right, where it stuck in the soft dirt short of the railroad tracks. The shouting, bawling people inside scrambled out and ran back down the road. Seeing the fire, not stopping to ask what their options were, other drivers began to turn around as well as they could in the space. The road became filled with vehicles turned against each other with shouting men and women trying to help in the turning, while boxes, pans, mattresses, bits of furniture were jettisoned to make the flight faster. Women carrying crying babies fled on foot down the road, to be picked up when their men caught up with them. The third and fourth cars, locked together and abandoned after their collision, stood stranded and empty of people. The fire flirted along the asphalt, taking its time, waiting for an encouraging splash of gasoline or drifting piece of paper to help it along, until it licked its way up into the two stalled cars. It caught the contents first, the rags of clothing and the bedding, a mattress that had slipped down from its place on the roof. Then, taking a leisurely course, the fire found the gas tank of one car. An immense bang, out of all proportion to the puny vehicle, cannoned into the night. That explosion was followed by the second a few moments later, and flame shot up into the trees where it caught dry leaves and oily bark. If it wasn't the fiery sword barring the way back into

27

Eden, it made a good facsimile. The sounds and the spectacle threw hysteria into the Okies trying to turn their cars or get out of loose dirt. They jumped and fell from the jammed cars, and the highway south became filled with running, screaming people, leaving the tangle of machinery to whatever power it was that had defeated them.

So ended the first war of Red Branch. Lee Roy Stagg was elected to the county council at the next election, Mort Thomas held his office for life, and Sheriff Atwater was invited to be the guest preacher at the Methodist Church anytime he felt the call.

II

only legacy of the war. Those who had a conscience pricked by the outcome of the Okie war spread a balm of charity on it with clothes and food for the people in the River Road shacks.

East of the town was the long, dull stretch of road that parted the wheat fields in pursuit of the Santa Fe Railway tracks. Having passed the two-room station that sat high up beside the tracks, the main road kept on its way, now going for the foothills, content to be swallowed up in billowing miles of grain. Another, smaller road branched off to the south just beyond the tracks and followed the line of them until it turned diagonally east. At the turn, between the road and the tracks, huddled down so that as few people as possible would notice and remark on them, were huts made of scrap wood and tarpaper. By accident the people who first sheltered here had found a piece of land that had been left off the map. It had been destined to belong to the railroad, but it failed to be drawn on a plan of their right of way. As usual, however, if something was even thought to belong to the railroad, everyone else gave it a wide berth. Everyone, that is, except people who had been thrown out of every other place that promised a chance to stop wandering, by officials with no less power than the railroad's attorney. From a chance settlement to a secret and undisturbed village had been an astonishingly easy progression for these people. Who and how many the women and children were who lived here was not clear, since they never went out and were not permitted by their menfolk to shop, go to school or have anything to do with the outside world. The men worked at farms just as if they were single men, making their own arrangements for accommodation. When they left the shanty town in the dead of night for a job, they carried a bedroll, a frying pan and a coffee pot, so that they could sleep in a dry river bottom or hobo jungle somewhere, pretending to be itinerants with no roots. These were the leftovers, as distinct from the survivors, of the Okies who had lost the first war with Red Branch. Like those on the

River Road, they had not gone back south to the government camps. Instead, they had hidden well away from the highway until the fuss had all died down, then had filtered east by stealth and built this colony of some two hundred men, women and children.

You didn't see the tarpaper colony except by accident unless you rode the Santa Fe Railway. Since Santa Fe trains didn't stop out there in the middle of nowhere except in emergency, Red Branch people always rode the Southern Pacific and most of them genuinely had never seen the black, flapping huddle of huts. As for those who had happened upon it, intimidated by the secrecy of a place which wrapped itself into itself like a nautilus shell, aware almost by vibration of the fear and consequent hostility of the unknown people sheltering inside it, they preferred not to know about it and Red Branch in the mass concurred. In a sense the shanty town just didn't exist.

To paraphrase a famous king, beware the secret borer which is making your crown into filigree. Even if they had read their Shakespeare with more understanding than was the case, people would still have missed the lesson. In a practical sense, Red Branch was dependent on the men from the shanty town and didn't know it. It was this small army that the farmers on the west side depended on for the important part of any crop harvest. They were fast workers, experienced and dependable. They knew when they would be needed and turned up to sign on at the right times. If a farmer needed someone for a special job, he got in touch with a man who had come with the Okies but given up working on the farms, Albert Baines, who now worked in a garage in Red Branch and had a son Billy in the grammar school. Albert said merely, "Let me know if you need a good man," and the good men turned up every time. They didn't drink or fight, and they didn't hang around, just disappeared at the end of the day after they had clocked in their time and washed down, stripped to the waist, under one of the irrigation pipes. At each farm they were part of the mechanism of the place, part of its fabric, with the farmer in each case having no responsibility for them except to pay their wages on Friday night promptly and in full.

There was another reason to be grateful for them that didn't come in for much discussion. In 1939 the war began to be real. Young men who had worked from childhood in peach orchards and grape packing stations, sons of men who had done the same, people who had dreamed of their own orchards and vineyards but who had never had the money at the right time and who didn't have the security the bank wanted, decided the Army or the Navy had something to offer called excitement. Quietly but increasingly they left the land to join the pre-war buildup of the armed forces. The gap was filled by these itinerants. They became the departed sons, without the blood ties and the attendant complications. Since they lived in a place that didn't legally exist and their families were unknown to any local government agency, they were non-persons. No Selective Service registration notice would ever arrive in their shanty town, and even if it had done, it would have been handed to a woman or child who couldn't read to be given to an unnamed man who was not at home. Dependable, experienced labor that was made available to the employer with no obligations and no strings attached – the offer was irresistible.

2

The first stories about the United Workers Union appeared in the city newspapers, north and south, as if the union was a curiosity. It was on the face of it naïve, provincial and presumptuous to say that any union represented the united workers. What workers? Doing what job? Who had ever heard of workers being united, anyway? You could laugh the union idea off the page without too much wit or even malice. And yet the stories were getting space regularly. The news value was in its leader, Cappy Petrillo, who had swallowed too many chapters of social history. "Cappy Stalin" was good copy, content to be called a communist, or even a Communist, as long as he could get the publicity. In the photos in the newspapers he was shorter than the people standing around him, but their eyes were on him. His eyes, on the other hand, were on the lens of the camera. He dressed well without being too custom-tailored, his clothes a degree or two more casual than those of the men he was dealing with, a bow tie instead of a four-in-hand, brown shoes instead of black. There was a mystery about his background, some reports making him the son of migrant workers, others saying he was the son of a winemaker from Sonoma County who fell out with his family and left for a bigger career. Again and again there were references to his smile. There were no good reasons for it to be so electric or so constant, he didn't ever not smile, so to speak. The rictus of the grave seemed to have taken over his facial muscles in life. To some, his smile passed the point of being a trade mark and took on the nature of a threat. Life was going to be good, Cappy would see to it, or else. To the public he was a character new on the scene that they wanted to hear about, to make up their minds whether to love him or loathe him. To potential opponents, just looking at his picture he smelled bad, the way trouble does. He was a man on the move, moving over whoever was in his way, his own people or his opposition. He was going up. Get out of his way.

Much more than the public face he wore, the truth about Cappy Petrillo would have made sensational copy for the newspapers, if he had not taken such great pains to obliterate it. For a start his Italian father had not so much emigrated as been exported to America. A smart young Sicilian who had got himself in trouble both with the police and the Mafia, he was shipped off by his family to Seattle, with orders to the vessel's captain that he wasn't to be allowed ashore until he reached his destination. There, he landed on his feet and his fists, in next to no time at all finding work as a strongarm man for a gang that ran a protection racket in the docks. This brought him to the notice of the dock owners, who gave him a free trip south across the states of Washington and Oregon, dumping him on the far north coast of California with the advice that the walk back to Italy was healthier than what he had been doing, with or without concrete shoes. He settled down and became a small-time conman, a husband, and soon the father of a boy, Sergio. When the boy was old enough to go to school, Petrillo beat his wife for the last time and then left her, taking the boy with him to the Valley of the Moon in Sonoma County. She made no attempt to find them, either then or later.

Sergio was taken into a Catholic charity home run by the Christian Brothers, who fell for Petrillo's story that he had been deserted by an alcoholic wife who took the family savings with her. The home, a group of Spanish style ranch buildings near Sonoma, was surrounded by vineyards, the effect of easy-going sanctuary somewhat spoiled by a high, chain link fence. Freed from family responsibilities, Petrillo began a life of gambling and petty racketeering, meandering through the larger towns of northern California while dreaming of the con of a lifetime that would allow him to live like the king in exile that he was somehow entitled to be. Young Sergio, resentful and rebellious because the Brothers had been the means of separating him from his father, grew up inside his father's dream, blistering any idealism with the suspicion that people with power, whoever they were and whatever the source of their power, were all usurpers of his, Sergio's, patrimony, and that someday he was going to reclaim the spoils of his father's dispossession. It made a sound basis for his later, mature, socialist philosophy, which was that knowledge of one's victimization was the beginning of political wisdom.

At the convent school where he was sent by the brothers, Sergio came under the care of Sister Benedictus. Her good right arm, equipped with a yardstick made of hardwood and brass, punctuated and underlined every lesson Sergio learned. Pain, his pain, accompanied all of Sister's triumphs on their way to a better life together. When she finished with him – and this life – four years later, her educational philosophy had fitted him so neatly into the elder Petrillo's fantasies that to Cappy, pain – preferably someone else's pain, needless to say – would always be the defining characteristic of each step in his progress toward his rightful place in the sun. Anyone who didn't want to get hurt would be best advised to get out of his way. By the time the boy was twelve years old, he was impatient, scornful, oversensitive, and also king of the boys in the home, their champion in all disputes with the Brothers. His father dubbed him "Cappy" as a Sicilian-American diminutive of "Capo" or chief, the old Mafia term for the gangster who has managed to rise to

37

the apex of the dunghill and stand off his challengers. Petrillo watched with awe as his son's ambitions, growing in step with his maturing grievances, shoved the father's petty criminality to one side as unworthy. Unable to stand the competition or keep up with rising expectations, Petrillo vanished shortly before the boy finished high school.

A few miles away from the Christian Brothers' home was a redwood grove that spread like a dark, tufted carpet up the mountains of the west side of the Valley of the Moon. Here the cool sea air met the heat of the valley, so that fog banks gathered until even the tallest of the trees were covered by the gray blanket, which then rolled down over the vineyards. In the depths of the damp gloom of the grove were hidden some buildings abandoned by the Children of the Moon, a utopian cult that had died when the millennium was postponed once too often. At the end of a rutted road that bent its way up a narrow canyon lay their huddled little settlement of four cabins and a bunkhouse. Two cabins were now classrooms, one was once again the kitchen and dining room, and the fourth, which had been a temple, had become a library where the twenty-eight painted faces of the mystic moon dreamed down upon the works of Marx, Lenin and Trotsky. This was the Jack London School, set up by some of Trotsky's disciples in order to create and train socialist activists so that they could politicize the proletariat in American industry and commerce. It was a training school for Communist fifth columnists, a dozen at most at any time, but still the stuff of capitalist America's nightmares. Ineffective, esoteric, self-serving, also secretive, threatening, subversive – the school encapsulated the Red Menace perfectly. To this shadowy college for articulate working class men with political chips on their shoulders, the young Cappy Petrillo gravitated as naturally as water flows downhill. As soon as the first Christian Brother told the boy to stay away from those Communists in that place of moral danger, he strained at the leash to be off, like any young dog worthy of his marrow bone. The same day that he received the blessing

38

of the Brother Rector as he left his home of eleven years, Cappy arrived on foot on the school's doorstep.

A year at the Jack London School gave a revolutionary shape to Cappy's personal grievances against the world. He learned that there was no good reason he should restrict the way he went about his vindication, since the end would justify the means. With several others he left the school as a furtive pilgrim making his way to Mexico, where he mingled in the intrigues surrounding the doomed Trotsky. What he saw and heard in Mexico disturbed him. Impressed by the evidence of Stalin's long, vengeful arm, he separated from his companions to take time to think about this. He paid his respects to Jack London by signing on as an ordinary seaman on a freighter, until he jumped ship in Galveston in order to work as a roustabout in the oilfields of the Gulf of Mexico. When he was ready, which was when an important point had been settled in his mind, he returned to the West Coast as a hobo, riding under a Union Pacific boxcar across the deserts and plains of the southwest, and back up to San Francisco.

The decision that he had made was that he was not going to let principles or ideals keep him from playing on the winning team, not ever. The winning team in the company he had been keeping was not going to be the one gathered around Leon Trotsky. So he enrolled at the Pacific Institute in San Francisco as a student of the history and politics of the Soviet Union. The Pacific Institute was in part a college for mature, working students. In greater part it was a front for the official – Stalinist – Communist Party, where men and women were groomed for roles as "sleepers", dormant party activists prepared to be or do whatever was required of them, submerged in the workaday world until they were needed. Already trained in the skills of a proletarian subversive, Cappy received at the Institute a grounding in Marxist economics and history, while a cultural seasoning was sprinkled on top like dried herbs over a casserole. When he had completed his indoctrination, a job was found for him in Harry Bridges' Longshoremen's Union so that he could get practical training as a labor union official. Once safely inside the union, using the platform of secret party connections which he shared with some of his new associates, he launched himself at the ranks of officials, smiling and self contained and strangely powerful, unashamedly bidding for entry into the circle at the top of the organization. Before long he acquired a wife, adding two children in due course and a home in the Sunset district of the city, where the houses all look toward the ocean and their know-nothing windows turn safely away from the boisterous, dangerous city.

After a few years, however, it was clear to longshoremen insiders that something was wrong. No one denied his importance to the organization, and no one questioned the necessity of his approval when there was a vital decision to be made. And yet the higher ranks of the union were filling with men who had been Cappy's steppingstones toward a crown which still dangled tantalizingly beyond his reach. He was going prematurely gray at the temples in his service to the union labor cause; he was strangely rich like all prominent and successful socialist union leaders; he was pictured in the papers as often as John L. Lewis, his smile almost rivalling the famous bushy eyebrows; and still he was the same distance from the top of the heap as he had been at the start of it all. What he didn't have was the trust of the men who mattered. However he savaged the lower orders, those above refused to be grateful. They knew what he was after, which was no different from what they themselves wanted, and they accepted that he had a right to aim as high as he pleased as long as he was prepared to take the punishment that came with such ambition. But they had been frightened by glimpses of his brand of ruthlessness as he reached for power. He was, as his father had said, by nature a Capo, and to those close to him it showed. There was too much blood in his eye.

According to the handbook of successful subversive behavior, Cappy should have modified his tactics and at least put on a show of patience, displaying less exalted ambitions while giving the appearance of waiting for a lucky break. Being a brigand, however, he packed up and left the union and the city, opening for business in a suite of fancy offices next to the State Capitol in Sacramento. The business had to be a union, of course, the only kind of business he knew, but which union didn't matter. He cast around for a niche that needed filling, marking his place in the firmament with his nebulous United Workers Union until he could find a star role. Meanwhile he reverted to his experience as a seaman and cleared the decks. First he visited Sonoma, where he paid for a new chapel at the Christian Brothers' home in exchange for a vow of silence. With some difficulty he located his father rotting in a transient hotel in Los Angeles and moved him to an old people's home, which bore some resemblance to a luxurious prison, located far from anywhere in an expensive oasis of the Mojave Desert. He left his family where they were, settled, nicely housed, and out of his way.

At thirty, now forceful rather than aggressive, suavely threatening rather than callously overbearing, Cappy Petrillo stood up and smiled, and with that smile announced that he was ready to be counted among men who mattered.

All he needed was an opportunity to prove his point. Cappy zeroed in on the farm workers. They were the workers who needed union organization more than any other, he told the newspapers. They were not only exploited shamelessly, they were denied the decencies of a normal life because they were forced to migrate from crop to crop, harvest to harvest, as though time hadn't passed from the days of the hunter gatherers in the Stone Age. It was the farmers, he said, who were in the Stone Age. He could correct the situation at a stroke – he was starting right now to lead a campaign to gain for the migrant workers the right to strike. The reporters gave the story full play, along with photos of the smiling Cappy standing knee deep in carrots in a packing plant.

Even when the name of his union was changed to the United Farm Workers, Cappy received less than belief from

41

the farmers in and around Red Branch. The reality was that there was work, a man came and asked for a job, he got the job if he looked the right man for it, he worked the hours that were needed to get the job done, and he got paid the going rate for the job. It was practical economics. The farmer employer held all the cards, true enough, but that was fair. It was his land, his investment, his hard work that had built up the place. The frills that Cappy wanted to add to the system did an injustice to the horse manure with which it was usually compared. Manure may smell bad, but it is a great benefit in the long run, which is more than you could say for overtime, minimum wages, mandatory rest breaks, and all the rest of that, or so they said in the cigar store and the barber shop and the Rex Hotel bar. Farmers weren't going to negotiate a rate for a job with a union instead of a worker; it was a waste of time and breath. If a day's work was seven hours or twelve hours, it didn't change the rate of pay; it was the job that needed doing that set the rate, not the man who was doing the work. Overtime? No such thing. All farming was overtime, that was part of the job.

It was Lee Roy Stagg who pointed out the part of Cappy's argument that was really the work of a Communist. That was this business of having the right to strike. He was in Mike and Gene's on a Saturday morning getting his weekly shave, and the conversation had been all about the first forecasts – it was March – of the new crops and the prices they were likely to get for them. You get a few farmers together and you're going to get shop talk, so the topic had switched to changes coming up, new equipment, some promise of better prices if the farmers would get more efficiency into grading their produce, new silos and storage facilities, all that sort of thing that bores and irritates a non-farmer stuck in a barber shop full of farmers to the point of wanting to wad up the newspapers and stuff them in their flapping mouths. Lee Roy slipped in the comment that if the workers went on this strike that the union was getting ready for, all this improvement wouldn't amount to much because a crop was ready at an hour on a day, and if you missed it you missed your big profit. Everyone nodded and grunted and said "Yeah" and finally somebody had the courage to ask, "What strike, Lee Roy?"

So Lee Roy told them about a story he had read in a newspaper.

"There was a man up north," he said, "who was the cautious type of person, good farmer, decided to change the habits of a lifetime and go in for tomatoes last year, tomatoes all the way. Some buyer had talked him into it, I guess. Anyway, you remember that heatwave we had in June? They had it twice as bad up there, and the half of the crop was ready all at the same time. He'd lined up tractors and trailers for the fields, and trucks for the haul to the plant with a big contractor, and told them the day and hour to turn up, and then they didn't show up. He got to calling around and found out that another grower up there had bought out the contractor, bought him out right out from under the other farmer. I don't know if he bought the company or the contract, it didn't say. Anyhow, the first farmer had to wait for the transport while the other farmer used it to get his own tomatoes to the packer for the premium price, and then had to pay the man who'd sold him down the river to get his crop moved, and then he had to take the price for over-ripes, rather than primes, and he lost the payment on his new tomato grading machinery in one day. Now that's what can happen to you if your labor goes on strike, same sort of thing, and it's only union labor that goes on strike. Like this strike Cappy Petrillo's planning right now. Hire union labor, miss a crop, and you're broke."

Mike had stopped the shave he was giving in order to listen to this horror tale and stood, razor in midair, thinking about the unthinkable, the specter of bankruptcy that still hung over him as well as most of the people there. Gene jogged him, "Come on, come on, they want to get out of here someday." The story had hit Mike's secret fear so

43

squarely that he couldn't get mad at Gene for chivvying him up, and his unbidden demonstration of the power of that fear was the only thing that set him apart from the others, who had also gone to zero at the bone at the thought of it but were damned if they were going to show it.

There was a general clucking over Lee Roy's story, avoiding the union labor side of things, being concerned to appear among these friends to worry mainly about the risks in doing business with people who had enough money to do dirty tricks to you. Henry Proudfoot, whose grandfather had been an Indian, listened to all of this and said nothing – which he often did, and which was taken to be the Indian in him. He was willing to show what worried him, unlike the others, when he steered the thoughts of the farmers back to the idea of strikes with one sentence.

"We're okay if there's plenty of labor," he said, "but if it's short, none of us could last out a strike. We're only okay as long as two people want one job."

A muffled voice from under a towel said, "Labor's already short around here, and it's getting worse."

Gene said, thinking he was making a joke, "Don't let Cappy Petrillo hear that."

"Oh, he's already heard, don't you worry about that," said Lee Roy. "He's no dummy. He knows. Why do you think he's pushing this union at us? We're the most vulnerable place in the state."

This wasn't true, any more than Henry Proudfoot's analysis of the management style of the agricultural industry was true, or that it was true that labor was scarce. The migrant workers hadn't even come north from the Imperial Valley yet. These were farmers indulging in overstatement, as usual. They were over-committed at the bank, in debt to fortune in that a good crop was their only real guarantee of security, and they had all been badly scarred by the Depression. The word insecure merely scratches the surface of their feelings. If only for the sweating, sleepless nights of tortured worry, there should be a better word for their predicament. Now, with the specter of union labor being raised, they were moving their nightmares into the daylight hours. Irrationally, senselessly, like kids telling each other ghost stories that they swear are absolutely true, or old people picking at scabs on their veined shins, they were making their fears into destructive fact.

The same general conversation worked its way across the railroad tracks into the town center by a process that could be compared to a spreading stain. There was another element in the idea of a strike by farm workers that had the ability to frighten these hard men silly. It was the first time they had come up against the idea of an underclass in a mass at a time that power might not be in their own hands. On the following Tuesday at the shoeshine stand beside the sidewalk in front of the Mariposa Hotel, Henry Proudfoot repeated his cautionary sentence as he was getting himself cleaned up ready to see the branch manager at the Bank of America. "None of us can last out a strike now that labor's short," he said. "We're only okay as long as there's two people for every job," he insisted to Orville Hayes, supplier of fine men's clothes, who was next in line for a shoeshine. The comment was heard by Clarence Gump from the grocery store next to the shoeshine stand, who was gossiping with Jubilee Hubbard, the shoeblack, when Henry came for his shine. All that day Clarence used it as a conversational gambit intended to warn his customers in plenty of time that he couldn't support the charge accounts that would be needed if there ever were to be a strike. Henry himself had a chance to repeat it after he decided he might need a change of socks and, disdaining Orville's expensive brands, crossed the avenue to J. C. Penney's to buy a pair. From there it travelled to the Sunlite Bakery and on to the five and dime store next door to that. The people who worked there weren't too worried, in either of them, since they never gave credit anyway, but they passed the story on. Henry Proudfoot of course repeated the sentence when he met with the bank manager, because the purpose of the visit was to test the current climate of financial opinion concerning further investment – in shorter words, he needed a loan for some fruit packing equipment. When he was turned down, he crossed the avenue the other way to the Rex Hotel, where he had a lemon Coke and complained that no one could see that the only way to beat this strike that was coming was to buy equipment that would let you do without labor. Mr Norby heard this, and after he had finished his bourbon he walked back up the avenue to the Regency Hotel for his lunch. Over lunch, which he had at the counter in the hotel coffee shop, he said to the waitress, Imogene Simi, how glad he was to hear that the spring snow in the mountains was melting fast because he would be relieved to get back to his lumber mill in the mountains and away from this farm workers' strike that was coming. Imogene had just been told by a traveling salesman who had been in Gump's that the labor situation for the farmers was looking bad, and she added the two of them together when she went into the drug store later that day and stopped at the soda fountain for a cup of coffee, passing on the sum of her information to her boyfriend Jack Wheeler, who was the soda jerk there. When he went next door to the cigar store, through the back door because he was under age, Jack eased the always tense transaction of buying cigarettes illegally by repeating the news that there was a farm workers' strike coming, adding the embellishment that it was being organized by that new farm workers' union, in his opinion. He repeated the by now firm news that the new farm workers' union was calling a strike in the Red Branch area when he went into the pool hall to wait for the movie to start at the Aragon Theater next door to it. Mr Benjamin, taking a break from printing pornographic photos in the suffocating darkroom of his photographic studio next door to the pool hall, was sufficiently disturbed to stop his afternoon's ogling of young men's backsides as they bent over the pool tables. Fantasy was all very well, but the sobering prospect of his farmer customers no longer having the cash for their annual studio photographs was a more pressing matter.

Karl Whichell, a dealer in orchard fruit futures, was staying at the Mariposa Hotel that week. Noticing the prices slumping, and therefore moving in his direction, he was pleased but puzzled as to why the farmers were in a "take the money and run" frame of mind. It was too good to be true, and tight lips instead of loose talk were the order of the day, none of the usual talking and swapping of stories. It made him nervous. For the most part they said they needed the contracts and the advance payment on deliveries in order to get the bank to underwrite equipment purchases, but a little bit of checking showed Karl that they weren't buying equipment that anyone knew of. By Thursday morning his clients had all settled and signed. All he had to do was pack his suitcase and walk a hundred yards to the train station. Instead, he confirmed his room reservation for another day and walked to the station to send a telegram to his office, saying he was staying another night. He walked down to the bus depot for a newspaper, then back up the avenue to the shoeshine stand where he climbed into the chair and waited for Jubilee to get out his box of polishes. In the warm morning sun, with the pleasant feeling of someone massaging his feet, his nervousness seemed silly. He had wasted a day for no good reason, he felt.

He spoke to Jubilee just to greet another human being on a fine day. "It's a nice town, isn't it."

Since this was a statement rather than a question, Jubilee responded noncommittally, "Yes, sir, it's a nice place."

Karl wanted more than that. "Where do you live?"

"I got me a house out Mexican Town," he said.

Karl laughed. "A black man living in Mexican Town?" he said. "They'll have to change the name."

Jubilee hee-hee'd and shook his shoulders. "That's what everybody say," he said, "but some of them as black as me, nearly. They don't mind, I don't mind." He laughed again.

"Hey," Karl said, "you trying to tell me you're one of a

47

kind around here? Aren't there any other negroes?" When Jubilee shook his head, smiled and grunted "uh-uh" Karl continued, "Who do you find to talk to?"

Jubilee stopped smearing on the polish and looked up at his customer for the first time. "Well sir," he said, "that's a difficulty. That's why I got me two jobs. You see, my real job is garbage man, and there ain't but a few of the little children in town who talks to a garbage man." He paused and studied the effect of this on the dapper city man before him. When there was no reaction he said, "Generally, I smells too bad."

They both laughed heartily, with Karl adding, "I don't notice it from up here."

Jubilee took him seriously. "No, sir, you wouldn't. I do the garbage work in the evening and night, when it's not much traffic this time of year. I do it the middle of the day in the summer, when nobody else goes out." He pointed to a small sign listing the hours the shoeshine stand was open. "Them hours is all messed around to fit in with the garbage. Ain't no other black man in town to do the shoeshines, so I got to do both. Ain't but one shoeblack in town, now the young one's gone from Mike and Gene's."

He went back to work on Karl's shoes before he added, "Down here, I gets to talk and listen. Keep me going."

Karl struck when he heard that. "What are they talking about these days?"

"Not much until this week," Jubilee said. "Now it's all this here strike. Fruit pickers, cotton pickers, grape pickers, all them kind of people going on strike. That's what they all saying. Big trouble coming, that's what they say."

"Oh, for Christ's sake!" Karl swore.

Jubilee straightened up once more. "Please, sir, if you can, please, I'll thank you not to take the name of the Lord in vain. He's mighty good to me, sir, and I can't afford to forget it. If you don't mind."

"No, I'm sorry about that. Just finish me up now," Karl said.

48

"You ain't mad at me, please, sir?" said Jubilee.

Karl said, "No, I'm grateful, really."

Back in the Mariposa Hotel, Karl laid a two dollar bill on the counter in front of the day manager and asked him if this story of a strike by farm workers was true. He was told that there was no confirmation, but the story was so strong that there had to be something in it. "The farmers are worried sick," the manager added.

"So am I," said Karl.

He went into the lounge and sat at a writing desk, where he roughed out another telegram to his office. He worked at it until he got it right, then did a fair copy and took it with him as he walked back to the train station to the telegraph counter. Karl studied the operator behind the counter, a man with an eyeshade, rolled up sleeves under a black vest, skin like parchment, small blue eyes lost behind thick glasses in silver wire frames. He decided he could be trusted. "Are your telegrams confidential?" Karl asked. "I mean, really confidential, you know what I mean."

The man took the paper from him and began to copy it onto a yellow Western Union form. "They always are," he said; "it's your money and your message. I don't give a good God damn."

It was an expensive message to all the partners in the business. It related the information that he had collected and advised that someone get in touch with Cappy Petrillo to see what was going on, and do it quickly. The farmers had got contracts from Whichell that guaranteed them a partial payout, now that he thought about it, even if their workers were on strike – they had their insurance at his risk, and now he understood their readiness to sign at low prices. If there was going to be a strike, of course, prices would go sky high, but only if there was anything to sell. As commodities brokers, his company could go broke or they could make a fortune, depending on the timing of the strike. If Cappy Petrillo could be persuaded to cooperate, they would be rich. The farmers had tried to screw them, all right; now

49

they were out on their own, they could look after themselves.

This was the gist of the message that Al Peart, the telegraph operator, passed on to Lee Roy Stagg that night outside the post office where he had arranged to meet him.

In this way Cappy Petrillo got a message from Karl Whichell's office indicating to him, as a union leader looking for a place to establish his authority, that Red Branch was ripe for a strike, a good one that would take place in the closest thing to a blaze of national publicity that he would be likely to get, short of burning down the offices of William Randolph Hearst.

The other general in this war, Lee Roy Stagg, was a man who had already waved the blazing sword of the Lord's righteousness in the face of the unbeliever, and he would happily pick it up again.

3

The city man who had had his shoes shined so early that morning had got Jubilee Hubbard started thinking about himself and his life. It was true, he considered, that he was all by himself, and it was also true that he never thought of himself as lonely, because he had got his Lord Jesus to keep him company. When he went back to his three room house that night, he said hello to the Mexicans who passed him and they said hello back, but no one was very interested in how he was and what he was going to do with himself. For that matter he wasn't very much interested in their interest, when he thought about it. Maybe he was going to end up one of those holy hermits, but living in among people instead of being out in the desert living on a pillar or whatever it was. Some days he smelled so bad from the garbage that he could understand living on a pillar, just to get your smell away from other people, but he didn't like to think about the other problems of living like that, things like the toilet and food. Maybe, however, that was something like his destiny, since his life was ruled by being unacceptable to somebody or other in one way or another. His last wife – his only wife really, not that he was right down married to any of them – Saralene, she had stuck with him in spite of his garbage smell as long as she could. It wasn't the smell so much as having to wash his coveralls every day by hand, except on Sunday. With that and the children and a house that was too small, it was just one thing too much, the washing, especially when he didn't really need the job. The shoeshine stand would have been enough for them, if he'd done a little more begging and got the tips rolling in better. In the back of his mind there was another reason why she took the children and left, as he knew, but it wasn't something he admitted to himself. In an admitting mood now, he went back over his life as a Presbyterian, all two years of it, expecting to find it at least an enriching experience despite the hurt of the way it ended.

He had every reason to want to be a Scottish Presbyterian, if he had known about them ahead of time, with their ideas about being different from other people. He and Saralene were the only negro couple in Red Branch, and there was only one negro man other then Jubilee, the shoeblack from the barber shop who called himself Ace. He had no reason ahead of time to pick out the Presbyterians, he just shopped around. The Methodists sang all the wrong songs and came from the South, so he didn't fit in there. The Episcopalians thought they were Englishmen who happened to be in the wrong place and looked over him and around him or through him, until he understood what they wanted and quietly left. He couldn't beat the color bar at the Baptist Church. They were glad to take his money, but there was no chance he was going to get baptized when they were the same people who wouldn't let anybody who wasn't white go in the town swimming pool. By the time he got to the Presbyterian Church, after a short blast with the holy rollers at the Pentecostal Church, he was good and ready to consider himself one of the unelected elect.

He went there for the first time on a very gray morning in wintertime. He sat in the back row, he remembered, in the middle of the pew so he wouldn't take anybody's aisle seat. Reverend Ward was preaching about the way the Lord's mercy strikes you unawares, when you least deserve it, when the sun decided to shine after all and a warm, clean beam of it came through the big window and lit him up. Just him, not the people sitting around him. He knew it was a sign, not an accident. He sat in that same place for over two years, and people expected him to be there, he could tell that from the way they nodded to him as they went to sit in their usual places. He felt he belonged, even though no one ever came to sit beside him.

Maybe if Saralene had come to the Lord Jesus when she was a girl, the way he had done when he was a boy, she would have been able to see why he needed his church. She always said all he needed was a Bible and a half hour for his mumbling, that was what she called his praying, and he could go on living like anyone else. "Where's the need for any old church?" she said. What was right for one man wasn't enough for another. He had to respond to his Jesus. That was what finished him at the Presbyterians. He couldn't sit there quiet and not say an Amen or a Hallelujah, especially when the preacher got worked up about something that he agreed with. He hadn't been aware that he started to say them out loud until the man with the long fingernail turned around to look at him several times during one sermon and he figured out what he had been doing that annoyed other people, especially that man, so much. Unfortunately the dam had broken that day, and the Amens came crowding over his lip from then on, and when he let loose with a Hallelujah it came unbidden but undenied from his bowels up and shook his soul. He could no sooner have squelched it than he could have stifled his wind. The Amens and Hallelujahs came out after Saralene had run off with the children and Ace. Why he had to shout to his Lord when his family had mistaken Ace for Moses and a city for the promised land, well, who knows? Not him.

After that, he couldn't go to church. If he couldn't keep his mouth shut, he wasn't wanted. There wasn't a new one to try, and he couldn't go back to any of the others. Besides that, he wasn't worthy any more. He got the ache on him

53

without Saralene there, and every three weeks he couldn't take any more of it and rode the bus on the Saturday to Placid City. Across the railroad tracks, beyond the freight yards, was a Basque restaurant where the Spanish sheepherders went for dinner when they were in town. Next to it was a hotel where you could pay for a bath in a real bath tub and soak until you felt good and clean, then you could go upstairs and find a girl who didn't mind coloreds and pay for her by the hour. A good cleanup, an hour with a nice girl, and a big dinner, and he was too big a sinner to go sit in church the next day. He had always had a clear sense of his own unworthiness, but he knew it now so strongly that he felt if the time came, he could be a preacher.

The difference wasn't that he was doing his stuff with a girl instead of with his wife, because he and Saralene had never really been married except in the eyes of God. It was that he did it there in Placid City without the blessing of Jesus. That was what Saralene hated, what drove her to Ace, she said. She said the praying made lovemaking too complicated. She was his wife so she would do it, but that didn't say she liked it, she told him every time, which was generally three nights a week and a special one to celebrate Sunday. Sometimes when they'd taken their clothes off and knelt down naked for him to start the Bible readings, one of the children would cry, and that would be it for that night. Other nights he would get into it real good, the praying and the hallelujah praise coming so naturally out of him that he would be really, truly ready for Saralene when they couldn't wait any longer. You couldn't do that with a girl in the S.P. Hotel. For one thing he'd have to pay for another hour, which would mean he could only afford to go every four or five weeks, and waiting three weeks the way he did now was almost too much to bear. More than that, the girls there were all Mexicans, with pictures of the Virgin Mary in the rooms, so they were Catholics. He couldn't see doing real religion with a Catholic.

When he looked at his life like this, Jubilee knew that

there was nothing to keep him in Red Branch except his little house and his jobs. He could find work somewhere else, and he didn't really need a house to himself unless he got married again. A room anywhere would do. But he felt he wasn't ready to leave Red Branch. There was something here for him to do; exactly or even vaguely what that was had yet to be revealed. Jesus would tell him.

III

Five Excerpts from
The Annals of Red Branch

In which the point is made that the diversity among the good
people of Red Branch served to hide not a microcosm but a
microcivilization, and that what might at first appear to be
the healthy eccentricity of a well rooted culture is actually
the implosion of a cultural bubble which maintains its surface
tension as its nucleus diminishes. Oh, what a thing is man.

To Change the World

When Nettie Atwater was fairly certain she was going to die, she made her will and called her housekeeper in to witness it. It was not an unusual will in any way, the housekeeper said, except that it cut her favorite grandsons off with a memento (a photograph of her in a silver frame) and a book each. To Casper she gave the family Bible, and to Jasper she gave an inspirational book entitled *Learn to Aspire*. Of course, they didn't know this at the time.

When Nettie was absolutely certain she was going to die, which was just short of two years later, she called everybody up to the big, old house at the end of Greenfield Avenue. The members of the family gathered in the huge drawing room, where the gloomy tapestry curtains had been pulled back only enough to protect the visitors from the hazards of furniture. Then she had herself wheeled in by her nurse, seated in a big, upholstered chair that had been her own grandmother's and had been fitted with wheels so she could interfere with everybody's lives no matter in what part of the house they tried to take refuge. Nettie surveyed the clan in a sweep of her eyes that recalled Bette Davis in her spoiled heiress mood. She withered her cousin, who was sniveling, with a look that was like a twelve-volt flashlight cutting through an attic.

Then she spoke. "You have all been taken care of, and I expect you to be grateful. Casper and Jasper, come here."

The twins were only eleven at the time, not yet old enough to enjoy this kind of show. They came forward very solemnly. As befitted the two boy sopranos of the Atwater Gospel Quartet, however, they kept their heads high and didn't let the big occasion overwhelm them.

"I've left you nothing for now," their grandmother said, "except something to remember me by. Casper, you are going to be a preacher. Jasper, you are going to be a teacher. You boys are going to change the world. When you've changed it, the Red Branch Bank will pay you a reward from my trust fund."

She waved a hand upward, while she kept her eyes fixed on her grandsons. "Wheel me back," she told the nurse, who took her back to her bed, got her into it and arranged her head on the pillows. Nettie gave a little gulp and quietly died.

The twins were changed people after that. As twins they had always been close, but now they were two sides of the same dollar bill, together in everything they did. Herb Atwater and his wife Suzanne tried every way they knew to get their boys to separate their lives, but it was no good. The boys had dedicated themselves to their grandmother's prophecy, not for the money that was to be their reward, as they said, but because that old woman on her deathbed had been able to see their destinies. Overnight they turned into straight A students in school. When they went to college, Casper majored in theology and Jasper majored in education, and they followed that up with a year in graduate school. Then they went to Placid City, where Casper got the job of understudying the preacher of the Free Methodist Church and Jasper went to the high school to teach social studies. Right away they began to make their mark – in Placid City.

And that's where the doubts began. Placid City was not the hub of the universe, more like one of the shabbier spokes

61

of a spare wheel of fortune. So it came about that finally someone back in Red Branch said it out loud: "It's a mercy Nettie Atwater didn't live to see her prediction mocked." And wise heads nodded grim agreement. They had hard evidence: Neither of the twins had the gall to approach the bank manager to get the trust fund to pay out; the world showed no sign of change.

The Regency Hotel in Red Branch has always been the setting for important events. One warm April night Casper and Jasper arrived there with two blondes impersonating Hollywood starlets of the kind regularly photographed doing silly things. However, the boys (well, men) hadn't come to Red Branch to show off their fancy girlfriends to their former neighbors. What they had in mind was roughly the other way around; they had brought the ladies to see the little old backwater of a town they had left, the idea being to demonstrate their rise in the world, and shore up their sagging confidence. After the grand tour, they had brought the girls here for drinks and dinner. It was generally held to be those drinks that did it. Casper made a reference to the prophecy, and Jasper tried to shut him up, and the girls insisted on hearing the story. They heard in silence how their escorts were meant to change the world, then collapsed in laughter until they had to go re-powder their noses. One of the regulars in the dining room heard one girl say, when they returned to the table, "Are you serious? Change the world?" Her friend added, "You looked so funny when you said it. I don't even know what you mean."

Out of the mouths of babes, so to speak. The idea that it looked as though they were the butt of some kind of cosmic joke had never occurred to the twins. They were thunder-struck, or at least struck by something pretty close to thunder. The four of them left the Regency Hotel in a hurry, and in a matter of weeks Casper and Jasper left Placid City for someplace out of state, which to Red Branch was the same as dying. Their resurrection came when Mrs Joe Garbett identified them as the new people on the radio evangelists station that came through clear but crackly on Saturday nights. There from the ether itself were the twins, reborn as the Atwater Gospel Duo, Casper preaching away as though he was running for the title of Most Compelling Evangelist of the Year, Jasper pleading in a folksy, sincere way as the most trustworthy collector of offerings in the whole Jesus industry. It took them just four months to get the money from the faithful listening public to build their gleaming new Atwater Gospel Temple.

They came back to Placid City in the year of their triumph for a weeklong revival campaign, and Red Branch emptied to go see them and shake their hands and remind them who it was who was shaking those famous hands. The bank manager, Roger Preece, went along too. When he finally was ushered into their presence, he asked the twins if, with all this fame and so forth, they thought they had met the conditions of their grandmother's trust.

Casper answered in a grand but humble voice, "I think you can trust me to put Grandma's money to the best use." Jasper sighed a little sigh as he gave the question careful consideration, then said, "A check will do just fine."

Except for the use of the term "Grandma," which no one would have dared apply to Nettie Atwater while she was alive and able to shout "Grandmother!" in correction, what Roger had heard sounded pretty familiar to him. In fact he heard it every day of the week – "Just give me the money and I'll make use of it."

He thought a minute, and then cleared his throat a couple of times and settled his trousers on his hip bones, and said, "I hope you don't take this wrong, boys, but, speaking for Nettie Atwater, I think you've made a mistake. Even if we all thought that prophecy was nothing but an old woman's foolishness, a trust fund is what it says it is, and I've got to carry out my trust. Now, correct me if I'm wrong, but I think you boys didn't change the world after all. It changed you."

Inevitably the matter of Nettie Atwater's trust found its way into a courtroom. Almost as inevitably, Roger Preece was overruled. Well, not so much overruled as sidelined. As the judge said when he arrived at his decision, Nettie's idea of the world was endearing, but it wasn't to be taken quite so seriously as she intended. Two people couldn't change a world that was hellbent on change already. They might even have trouble getting safely out of its way. It was a judgment that accorded oddly with Red Branch; people nodded and agreed. That's not to say anyone was pleased when the trust was dissolved and Roger Preece had to put a check in the mail to the Atwater Gospel Duo.

The Cow and the Trick Cyclist

Doc Hawser was the best vet in the county – for farm animals, that is. He couldn't so much as look at a dog without getting fanged, but cows loved him. He worked from a nice little bungalow style house halfway up the south side of Greenfield Avenue. Although the avenue ran out of chic at just about that point, nevertheless it was the broadest, grandest street in the town and you didn't think a vet would hang out his shingle there. It said something about Doc that people shied away from analysing. Probably somebody should have thought more about it, because for twenty years of his life Doc went on some of the wildest, craziest, most destructive drunks that people could remember.

As Doc mellowed into middle age, his drinking sprees fell into a definite pattern. He would start out at the Rex Hotel, drinking at the back bar with one or two of his farmer clients, and then move to the front bar which had windows that gave right onto the street. When you could hear his voice above all the others, you knew he was set for a big one. Sitting there in the window, inviting the town to witness his trangression, he drank as though he wanted above anything in this world to become insensible. Just before he got that far, he would get up and bull his way out with his jacket pockets crammed with half bottles of bourbon, get

65

into his car, and point it toward home. Mort Thomas, the police chief, who always got wind of events by that time, discreetly shadowed him home. Not to arrest him, just to see he got there without any difficulties. Once home, Doc went into his office at the front of his house and drank steadily, with the lights on and the window shades up so that the whole town could see what he was doing. Traffic along the avenue would pick up while cars cruised by for a look, until Doc went into phase three. At this point he moved his drinking out onto the front porch and bellowed at anyone within range, and cars would get very scarce. What he bellowed about was the sins and shortcomings of his wife Dottie. When she couldn't stand it any longer, or maybe when she felt the sensible thing to do was to get it over with, she went out onto the porch to try to calm him down. That was when he swung on her. If you were hardened to it, you might have placed bets on whether Dottie had timed it right. If she had, Doc was so drunk he swung and missed and fell onto the floor, where he stayed for the night. If she had miscalculated, her latest black eye was the talk of the town the next day.

What lifted this dismal pattern out of the squalid into the pathetic, if not the tragic, was that Doc's complaints about Dottie were all about Dickie Hawser, their son. He was a big, handsome boy, over six feet tall when he was only thirteen, with two older sisters who had married and left Red Branch. Dickie was feebleminded, apparently damaged at birth. To Doc in his alcoholic rages his son was in some way a diabolical plot by Dottie to humiliate her husband. The boy was, and had always been, a living reproach to his father, and the fault alighted on his mother.

It was not merely the feeblemindedness at issue, either. Doc had so thoroughly got on the wrong side of Dickie that the boy over the years found ways of retaliating against his father. He smoked cigarettes from the time he was nine, he regularly drove his bicycle into cars after arguments with his father, and he sat on the curb outside the house imitating his

66

father's curses when there was a family argument going on inside. When he was thirteen, he discovered the ultimate weapon of humiliation – if Doc began shouting at him, he went out and sat on the curb and exposed himself to passing cars. Those who didn't look away quickly enough said Dickie was prodigiously endowed. When the person who commented to Doc along the lines of a comparison to a stud mule was laid out with a right hook, the subject became unmentionable, kept alive only by younger boys who traded a peek at the fabled member for a cigarette stolen from the pack their mothers kept for visitors.

All life and experience, in Red Branch as elsewhere, points us in the direction of a single revelation that climaxes and sums up our existence. Doc Hawser was called out to Cadwalladers' dairy herd on the west side of the valley late one afternoon. One of their best cows, heavily in calf, was in distress. Doc investigated and decided that there had been some unnoticed eating of something completely wrong for an expectant cow, and the answer was a pretty violent drench. The animal was sick enough furthermore to warrant a manual administration of the laxative. Tomorrow, in the normal way, might be too late. So Doc prepared the potion, greased his right arm, greased the cow's anus, and very shortly was standing behind the cow with his arm inside it past his elbow. Judging from the symptoms he observed in his passage, he was going to have to be patient and wait for developments.

There is something about a man standing with the best part of his arm inserted into a cow's anus that can lead you to believe that the man is somehow neutralized. Young Allie Cadwallader felt this when he came around the barn and saw Doc pinioned there. Another time, probably many other times before, he had not felt he could talk to Doc about what was on his mind because, well, Doc was a force to beware of. Now he could. He began with pleasantries, then veered to his theme.

"Doc," Allie said, "about that boy of yours, Dickie –"

Doc hummed a tuneless song and didn't reply.

"My Alec was in town for a haircut one Saturday," Allie persisted, "and met up with Dickie behind the drug store. The new one. Alec says Dickie said he'd show him something important if he got him a pack of Camels."

"I know Dickie smokes, Allie," said Doc, trying to shut him off and not very happy about Allie getting around to where Doc couldn't get a good look at him to see what was coming next.

"Yeah, well, Alec used his haircut money to buy the damned cigarettes," Allie continued.

Doc said, "When I've got my hand free, I'll pay you back what you figure it cost you."

"No," Allie said, "that's not necessary. You can knock it off my bill. It's what come after that I think you ought to do something about. What Dickie called 'something important'."

Doc hummed again, and Allie continued, "He opened up his pants, you see, and showed Alec his tool."

"You ever told that boy of yours the facts of life?" asked Doc. He moved his arm as well as he could until the cow kicked. "Arm's going to sleep," he said.

"Hell, Doc, he's only eight. He knows what he sees on the farm, but that's not the same as men and women. And Dickie's is so damn big, Alec got scared. So he started to walk away, and Dickie said to him, 'This here is what you come from!' and spooked the hell out of Alec."

"Oh my God," said Doc.

"He thought Dickie had, you know, made him, Doc, and I've even showed him mine to try to get it out of his head, but he's all messed up about it. I don't think Dickie ought to do that to little kids, Doc."

Doc was mad and embarrassed and totally forgot the business at hand. He wrenched his hand out of the cow intending to wave it in Allie's face. It never got that far, because the cow loosed the pent up nastiness of three frustrating days all over Doc. Allie said afterwards it was like Doc was spray painted by a brown explosion.

Doc borrowed an old saddle blanket to sit on so that he could drive himself home. There he got out of his car and walked up to the back door, where he took off all his clothes and started sluicing himself down with the garden hose, all the time shouting for Dottie. It was Dickie who first came to see what all the noise was about, however, and Doc let fly at him with every malediction he had ever heard or thought of. Dottie came along and heard it all, and gradually worked out what had happened. She could see that Dickie was deeply offended, and she tried to get Doc to calm down.

"Please, Doc," said Dottie, "stop it now or you'll have Dickie doing something a lot worse."

"Yeah, a lot worse," said Dickie. "I'll ride my bike no hands."

This was the wrong thing to say. Doc started off on a fresh wave of invention and added a few threats. Dickie saw what was coming and walked away. He got his bike from the shed and took it out to the avenue. There he took off his pants and shorts, lit a cigarette, and rode out into the late evening traffic. Doc forgot completely that he was stripped raw and ran after Dickie, only to see him calmly riding no hands out on the avenue in big circles and loops, smoking his cigarette with one hand, and flapping his shirt tails provocatively with the other, showing off his nakedness.

Doc stood on the curb and shouted in a voice that rocked the planet, "What the hell do you think you're doing!"

A car had stopped near him, out of fears for Dickie's safety. From its interior came a man's voice, "Looks like he's doing about the same as you, Doc."

Doc was struck still as a statue – a slightly brown, completely naked statue without so much as a fig leaf for decency.

A woman's voice chimed in, "Huh! Like father, like son."

Though Doc was the only person who saw it, the sky cleft as he realized that the voice of revelation had been heard in

The Curse of the Fat Spaniard

Ledyard Job was a living proof of the axiom that there is no significance in a name. "The patience of" had nothing whatever to do with the temperament of this particular Job. From the earliest days in Sunday School he was the nameless terror of which they dare not speak – the Sunday School teachers, that is. And it didn't take the Shadow to know that, because it was the talk of Red Branch.

If this was common knowledge, why was he allowed to get away with it? Reason One, his mother was formidable in conversation and unswerving in her belief that Ledyard was incapable of doing the deeds that had just been brought to her attention. Reason Two, his father was the area manager of the district's biggest employer, liked and respected and even admired, but also empowered to hire and fire more workers than anybody else north of Placid City. Reason Three, Ledyard was a master of acts of ambush and humiliation that hardly bore thinking of, even when he was a small child.

It was Reason Three that mattered most. One famous example of his genius for revenge came about after he had an emergency appendectomy, when he was only four years old. The nurse assigned to him at the hospital coped very well with a half-sedated near infant. When his hospital room

71

was needed for a new emergency, he was taken home and the nurse went with him. With him also went his appendix, pickled in formaldehyde in a specimen jar, as a get well present from the surgeon.

Back at home among familiar surroundings, the natural Ledyard surfaced again when the nurse began giving him orders under the guise of "little requests". He exulted in the discovery of a worthy enemy and waited his chance. Nurse had that annoying hospital habit of opening the window wide in the early morning in the strange belief that the air outside needed the heating more than the patient. The consequently freezing room made Ledyard get down under the blankets when he would have much preferred to be sitting up reading a pop-up book. After fifteen minutes of this blast refrigeration, every morning without fail, nurse charged back into the room and slammed down the window in a rush saying, "Oh, that's much better!" One morning when nurse opened the window, he took the appendix jar off the night stand and stood it on the window ledge. Nurse bustled in and slammed down the window without looking. Yellowed formaldehyde and used appendix, now well and truly ruptured, splattered all over the bedroom. As soon as she had cleaned it up, nurse left.

By the time Ledyard entered kindergarten, however, the other children as well as the teachers were already wary. He therefore developed another tactic altogether, that of the amusing but destructive comment, innocent enough on its own but wounding in context. All kindergarten children had to bring along a small blanket to spread out on the floor when it was time for a nap. Natalie Krebs, daughter of Red Branch's most notorious tightwad, came to school with a piece of flannel that if stretched might have measured up to a tea towel. At nap time when teacher tried to spread out Natalie's blanket, it was clear there was a problem, and the little girl was mortified. Quick as a flash Ledyard asked, "Is kindergarten half price, teacher, if she sleeps sitting up?" It was another four weeks before Natalie's mother could get her to come back to kindergarten in something less than a state of hysteria.

Flushed with success, Ledyard extended his repertoire and used it with grownups. Before he was even in first grade he delivered a notable remark when old Mrs Koenig, feeling unwell but determined to go to church nevertheless, stepped off the sidewalk in front of the Courthouse and fell into the rose bed stone dead. Ledyard was the first to speak, telling his mother, "I think she's going to be very, very late for church, Mommy."

You could sum up Ledyard's gift by saying that he had a highly developed verbal facility but a lower than average awareness of the effect of his words. He was a prodigiously mouthy little oaf.

When Ledyard was six, his mother agreed to let a new high school teacher stay in their guest bedroom until her own apartment was ready. Miss Hall was the new Spanish teacher, with the exotic qualification of actually being Hispanic on her mother's side. She had taken her heritage seriously and spent the whole of her summer vacation in Spain, polishing her pronunciation and attending dance festivals. She had turned up for her new job possessing not only enthusiasm, but also castanets, a flame red flamenco costume, and the requisite thunderclap shoes. These she unpacked as a special treat for Ledyard on her first night with the Job family, putting them on in order to model the Spanish way of dance.

The problem was that Miss Hall was about two and a half times the size of the lithe, sensual, dextrous Spanish gypsy that she saw as herself in her imagination. In her costume she looked like the proverbial fat girl with a thin one in there with her struggling to get out, and every round of the struggle was visible. The bodice writhed in its efforts to contain her generous trunk, and each gypsylike twitch of the skirt brought into view the kind of legs that underpinned weight lifters on the covers of the health and strength magazines in the Greyhound depot. Suddenly, with a clacking of castanets, she began to dance. The dance started serenely enough, with a great deal of that haughty posing that seems to have been invented to go onto postcards. Soon, however, it became passionate, this emotion having somehow transmigrated from the soul into the feet. The club heels beat a tattoo on the oak floor, leaving heel marks that can be seen to this day. As the noise increased, Ledyard's smile spread wider and wider until finally, when the flamenco dancer seemed about to throw caution to the winds and scream enchantments over her heaving shoulders, Ledyard fell to the floor and pressed his ear to the wood. Miss Hall stopped in mid-clop, but before she could bend down to see if emotion had overwhelmed the lad, he lifted his head and cried out, "It worked, Daddy! I can hear all the termites leaving!"

There was a stunned silence; dark, half-Spanish eyes glared; the flamenco skirt dropped like a theater curtain to cover the dancing feet. Miss Hall said, "Be careful, young man, with your insults. We Spaniards never forget."

In a riposte that would haunt him the rest of his life, Ledyard responded, "Neither do elephants."

Miss Hall swept into her room, slamming the door after herself. At breakfast time the next morning, she came out with her bags and boxes packed ready to move anywhere rather than stay with the child another evening.

"His mouth will be his downfall," she predicted to Mrs Job as she left in a taxi.

To make the dismal story short in the telling, she was right. Ledyard's remarks lost their humor and became simply malicious, but he couldn't stop them coming out of his mouth. He and his family were appalled at what he was doing, and yet he kept it up. When he graduated from high school he was voted least likely to succeed, though the principal managed to keep that from being printed in the yearbook with the other superlatives. Shortly after graduation he accepted his fate and moved to the big city, where he parlayed his talent for the killer quip into a job writing

74

prepared ad libs for second rate night club comedians who had to insult their audiences to keep going.

One day, very down and almost out, he stopped by the office of the scriptwriting agency and was given a cup of coffee by the kindly typist. She asked him the question, in the guise of a professional inquiry, that many others had asked him all his professional life: "You're a nice person, really. Where did you get your nastiness from?"

He answered as always, "I was cursed by a fat Spanish dancer."

She looked at him, puzzled. "A fat Spanish dancer?" she repeated. "And you think you're the one that was cursed?"

Ledyard shouted with delight, danced with glee, kissed her with passion, and fell to his knees in thanksgiving. "At last!" he cried, "I'm free of it at last! Someone has finally topped that gag! Marry me." And she did.

Who Killed Posy Olson?

Glenn Olson and Eunice Kestner were hand holders from the third grade. They were a little old married couple as soon as they saw each other, which was right after the Olsons moved into town from a ranch in the foothills, when the government announced that the new dam on the Red Branch River would flood their shallow valley. Coming from up there where all he saw was the sky and the other Olsons, Glenn was badly in need of a friend, and Eunice took him into her charitable little heart. And never after that did she once let him go. When they went to high school, they weren't so much sweethearts as Siamese twins.

There was always something risky about high school sweethearts in Red Branch. They spent their salad days locked in each other's gaze, miming wedlock with a lot of lock and no wed. It was assumed that the kids were only lovers up to a point. That point was the one at which there was a sudden and previously unexpected marriage.

What followed was a honeymoon period not only for the couple but for the whole town, while people studied the girl's figure in profile to see if what had driven them to marriage was the young people's natural frustration or the satisfaction of it. If the first baby was full term, everything was fine. If it was premature, the euphemism for having started a family before starting for the wedding, the reaction was more complicated. Some moral censure, of course; but there were also some misty eyes, not because of this new demonstration of young love, but because people in this sort of town know that youth lasts only a short time, and bringing up a baby is a very quick way to use up what youth you have.

If one of the youngsters, Glenn or Eunice, simply thought it was more honest to get married, or if there was a better reason, no one ever knew. They had been in high school less than two years when they got a license and got Judge Cooper to marry them one Saturday morning. Eunice turned up in tenth grade English at 8 a.m. the next Monday wearing a wedding ring, and that was as much announcement as they ever made. The parents had to sign pieces of paper saying they knew and approved, and then the two of them were just high school kids again, for as long as Eunice didn't get pregnant. She didn't, and Mr and Mrs Glenn Olson graduated with their class two years later.

They sprang another surprise then. For two people who had been inseparable, it was quite a shock when Glenn took a job with the Valley Grain and Feed Company as a travelling salesman, with a territory that required him to stay on the road away from home about three nights out of five. Eunice, who had never taken care to cultivate friends any more than her husband had, was on her own the best part of every working week. The solution was a typical one for shy or lonely people – they got a dog. Tippy was a friendly little sheep dog with none of the instincts of that breed, who took to wandering all over town instead of being his mistress's companion. When he was barely two years old, he was hit by a furniture van on the main highway and buried in a flower bed in the park next to the granite monument to the Native Sons of the Golden West.

The sensible solution now would have been for them to have a family and keep Eunice occupied and happy. It was time for yet another surprise. Shortly after Tippy's accident,

Eunice went shopping at the Safeway store carrying a glove puppet. When she went up to the cash register, she had the puppet on her hand. After she let it hand the money to the cashier, she introduced it to the girl as Posy, "Our new daughter." Later on that afternoon she went to the library where she introduced Posy as her daughter to Mrs Ganz, the librarian, and said that her baby had begun to talk. While cradling the doll in her arms, Eunice put on a whiny little girl's voice, full of lisps and giggles and hesitations. When she returned the books after their two weeks was up, Eunice didn't speak to Mrs Ganz herself at all. Instead, she turned her back, put Posy on her shoulder facing the other way, and talked to the librarian through the doll.

A few days later Glenn drove into the Shell gas station with Eunice in the seat beside him and Posy up on Eunice's shoulder. He was very matter of fact, passed the time of day and all that; when he spoke to Eunice, however, she referred everything back to Posy, and the two of them had a little chat about the subject at hand before Eunice answered. The gas station attendant was as embarrassed as Mrs Ganz had been, and yet the three of them in the car didn't seem to notice anything unusual. Little by little people discovered that Eunice had lost her voice permanently and it was only possible to talk to her through Posy. However, the truth was that not that many people talked to Eunice anyway, and while they may not have been comfortable about it, they adapted.

Underneath the adaptation, at home with the family behind closed doors, people in Red Branch let speculation rip. They all wondered what Glenn made of it. They stopped wondering when his sales territory was expanded and he had to spend all five days of the working week away from home. Everyone said it was a godsend. People next door to her said Eunice never stopped chattering to Posy all day long, and she was happy, so let her alone. In the warm weather, when everyone's windows were open, they heard what seemed like a nice, ordinary little family getting along nicely.

What changed it was the old lipstick on the collar. One weekend there was a lot of loud arguing about what Glenn got up to when he was away, and he slammed into the car and drove to the Regency Hotel where he stayed in the bar until after midnight. The next weekend when he took Eunice and Posy out shopping, he wasn't talking to Eunice. He would talk to Posy but not to Eunice. She got very uppity with Glenn for a while after that; then her face settled gradually into a look of plain old anger, and then something else was added into her expression that people couldn't quite believe. Anyone who didn't know better would have said she was jealous.

The weekend before Christmas at a quarter to one in the Sunday morning, Mort Thomas had a phone call at home. It was Eunice, calling from the jail, where she had gone to give herself up for murder. She told him the body was at home, and she would wait at the jail for him to come lock her up. She was guilty and had no regrets. Mort rushed to their house and found Glenn sound asleep in the spare bedroom. There was a butcher knife on the kitchen floor with parts of Posy scattered around, liberally sprinkled with Del Monte ketchup. When he saw the mess, Mort lit into Glenn, accusing him of failing to protect his poor wife, of abusing her and pushing her into mental illness, and now of being crass and unfeeling while she went through some kind of breakdown. Glenn cried a little, which seemed like a good sign at the time. Down at the jail, however, he wasn't crestfallen any longer. As soon as he saw Eunice, he shouted at her, "Why did you kill Posy?"

Eunice shouted back, "Because you loved her better than me, you lowdown . . ." – she hunted for the word – ". . . something!"

Everybody came in then, the district attorney, the county sheriff, the town's lawyers hoping to get a client. They all started asking Eunice questions. She wouldn't say anything, just smiled, and smiled, and smiled. Finally she spoke to Glenn and said, "Tell them if they want to ask me anything,

79

they'll have to ask you. Now Posy is gone, it's up to you to do my talking for me. You killed her, that's the least you can do."

Glenn opened his mouth to speak two or three times, but no words came. He looked like a man that had just dropped down a mine shaft and found the ladder to get back up was broken.

Eunice said, "Tell them it's time for everybody to go home and get some sleep."

Glenn repeated, "Eunice says it's time for everybody to go home and get some sleep. Okay?"

Almost a year later the town's oldest surviving telephone operator died at her switchboard. The telephone company sent a man to talk to the women who wrote in when the job was advertised in the *Red Branch Herald*. One of them was quite a surprise. Eunice Olson had applied for the job, asking for her interview to be conducted in her own home. It wasn't an auspicious start to a successful career, but the man decided to humor her and went to see her. She turned out to be a very bright young woman, he said, who answered all his questions correctly about how you deal with different sorts of telephone calls. She seemed to have thought through how to work with a mechanical device in order to communicate with people, he said. In his report to the telephone company recommending that Eunice should be hired, he said that she had told him that she didn't speak to people, she couldn't. It was the result of a terrible sadness in her life. But she could talk to the telephone better than anyone else, because the person on the other end didn't get in her way.

On her application form Eunice had written her name as Posy Olson, but they got that straightened out without any trouble.

I'd Know Your Face Anywhere

Red Branch High School always had a surprising number of teachers who were pacing themselves down the retirement track like a stagger of marathon runners, the kind that brought up the tail. They had come there on the way to bigger towns and greater things, and then without planning to they just stayed on. With some it was inertia, with others it was fulfillment, and with all of them after fifteen years it was difficult to say which were which.

Fred Prout was one of those. Just reaching sixty, Fred was very proud of his time teaching English and history at the school, and he was especially proud of the fact that he never forgot a student, however ex-, and could remember the face and the name that went with it through any number of class reunions. Never having been a drinking man, at the reunions he was the older man with the glass of violently pink punch who was watched with secret terror by everyone, because Fred's favorite trick at one of these celebrations was suddenly to stride across the room brushing people aside until he had come upon his quarry. Then, extending his hand, he would say, for example, "You're Jimmy Fontini, class of '31!" And he would be entirely correct.

Jimmy Fontini had never been a student of his, and had not realized that Mr Prout even knew who he was, in fact had prayed that he should remain forever unknown. The reason for the prayer lay in what followed the recognition. In this case Prout added that he had never forgotten that ancient Chevy that Fontini drove, and the noise it made when it pulled out of the parking lot to get its driver and passengers safely out of school grounds so that they could light up their "special cigarettes". Suddenly James Fontini was seventeen again, all acne and resentment, and no longer the area manager of America's most dependable insurance company. Suddenly, too, the Red Branch Boosters would have to look elsewhere for an up and coming alumnus to head the campaign to rehabilitate the boys' locker rooms in the basketball pavilion. Fred Prout himself had few boosters.

No simple technique explains how he did it. Partly it was the result of many nights spent poring over old yearbooks. He read and reread them the way other people do the *National Geographic*. But he didn't learn from a yearbook about Jimmy Fontini's Chevy and the other skeletons that he had rattled for the many others he had greeted. For this there was always gossip, as in any other school. Prout went to a lot of trouble to verify the stories floating around, and then cardfiled them in his mind. There they stayed, waiting. More of a mystery was why he did it. He wasn't even sure himself. He didn't really enjoy the writhing or the anger, certainly not the hatred that his recollections earned. And yet his face looking into his victim's was as set and implacable as a camera, recording the recoil, the blanch, the attempted smile, the sweaty blush. It satisfied something within him when Prout was back home on his own – deep in his very private life, he sat examining photo images in his mind of former students coming face to face with their disgraces.

Time advanced, and so did Fred Prout. He was only four years away from retirement when he began to demonstrate his powers of destructive recollection and thumpingly embarrassing detection at other gatherings. He first displayed this when he represented the senior members of the high school faculty as a guest at a Rotary Club luncheon. Having arrived late and missed the introductions, he spent the first course staring at the prosperous men at the officers' table. Midway through the roast Cornish rock hen, he got up to greet the president with, "Howie Dabney, class of '23, the first graduate of our high school to go to your baby's baptism before you went to your own commencement. I was sure I knew your face. How's the family?" No one could remember afterwards what the dessert had been. Rotary Club support for the faculty scholarship fund failed to materialize that year.

Things came to a pretty pass when Fred began to direct his memory, or whatever it was, to the opposite sex. And the sex was very opposite when greeted with remarks such as, "You're Lori Knight, the cheerleader who bounced out of your sweater at the football game against Roosevelt High. What do you do for excitement these days?" So it was a matter of immediate local gossip amounting to open rejoicing when he approached a frail looking, middle-aged, attractive brunette at a Civic Pride ball with, "I never expected to see you again after all these years," and she replied, "And you still haven't. I've never seen you before in my life. Go to hell."

To be fair, Prout didn't hear her add to her dancing partner, "When an old flame's about as exciting as cold ashes, he's forgotten." Maybe if he had he would not have reacted as he did. It was soon plain to everybody that he had been deeply gored. His power was gone, and he was a husk of the social irritant he had been. He established a solitary routine, working in his classroom at the high school every afternoon until six, then walking to the Regency Hotel where, having taken up drinking, he had a double Manhattan without ice before walking home and disappearing into his small apartment on East Clydesdale Drive. There, anguished yawns could be heard issuing from him until late at night. It was just as bad at school. When he took roll call in class he would pronounce each name silently to himself, then aloud,

83

then examine the face of the person who had said "Here," to verify that a face and a name actually accompanied each other. But the next day he would have to repeat the process, as though he had no power of retention whatever.

The change in his life came with the accidental suddenness of near disaster. It was spring, vibrant for everyone else, bleak for Prout. As will happen in spring, odd couplings occurred. And in the town of Red Branch, if a coupling was odd, the trysting place was even odder. Garfield Memorial Park was an oasis of shade on a hot day. The giant sycamore trees made the part of the park behind the bandstand as dark as a virgin rainforest. In the gloom could be found some cages of various sizes, with a peeling green sign that said this was the O'Connell Collection of Fauna. It was what was left of a little zoo, the remnant of a measly benefaction left to the town by an Irish immigrant who was stung to the nationalist quick when Red Branch was given its handsome Carnegie library by that famous Scottish benefactor. Here among the remnants of mistaken Celtic rivalry, while his ego struggled to find its identity, Prout walked every lunchtime, past the alligator the color of his slimy water, past the gloomy little hill rumored to be inhabited by prairie dogs, and on toward the two parrots in their cages, one bird gray and perpetually moulting, the other blue and in a similar state of feathered rot.

This particular lunchtime he had passed the wire mesh of the prairie dogs' cage when he glanced up toward the grey parrot's enclosure just in time to see a man, caught in the act, trying to disentangle himself from a much younger blonde woman. In doing so the man put his hand on the wire cage to steady himself, since the entanglement had been somewhat athletic. The parrot, great in age and wise in tactics, saw his chance and fastened his beak on the two fingers that extended into the cage. The man's jaw dropped, his eyes bulged, and his lungs released a shout that would have rivalled Jonah's greeting to the whale. He grabbed for the cage of the blue parrot to give himself support as he tried to drag his fingers out of the gray parrot's beak. The blue parrot obliged by seizing a finger of the other hand. The effect was of a man suspended between two live electric wires screaming bloody murder.

Fred Prout loped into action. He waved his newspaper and shouted at the parrots, "Release Jack Harper immediately! He was the only decent student council president we ever had, even if he cheated in his English final exam!" Understanding exactly what was being said, the parrots unclamped their beaks and crabbed along their perches, grumbling slightly.

Harper, who had been accurately identified, allowed the blonde to wrap his fingers in shreds of Kleenex before turning to Prout. He was in too much pain to believe he had heard what he thought he had heard, so he ignored the part that he had never wanted to hear. "I don't know who you are, but I want to thank you sincerely for coming to my aid. Did I hear you say you know me?"

"I'm Fred Prout, from the high school, remember?" And he beamed.

Harper stared at him. There was no sign of recognition on his face. "I'd know old Prout anywhere, and you sure as hell are not him." He moved Prout into less gloom and stared again. "You couldn't look like Fred Prout in a million years. What's the deal?"

Fred stumbled out of the park in a daze, crossed Greenfield Avenue to the Shell gas station, went into the men's room and locked the door. He double checked the door to make sure it was locked, and then he turned to look at himself in the mirror. He could not remember what Fred Prout looked like, but he was certain Jack Harper had been right and this wasn't the face of Fred Prout looking back at him from the mirror. Given time, he felt he would recall whose it was. He had a gift for remembering names and faces, after all, and it would surely come back to him.

1

It was about as normal a spring as you could possibly get in that part of the world. The sun began to bleach the blue out of the sky, and every day was greener than the one before. The town swimming pool opened on the fifteenth of April, the signal for the bolder kids to start nagging their mothers to let them go to school barefoot – out of school, and out of sight of their mothers, they were already showoff barefoot, except those who had scraped their bare ankles or caught their unshod feet in bicycle accidents, who now had to wear tennis shoes until the wounds healed. The flowers were coming on well and would be ready for Memorial Day, when buckets of them would be picked to decorate the graves. A few people in town still called it Decoration Day, but they were disappearing.

The only thing that was at all unusual was the shortness of tempers among the farmers and their friends in the town. You might almost have said they were disappointed that their worst fears had not been immediately confirmed. There was absolutely no sign of activity on the strike front. Harold Stoll at the bus depot had been keeping an eye cocked for any comings and goings involving a small, smiling man dressed like a disguised politician. Harold was a good man to choose, with his ability to watch traffic, keep the kids'

89

hands out of the candy trays, get the right brand of cigarette for his regulars before they had to ask, and relate the latest news in tidbits to help you choose which newspaper to buy, all this while getting people on and off buses with a minimum of consternation. Lee Roy Stagg was sure someone local, a surprise to everyone, would turn out to be Cappy's agent. There had been too much talk. On the grounds of no smoke without fire, it was certain to him that someone had been setting everything up under their noses. If anyone could spot the fifth columnist, Harold could, so you would have thought. This time, however, he had missed a trick, helped by the fact that there wasn't any agent.

At some time of one day or night, Harold hadn't seen Cappy Petrillo drive himself slowly through Red Branch sizing up the town, cruising his car along a few streets until he had a feel for it, then driving on in the direction of Placid City. Exactly what he did in or near Placid City wasn't clear until much later, but the effect wasn't long in coming. When the migrant workers started coming up from the south, moving north as the crops ripened, the union agitators were already in among them. The fifth columnist wasn't a local man at all. He was a hydra, every head different but every message from every mouth the same – keep quiet, stay united, wait for the word from Cappy. The impact on the farmers was the same as if station KPLA had started broadcasting the farming news at random times of day and night without any prior warning. They were jumpy and edgy, hard to live with, changeable and therefore hard to work for. The advice from the union agitators remained the same, even though there were plenty of small provocations that could have been used to produce some friction. As the migrants moved steadily into the area, filling the camps and the shacks and even the tent sites on the west side, as the sun got hotter and the crucial picking days came closer, everything looked set for the quietest, most profitable season ever, and the farmers were worried sick.

Mary Parsons was almost as dependable a harbinger of

spring as bare feet on the boys, quitting school as usual on the first convenient day after April first. She wasn't going to quit on the first and be called an April Fool. This was her third year of being in the high school for about half the year. Starting school only late in October, she didn't get credit for any courses in the first semester, and leaving early in April, she didn't complete any courses in the second semester. She had learned a lot in high school, but she was still zero in credits toward graduation and had just about used up the teachers and subjects that had interest for her. She thought this would turn out to have been the last year of school for her. Sometime during the summer, she thought, she would decide if she wanted to go ahead and be a prostitute, or settle for a husband. Life was all right for the time being, she felt, happy in knowing she was in charge of her life and could make a change in it anytime she chose to.

She took the first day after her amputated school year to bleach her hair as close as she could get it to platinum blonde. Then she sorted out last summer's clothes until she had her basic good time girl wardrobe that she could add to when she had the money. She practiced putting on her lipstick and rouge and posed in front of her mother's big mirror. Fashions were a little bit bolder this year anyway, so she altered the blouses to show some more of her chest and tightened the skirts until the shape of her backside was unmistakable. When she had packed all her things in two suitcases in preparation for her mother to throw her out, she was ready for her annual emergence as Louella. She couldn't remember who had first called her Louella, after the famous Hollywood movie gossip queen, but she liked it. It suited her second self. She could roll Louella around on her tongue when a strange man asked her what her name was, and if he didn't think it was sexy, adding Parsons was a good way to break the ice and start a laugh with him. It always worked.

When her mother found out she had dropped out of school again, that is after a week when she finally noticed that Louella had re-emerged, she duly threw her out of the house, at which point Louella again rented the little room above the dentist's office, even though she hated the drill sound that came through the floor and had to get out if a little kid got in the chair and started shouting in fright. It made her spine curl. She had enough to pay the rent for a couple of weeks, and after that one or another of her men friends would pay it, if they wanted to come to see her again, and they usually did. Then she made a nice, gradual return to her Louella life, going to the soda fountain for lunch and taking all the time in the world to eat it before scandalizing the women peering out from behind the counters and shelves by lighting up a very long, filter tip cigarette. It was funny how they could still be scandalized, having seen the same thing for the past three years, she thought. Then she strolled slowly down to the highway and walked south the three blocks to Nick's Diner, looking in a kind of astonishment at the spectacle of her schoolgirl feet in high heel shoes, getting back the feel of being dressed for men, placing her feet carefully in positions that made her swing her body just right. When she got to the diner and asked for her summer job back, Nick patted her on the fanny, said she was as good as ever, and she could start the next day, six-thirty sharp. It was reassuring the way things didn't change, she thought, as she waited for the news to get around to Calvin that she was back at Nick's.

Nick's was an important part of the Red Branch intelligence network. Nick the Greek, Mike's brother, ran a good cafe, popular with local men for breakfast, equally popular with truck drivers for breakfast any time of the day, or lunch if that was your preference. Louella was an added attraction. What people came in for was the news. Nick listened and talked, and if he didn't know what was going on up and down the whole length of the valley, he knew a truck driver who did and who was due to stop in Red Branch within the next day or two. If he was busy at the grill or out in the back fixing up the à la carte for lunch, Louella filled in for him, listening and adding in what had been said earlier that day, then passing it on to Nick. Nick and Mike had long telephone conversations almost every night, the sensible thing to do since they didn't get along very well when they met face to face. They traded news and kept off family topics when they were on the phone, and it went off all right that way without wives to set them at each other about old grievances and rivalries.

From Nick's the line of communication went to the Rex Hotel bar, frequented in the afternoon and evening by the people who either ate breakfast at Nick's or who had missed having breakfast there and wanted to catch up on the news. Louella helped the process along, since this is where she met her men friends. She had a good memory and a nice way of salting her retelling of the morning's gossip that fitted with her adopted name. When the men were swapping stories at the Rex Hotel, she could be counted on to add the detail that made the difference. Old Gomez, the owner of the Rex Hotel, liked her and found her an asset to his business. He ignored her age – she looked older than seventeen – and gave her a free drink every once in a while to encourage her to use the place. Once he had asked her if she would like to move from over the dentist's to the top floor of the hotel, but she knew what that meant and preferred to play the field. Mort Thomas, the police chief, never went to Nick's except to get information on an official basis. No one knew why. Rumor said there had been some remark passed by Nick when he was still fresh enough in Red Branch not to understand the kind of reticence that balanced friendship and respect for a police officer. On the other hand Mort on duty as a policeman was a regular at the Rex Hotel, where he listened carefully and watched the customers as if he was in the business of memorizing faces. He had a way of lifting his belly onto the edge of the bar just before he was going to say something that was worth hearing, producing moments of hush that were unsettling to strangers, followed by a brief growl of a comment that was always worth taking note of.

From the Rex Hotel the line went down the avenue to the cigar store. The rich smell of cigars, chewing tobacco, spit, male sweat and the cleaning bleach needed to deal with the effects of all these belched out the door whenever it was opened. Always hot and gloomy, impermeably male, it was either a sink or den of iniquity, depending on the vehemence of the female speaker denouncing it. It supposedly existed on the sale of cigars and cigarettes, priced so as to give the buyer the opportunity of relaxing in the leather chairs and enjoying his smoke without any contribution from the opposite sex. On that basis, as necessary as the recreation might have seemed to many of the men, the business should have been bankrupt years before.

It had two secrets of commercial success. One was the telephone and the other was the back room. The telephone was polished brass and sat on the counter near the window. Tom Potter could answer the phone and keep an eye on the whole place from there. He also took calls there for regulars, who picked up the phone from the counter and stepped back a few feet into an alcove with a door that Tom slid closed. It was soundproof, of course, but it also was effectively monitored. Tom knew who didn't want to take calls from whom, who was likely to be an important caller, whose wife had to be lied to, everything a good personal assistant should know. A dollar bill on the counter took care of a lot of assistance.

A regular five dollar bill took care of a whole lot more, with the back room the scene of events. The back room was known throughout the valley as neutral ground. Men came in by car or on the train, went straight to the cigar store, met their appointments, and left as soon as possible. It was here that the politician met the police chief, the newspaper editor met the bank manager, the tax investigator met the racketeer. Tom Potter took no interest in the use to which the back room was put, so long as no women were involved. It was, however, opened only to people who had the right credentials and who knew what to do with a five dollar bill. If the purpose was a blue movie or a poker game that was going to go to the death, something more substantial than the number five was required. The movie would require a

bill from every viewer, and the poker game would pay a
hefty ante from every player to the house. Sometimes,
rarely, the word would get round that a professional game
had been set up. Men in felt hats and business suits would
arrive on a morning train and check in at the Mariposa
Hotel, then go out and walk the streets singly, coughing and
squinting in the sunshine. When their rooms were ready,
they would go to bed, leaving a call for six or seven that
evening. Dinner at the Regency Hotel and maybe a drink or
two at the Rex Hotel were followed by a drift toward the
cigar store, where each of the men stood and glanced up and
down the street before going in. There was always some
local fool who wanted to buy into the game, followed by
another who imagined himself luckier than the last, and so
on, until the out of town gamblers got down to serious poker
and found a winner among themselves. If you wanted to
watch the game, you had to be approved by Tom Potter,
which would cost you ten dollars and a guarantee of no
monkey business. The gamblers all carried guns. In the
humdrum months between such excitements, the business of
the town went on being settled in the back room, with the
cigar store's telephone the private, privileged means of
securing the power to get things done.

By Memorial Day the temperature was ninety or above
every day in the most prolonged hot spell of the past few
years. The outdoor memorial service was rescheduled to
start at nine in the morning to beat the heat, but the Catholic
part of the service went on so long that there were a few
faintings and one fit. After the volley of shots was fired by
five riflemen wearing American Legion caps, and the boys
had scrambled for the brass shell cases, and after taps had
sounded eerily from the far side of the cemetery, the small
mountain of flowers was divided up and given to people
carrying new zinc buckets that flashed in the sun. The
seriousness of the occasion broke down in about two minutes
flat, demolished by kids laughing and running, carrying small
bunches of flowers to make sure all the graves were decor-

ated, competing with each other in the number of graves they had done and shouting the totals of the leaders until the winner emerged. A few grownups toured the graves to make sure the children had added water to the flowers so that these would have a few hours of freshness before wilting in the heat. Some of those grownups stayed after the crowd had left, searching the cemetery and reading the stones in an annual personal act of remembrance. The place was empty by lunchtime, when the picnics started at various places in the town with softball games stretching through the long, hot afternoon afterwards, to be followed by an open air band concert under the floodlights at the high school football field. By ten o'clock the preliminaries were over, and a hot summer was ready to begin.

2

When the pioneers first came to the valley, they hurried through the flattening heat of what was to all intents a desert. When others came back, it was early spring, and they saw the vegetation that goes with rich land, if it is given the water it needs. The first machinery imported into the infant town of Red Branch was equipment to drill wells. It was the vast lake of water that was found to lie under the valley that gave life to the land and its towns. Later on it was the grid of canals and irrigation ditches that sustained and extended that life and gave prosperity to the valley.

Long before June the effect of the drenching winter rains has been replaced in the groves and fields and vineyards around Red Branch by the miraculous upwelling of water through standpipes, or the transparent gush of it being diverted from ditches. It runs like a benevolent spirit through the tan soil, turning it dark brown and creamy until the leaves of the trees and bushes and vines lift and wax themselves so that they can stand up to the fierce heat again. Anyone wanting to observe the effect of the irrigation on fruit does best to examine apricots. The hard green nuts swell almost as you watch, to a size about as large as the inner palm of the hand, when they begin to flush away the green with yellow that enriches into gold as the days go by.

When the scent coming from the fruit is like that of a kitchen where bread has been toasted and a ripe melon has been cut, it is ready to be picked. By the evening of the day it is picked, it is ready for eating. If the fruit is to be eaten straight off the tree, the scent has to intensify to where the toast in that imaginary kitchen has had honey spread thickly on it.

Since the world is primarily inhabited by people who do not have apricot trees outside the back door, getting that toast, melon and honey smelling fruit to the consumer takes hard work and organization. In early July the men from the shanty town turned up at the foremen's offices in the orchards on the west side. They were put to work getting ready for the picking, flattening the irrigation channels to make primitive roads between the trees, setting stacks and ziggurats of boxes at the places they would be needed, clearing the loading sheds and storage bays so there would be no holdups once the fruit began to accumulate. The tractors, trailers and trucks that had stood unused over the winter were checked over to avoid breakdowns. The rest areas for the pickers were cleaned up and a few tables and benches brought in. At a discreet distance the men dug holes and moved the privies over them, then put up a screen of wood fencing around a standpipe so the women pickers could wash themselves with basic modesty. Under another standpipe they put a round wash tub and strung up a rope between some posts nearby, making a washing place so that one of the two sets of clothing the pickers owned would be rinsing and drying while they wore the other. In the part of the orchard where picking would begin, they unloaded galvanized iron boxes with faucets in them, which were set up off the ground on pieces of piping at intervals down the rows of trees. These would be filled every morning with fresh drinking water.

From early June the farmers had been regularly touring the places where the migrant workers were congregating. They sized up the numbers of people available and looked for familiar faces from years before, trying to get a feel for what the picking was going to be like. As the orchards grew in size and number each year, the day came closer when there would have to be gang foremen between the farmers and the workers, but not yet. For now, the farmers still went on these tours looking for natural leaders who could be used to get the workers organized and working as teams. By early July they had identified the men who, for a bonus of a few more dollars, would be their head pickers.

Sam Tolin had the farm farthest west. Beyond his land was the uncultivated hinterland, the huge block of land owned by a syndicate which was selling it off piecemeal as the markets for produce justified the kind of sale prices and mortgage terms that would interest these big city speculators. Being closest to the blasting winds that came off the western hills, Sam's orchards ripened early, and the eyes of the whole area's farmers were on him as the day came when he would take on labor. His kindest relative would have agreed he was the wrong man for the job. Sam was gifted with a natural insecurity that made him bolt for a solution like a trapped cat for an open door, a characteristic that in another age would have caused him to be called a pragmatist.

Sam had combined two Dodge trucks to make one fairly good one that he drove around the country. One had been white and the other black, giving the combination vehicle a piebald look. This alone was enough to make him a marked man. He drove into the big migrant camp near Las Cruces Slough on the morning of July 12. When they saw him coming, the men he had talked to before, ones who had all agreed to act as head pickers, came out to him and spoke politely to him, as men do when they know they are about to enter into a business arrangement with a superior who has not yet divulged the full terms of his offer.

"Get in the back of the truck and let's go someplace where we can talk," Sam invited them. About a dozen in all, they nodded and climbed up. He drove out of the camp toward what had been a hobo jungle during the worst years of the Depression, to where cottonwood trees shaded a small sandy beach on the less sluggish end of the slough. A few boys fishing for catfish gave way as the men got down from Sam's truck and squatted for their conference.

"Well, you boys know about as good as me what the terms are," Sam said, and laughed. No one laughed with him, so he went on to lay out the terms. "It looks like we start the end of the week, I'll know tomorrow. I'll get the price from the cooperative, and I'll give you the best price per pound that I can. Everybody works piece rate, and you fellows get a dollar an hour bonus on top."

A very thin, tall young man spoke up. He had declined to squat with the others. Tilting back the brim of his sweaty hat, he said, "We want twenty-five per cent of the price you're offered for the fruit."

Without hesitating Sam replied, "Yes, okay, that's fine."

Sam couldn't have told God Himself why he said that. It wasn't either okay or fine. You paid a picker by the pound, totted up when his box was weighed in. Twenty-five per cent? How did you do that? You just paid a figure, that's all. Sam was lost.

The young man asked, "What about the second picking?"

Sam hesitated. "What do you mean?" he asked.

"You want a first picking, that's fine, twenty-five per cent is fair. Second time over the trees is a lot of work for less fruit. We work the same hours but we don't get the same pay."

"Hold on," said Sam, a delaying tactic suggesting itself to him in his extremity. "How come you're the only one doing the talking? You boys all agree with him?"

An old man, the oldest in the group, spoke up. "We got us a spokesman. Done elected him. He's talkin' fer us."

"Oh," Sam replied, then paused to think about it. He wanted it over and done with. Maybe a spokesman wasn't such a bad idea. In the pressure of the moment, he forgot all he had been told by Lee Roy and the other farmers in the cooperative with him, forgot even about the United Farm Workers.

"What's your proposition?" Sam asked the young man.

"We'll pick by the pound first picking, but the second we work by the day." He paused before adding, "And we want one of our own people to do the grading."

"Gimme a minute," Sam said. He walked to his truck and climbed into the cab, sitting there and thinking, pretending to be working out figures on the back of a receipt that he found on top of the dashboard. They picked the first, top value crop at twenty-five per cent of the price set by the cooperative, he could figure that out somehow. The second picking they went over the trees and cleaned them of every useful piece of fruit, much of it for drying rather than shipping as fresh fruit. He got less for this fruit, and the pickers, having already taken about a third of the fruit off the trees, had less to show for their time. On the other hand if they didn't take the time on each tree, the fruit would be left to rot, representing a clear loss. Maybe working for their time wasn't such a bad idea, though offhand he couldn't think how to cost it. Someone had to grade the fruit, to see if the pickers were doing their job. Maybe graders coming from the pickers themselves could do it, but what happened if they found the quality was low? Would they tell their own kind, or would they cover up? He had always given that job to some women who turned up, friends of the regular farmhands, the ones working for him already getting set up for the picking. Well, what's the difference? he thought, one bunch you don't know and the other bunch you only half know. The only thing Sam knew for sure was that he was out of his depth, and he wanted to get this over with right now.

He went back to the men who sat silent and waiting. "Okay," Sam said, "I'll try it your way. But it better work." He had no idea what he would do if it didn't work.

He didn't question seriously the deal he had struck until he had let the men off at the camp. It was when he heard whoops of triumph and, looking behind the truck in his mirror, saw people congratulating the spokesman that he thought he might have been better off doing a little more thinking. He had no intimation even then that he had been talking to the union organizer, one of the planted agitators, and that he had been given the first installment of Cappy Petrillo's demands for the apricot harvest that year.

As he looked over his trees during the next three days, Sam felt good about having all the organizing done with. The apricots were fattening nicely, and he could see in his imagination the boxes of golden fruit stacking up in his sheds. He felt confident again, able, he thought, to take care of the bits and pieces that still had to be decided. He hadn't thought about talking to other farmers or to Lee Roy – well, he hadn't thought about it very often, anyway. There were too many things to do and think about. His whistle came back to him as his doubts fled to the back of his mind, where they didn't go away.

V

Saturday

1

It was Saturday when Sam Tolin drove back to Las Cruces to find the spokesman. "We start tomorrow," Sam said without so much as a greeting for a preamble. The man didn't like it and frowned. Sam added, "I'll have this truck and a couple of tractors and trailers over here at six-thirty. I'll need eighty people including you top pickers."

"Tomorrow's Sunday," the man said. "You're asking us to start on a Sunday. That's usually a rest day, but seeing as we ain't been working, we'll start tomorrow. Not next week, though. Not next Sunday."

Sam had the feeling he had slipped from the planet. Who was this man? What picker talked to his employer that way? He felt dizzy and grasped onto the only certain statement he could think of. "Six-thirty tomorrow," Sam said. "We'll see about Sunday."

He got back in his truck and set off for Red Branch. He could not get anything straight in his mind. No farmer who hired migrant labor had ever, to his certain knowledge, been told the workers wanted a rest day. Not just wanted it, either, expected it. A picking job was just that. You picked until the crop was in. He felt a zing go through him and his jaw dropped open in amazement that his memory had not clicked on when he had heard the tall man speak of a rest

105

day. This was that union business, it was sure to be that, and he had dropped right into their trap. What had he gotten himself into? Sam began to sweat, even though the day was not yet hot. On Greenfield Avenue, instead of driving uptown to the Safeway store, he turned right at the highway and went to Nick's.

Louella saw him coming and had a cup of coffee sliding across the counter about the same time as he slid between the revolving stools. He caught his shirt on the back of one of them, said "Damn!" and pushed it so hard it took the button off, and pushed his backside so hard down onto the other one that the air went out of it with a whoosh like a flyswatter.

"What's the trouble with you?" said Louella in a confidential voice as she pushed the cream jug across to Sam.

"I'm a worried man," Sam answered.

"I think you need some breakfast," Louella said.

"Yeah. Guess I do. Gotta do some thinking," Sam said. "Two eggs sunny side up. And toast."

"Bacon?" asked Louella. "Nick's got hold of some good bacon this week."

"Yeah," replied Sam, hardly thinking of his stomach. "I could do with some bacon, I guess."

She wrote an undecipherable note on a sales ticket and put it under a clip on a wheel that hung in the opening between the counter and the kitchen. She gave the wheel a spin until the ticket faced Nick at eye level in the kitchen. Nick called it his insurance policy, because no one could say they hadn't ordered what they got if it was written down, even if calling the order through the window would have taken a quarter of the time to do.

Louella went to the far end of the counter and lit a cigarette and looked at Sam, then put it down in an ashtray after a single pull on it and went back to Sam.

"What's wrong?" she asked. "Wife trouble?"

"Not that I know of," said Sam. "The only time I've seen her is yesterday supper time, and she didn't say anything was wrong. You heard something?"

106

"No, come on, Sam," Louella teased, "I just said that to be saying something. You look so worried."

"Don't give me more troubles than I've already got," Sam said.

Louella shrugged and went back to her cigarette, until Nick called the order and she took it to Sam. She carefully, too carefully, placed the knife and fork beside his breakfast, daintily placed his glass of water on a paper napkin, then added another paper napkin beside his fork, pulling it from the dispenser for him. As an afterthought, she put two wooden toothpicks from another dispenser on the napkin by the water glass, and slid the salt and pepper forward for him. Sam observed all this and felt ashamed of himself. Mumbling some sort of apology and thanks, he cut into his eggs with the side of his fork until he had enough runny yolk to dip his toast into, and finally settled down to eat. Louella leaned back into the cupboard that held clean coffee mugs without moving away from her customer.

After Sam had cut up his bacon into crisp bits that he could eat with what was left of his eggs, he spoke to Louella without looking at her. "Trouble is that I think I'm walking into some kind of ambush. I thought I had my labor all settled and now I get the feeling that it's just beginning. Tomorrow we start picking, and I don't know what's happening with my pickers. They're acting up."

Louella shrugged, both to indicate her attitude toward fruit pickers and to shake the neckline of her blouse a little bit lower. A man sharing confidences with her had that kind of effect on her every time.

"Get some different pickers," she said.

"Can't," Sam answered, the squeaky note in his voice indicating his frustration. "I've left it too late, I didn't smell trouble in time."

"Just start picking a couple of days late," Louella insisted.

"I don't know about that," Sam insisted. "What do I say to a bunch of strange pickers when they ask me why I'm coming to them so late? They aren't stupid enough not to see I had trouble with the last bunch. They'll want to know why. What do I tell them?"

"I don't know. What's happened with this bunch you've got?" Louella asked.

Sam was embarrassed now. He saw very clearly that he had rushed in without thinking and he had created a situation that had no sensible solution to it from his point of view. He decided to put his dilemma as simply as he could. "They're telling me their working terms," he said, "like we had a contract almost. I don't know where I stand any more."

He said this in a way that closed the subject, and Louella accepted it. She refilled his coffee mug, took away his plate, wiped a sponge over the counter in front of Sam, and pushed the toothpicks closer to him. She knew how to put a man at his ease. Sam lit a cigarette and had a puff before covering his mouth with one hand while he probed with a toothpick for an annoying fragment of bacon with his other. He turned sideways to the counter and thought hard.

Louella had finished her shift. She took off her apron in the kitchen and told Nick she was going, standing close to him so that he would look up from his newspaper long enough to register the fact that he was on his own until his lunchtime girl came on duty. He smiled at her and gave her his usual pat on the fanny. Reassured, she left to walk uptown to her room. Arriving at her stairway, however, she thought about Sam and his worries, and walked another fifty yards, where she turned in at the Rex Hotel. As she had hoped, Calvin Whitmore was there, on his own except for a couple of strangers.

"Hi," she greeted him, and gave him a brush kiss on the temple. "Just who I wanted to see," she said. "We've got to help Sam Tolin." She didn't know how or very much why their help was needed. It was just her nature to feel a call for help and respond to it, when there was no good reason not to. Louella was a kind girl, whatever else you might on better acquaintance be inclined to say about her.

2

The relationship between Louella and Calvin was a hard one to work around. Age and experience didn't indicate the correct paths to understanding. Louella was the experienced one of the pair, and was the youngster. Calvin was the innocent, yet was four years older. When they got together in the first place, it was nevertheless Calvin that made the running, and when they broke up what looked like being a settled and dependable relationship, it was Louella that made the break. What went on between them to create this reverse logic of attraction and rejection was their own business. Maybe Louella, being still a child, didn't value Calvin's innocence the way others might; and maybe Calvin, trying to acquire experience by the handful and catch up with his years, failed to see that experience of the world has little to do with chronological years.

Calvin had broken with his family and a strict upbringing the previous year and thrown himself at hedonism like a dervish gone to the devil. He came into the town from the west side parched and athirst for life. He found the Rex Hotel without trouble, and there he found Louella. He was attractive, young and not worried about her reputation as a man-pleaser, unlike the other young men of the town, who listened too closely to their mothers. It was attraction at first sight. When it threatened to turn into love, they both backed off. They still occasionally went on dates and spent the night together as if they had once been married and couldn't see anything wrong in reminiscence. They were just good friends, genuinely.

Now Louella sat down on the bar stool beside Calvin and turned toward him so that she could link her arm through his and still reach the ashtray and the Coke that Old Gomez (he had no other name that anyone knew) put before her in greeting. Her chest gleamed slightly with the sweat of walking from Nick's, and her long legs pushed themselves out from under her skirt as if they needed their freedom.

"You look like that Joan Crawford," he said.

"She's a brunette in her new movie," Louella answered.

"That ain't what I mean," Calvin said, and raised his eyes to hers. "You're off work early."

"I'm off at the right time," Louella said. "The lunch girl is always late. I didn't wait for her today."

"This Sam business?" Calvin asked. When Louella nodded, he continued, "What's he in trouble about?"

"Labor," she said. "Some sort of trouble with the pickers. Best I could figure out is that they're telling him what they will and won't do."

"That's Sam," Calvin said. "Got acrost 'em again, I bet. He don't think, that's Sam's trouble."

Louella wondered if she had been right to think there was something more to Sam's trouble than that. He was a very up and down sort of person, on top of the world one day and down at the bottom of the heap the next. When he was at either of those extremes, he always seemed to know why he had got there, however, and that wasn't what she had seen this morning from him. She poked a finger under Calvin's ribs, making him giggle and dip his elbow to move her finger away.

"I think it's more than that," she said.

"What does Lee Roy say?" Calvin asked.

"Nothing," Louella answered, shifting her weight and legs

110

so that she could look at her hair in the mirror behind the bar. "Sam's on his own with this. Nobody else knows about it. He's too mixed up to tell anyone yet. I think he knows he's made a mess of his pickers and he's ashamed."

"Well, he'll have to get unmessed in a hurry if he's ready to start picking," Calvin said.

"Yeah, but I think he thinks you're all in the same boat and you just don't know it yet," Louella declared. "And what's got him ashamed is he thinks he started everything off wrong for all you growers." She thought more about it, then gave up on the whole topic. She shrugged her shoulders, examining the emergent cleavage in the mirror and picking up the blouse demurely, then letting it fall just so over her breasts. "I don't know anything about it," she said, "it's you guys' problem not mine." She turned her attention to her fingernails, chipping away a piece of nail polish that had snagged and lifted.

"Today's Saturday, ain't it," Calvin said.

"All day," Louella answered.

"Lee Roy might be in the house," Calvin said. "Maybe that dumb old lady of his can get him to the phone. It's their day to shop. I'll bet he don't know nothing about this."

"That's what I told you," said Louella.

"I'll go use the phone. I'll see you later." Calvin was already moving toward the door when he said this.

Louella called after him, "You're in a big hurry all of a sudden. Why didn't you believe me in the first place?" She finished her Coke and stood up. She thought she could hear Doc Hawser in the back bar. He would come out front here when he was good and drunk, and before lunch he could be too much to take. She waved goodbye to Old Gomez and walked along the street to her room. Saturday mornings the dentist finished his appointments at eleven. She could read and rest for a little while without the sound of the drill to put her teeth on edge.

Calvin walked straight to the cigar store, where Tom Potter asked Eunice Olson, the operator, for Lee Roy

111

Stagg's telephone number and waited while she rang it. Mrs Stagg answered the phone, her voice thin and distant. Tom could picture her holding the instrument almost at arm's length as if something evil might crawl out of the mouthpiece at any second.

"Hello, Mrs Stagg?" Tom rushed on, not giving her time to reply. "I need to speak to your husband, Mrs Stagg."

Potter looked over at Calvin and winked. They both knew the reason for the lie. Calvin the sinner, a traitor to his very name, would be unlikely to be able to bring Lee Roy to the phone, because Mrs Stagg would have nothing to do with him simply on the basis of his reputation. It remained to be seen if Tom, the owner-keeper of an establishment which lived on smoking tobacco and made its real money on poker, would pass the screen of her disapproval. The mesh of virtue can be a very fine one indeed, to the virtuous.

Mrs Stagg sighed and wheezed a little, high-pitched cough. "I'm not sure he's in the house right now," she said. Even the virtuous can be liars in a good cause.

"Can you find him for me, please?" Tom persisted. "It's important." He quickly amended the sentence, "It may be very important to Mr Stagg."

"Who is it who's calling, please?" she said.

"Mr Potter," Tom answered.

She took in the significance of the name, and then tried a gentle pry into her husband's affairs. "I hope it's nothing personal, Mr Potter."

"He'd have to tell you that himself," Potter answered, glaring at the unseen enemy.

"I'll give him your message, then," Mrs Stagg said, suddenly speaking in a voice that was altogether more businesslike and definite. Potter guessed that Stagg had come into the kitchen to see what the call was about, and he profoundly hoped her question had been overheard. Even Lee Roy Stagg was entitled to a private life beyond his wife's snooping.

Potter struck. "Would you put him on, please, Mrs Stagg. It's important."

She started her whine again, then: "But I don't know –"

Raising his voice a few notches into the range where irritation strays into anger, and letting her know it, Potter cut in with, "It's your husband I want to speak to, Mrs Stagg, not you. He's there." In a softer voice he added, "Please call him to the phone."

For an answer there were some whispers and an ineffective muffling of the telephone. Tom held the earpiece out so Calvin could hear as a man's voice came through with a gesture at being the busy, decisive, interrupted but forgiving male of a thousand caricatures.

"Hello. Hello. Lee Roy Stagg here. Is that Tom Potter calling me? Can I do something for you, Mr Potter?'

"It's Calvin Whitmore, Mr Stagg, Mr Potter placed the call for me." Calvin broke the pause that followed by adding, "We was afraid you might not accept a call from me."

There was another pause with more whispers from the Stagg kitchen, and then an audible, "Just go out and close the door behind you!" Then a sterner Lee Roy spoke. "What can I do for you, Mr Whitmore?"

"Calvin, Mr Stagg, not my dad, just Calvin."

Finally certain that his wife was out of earshot and would not hear him conversing with this notorious sinner, Lee Roy said, "Well, Calvin, what's going on? I'm surprised to hear you on my telephone, I can tell you that. Tom Potter too. Something's going on, that's for certain sure."

"I think something's going wrong, Mr Stagg, if it ain't already gone that way. It's Sam Tolin. He's been in Nick's saying that his pickers have got him on the run." Calvin added mildly, "Thought you ought to know, that's all."

"How bad is it, Calvin?" asked Lee Roy.

"Don't rightly know. Bad enough so he's not looking forward to telling you about it," said Calvin.

There was a prolonged Mmmmmmmm from Lee Roy.

When he spoke again, his tone had changed and he was no longer concealing his alarm.

"Has it got anything to do with me?" Lee Roy snapped.

"You're the farmers' co-op man," Calvin said; "sooner or later it's your baby, Mr Stagg. Reckon it's yours about now."

The audacity of Calvin's challenge stopped Lee Roy in mid-bluster. His answer was sharp but collaborative. "What are we going to do, Calvin?"

"You and your missus are coming into town to shop, ain't you, Mr Stagg? I reckon that's where Sam's at, up at the Safeway very likely."

Lee Roy grunted his acknowledgment.

"If he ain't there, I'll scout around town until I find that truck of his, which shouldn't be too hard to do, and then I'll get him to where you can talk to him." Calvin stopped, aware of the snag he had just struck. None of the usual meeting places would do, since Lee Roy couldn't be seen in a place that served liquor, sold cigarettes or cigars, or even had an edge of luxury like a marble counter top to recommend it, which put the soda fountain out of reach.

"Where in hades do you meet people, Mr Stagg?" Calvin asked, curious as well as genuine in his concern.

"I got to come check my mailbox. I'll meet him in the parking lot, around the back of the post office," answered Lee Roy.

"You got rural delivery and a box in town both, have you?" said Calvin. "You got a secret life, Mr Stagg? Okay, Mr Stagg. I'll have him there in about thirty minutes for you, unless he's left town."

His answer from Lee Roy was the telephone clicking dead.

Calvin got into his own truck and drove to the Safeway store, where he toured through the parking lot looking for the piebald truck. When it wasn't there, he drove back to Greenfield Avenue meaning to turn uptown to see if Sam had parked on a side street. At the last minute Calvin confused the driver of a LaSalle behind him by turning west

114

on Greenfield until he got to a cross street beyond the canal, then left and left again to bring him into Park Street. Past the jail he found Sam sitting in his truck behind Garfield Park, taking advantage of the shade from the trees.

"What you doing, Sam?" Calvin said as he went up to him.

"Thinkin'," was the reply. "And gettin' nowhere."

"Lee Roy's comin' into town to help you straighten things out," Calvin said. "He wants to meet you in about twenty minutes at the post office. In the parking lot."

Sam flared up like a match. "This is my problem, not Lee Roy Stagg's!" he said. "What's he want to do, mixing in my business?"

"Because I told him from the sound of it, the pickers have started on you but they got the whole bunch of us growers in their sights," Calvin answered. "You reckon that's right? If I got it wrong, I apologize and I'll go call off the meetin' with Lee Roy myself."

Up-and-down Sam went down again. "Oh, I'll meet him, but I don't know what good it's gonna do me. You guys are sittin' back waitin' to see what happens to me, I know that, but I'm the one on the line. I'm the guy with the apricots."

"I'll allow I'm going to learn from you, Sam, but that don't mean I'm going to leave you hangin' out there with the rest of the wash," Calvin said. "That's why I called Lee Roy."

"Okay, Calvin," Sam said. "Okay. I'll meet him." He pressed the starter and pushed the truck into reverse as soon as the engine caught.

"You got fifteen minutes to make a two-minute trip to the post office, Sam!" Calvin shouted it over the noise of the engine as he backed off the running board.

"You made me feel better, Calvin," Sam said and tried a weak smile. "Reckon I can go to the toilet now."

Sam drove back to Nick's, where he parked and rushed in, shouting to Nick in the kitchen, "Got to use your facilities, Nick, thanks." That done, he drove to the post office and found the parking lot. This was strange territory to a farmer, since all their mail came Rural Free Delivery to a tin box on a post on the roadside. Mrs Tolin came to the post office every once in a while to keep them in stamps and check the General Delivery window to see if someone, not knowing their address, had tried to get in touch. Sam stayed away – it wasn't a part of his world. He wasn't averse to living in a town. When they retired, he and his wife intended to live in a nice little house in Red Branch, if the place wasn't too crowded by then. But he didn't like talking business in the town. Those regular visits to the bank manager were as much as he needed of the kind of business you did in a town.

Nevertheless, into the parking lot rolled Lee Roy Stagg in his black Chrysler car, a sober, rectangular, Godfearing car with only the wheels and their attendant fenders to break up the overwhelming impression of a set of polished black boxes made miraculously mobile. He was alone, being on a man's errand. He beckoned Sam over to his car and made no move to open the passenger door for him. By the time he got in and settled, Sam felt himself on trial.

Never a man for preliminaries, Lee Roy said, "Tell me all about it, Sam. What you got yourself into this time?"

It occurred to Sam to keep his dignity, get back out of the car, say nothing, and go his own way. He did nothing about this momentary glimpse of the power of positive thinking, however. Instead, he fixed his eyes on a part of the hood ornament that sent the sun's glare in a dazzling line that looked like a sword held vertically, and confessed.

3

Once Lee Roy had heard the whole story, the cross examination began.

"All right now," he said, "let's take things one at a time."

He went through all the facts again, getting all the detail Sam could recall. As he did, his resolution took a firm hold on Lee Roy. He was going to be easy on Sam. He was going to treat him with a reasonable degree of leniency, laced with a dose of realism. Sam was going to be made to realize before the conference was over that he was a jackass in sheep's clothing and had made a difficulty into a disaster unless people with more savvy than he had shown came in to clean up the mess. Lee Roy wanted both hands on the controls.

When he felt satisfied he had all the information, he went on to a more probing style, letting Sam know that he had missed far too many tricks along the way. "Who was this tall fellow you were talking to?" Lee Roy asked.

"I was talking to all of 'em," Sam answered. "We had a meeting at Las Cruces, away from the camp. Took 'em there in my truck myself. I told you that twice."

Lee Roy was determined to be very patient. "I know that, Sam, I understand that. But who was this young fellow, this spokesman?"

117

"Never saw him before," Sam answered. "Looked like Henry Fonda, not enough to hold it agin' him."

"How did he get to be the spokesman?" Lee Roy asked. "Did they say anything about that?"

"Said they elected him. Guess they did," Sam said.

"Or somebody else did," Lee Roy countered almost under his breath.

"Who else is there?" Sam asked.

"The union," Lee Roy said, and sighed.

Lee Roy was right. When Cappy Petrillo got that warning from the buyers up north and went to Red Branch to look over the situation for himself, he drove for an hour beyond Placid City to a town called Delphi. It was a one-street town made up of a double row of wooden stores and a few houses, ranged on both sides of the Southern Pacific tracks, set back from them about fifty yards. No trees showed their heads from backyards behind the houses, and where other towns might have softened the sun's fierceness with a strip of grass each side of the railroad tracks, here there were only tumbleweeds and puncture vine and a few stalks of dried out daisies to show there had ever been moisture. The town could boast of a wooden water tank for freight trains in trouble, a row of electric and telephone poles running beside the tracks, and an abandoned switching tower. It was like a movie set that Hollywood had given up on because it was too damned depressing to use for a family audience, the sort of place that made a man take up swearing.

On its southern edge, separated by enough empty ground to make it clear that it was located in Delphi by necessity and not by choice, was a collection of motel cabins. Some were of stucco and the other, better ones were built of wood with a porch running around all four sides. Cappy got there after midnight and went straight to a wooden cabin reserved and left unlocked for him. At about daybreak, before other people would be likely to be up, a little black Ford drove straight to Cappy's cabin. The tall young man who would

118

later be at Las Cruces camp got out of the dusty car and knocked at the cabin door. Sheltering behind the door because he didn't want to be seen, Cappy opened the door and the man went in.

The man called himself Vinnie Duffy. In the government camps and in the migrant workers' campsites he was known as Irish. He wasn't Irish at all, or if he was, that was a part of family history that he knew nothing about. He had been Vin Akerman, an Okie who came west with his family when they were blown out of the Dust Bowl. He had buried his father and seen his mother taken care of by joining up with her sister's family working the crops east of Turlock. Then he had gone south to Imperial Valley where there was good money working for farmers who hired Okies to keep the Mexicans out of the area. He had been driving a truckload of workers toward a part of the valley where the lettuce picking was due to start when a sheriff's deputy flagged him down. The deputy pulled Vin so far over to the side of the road that the heavily loaded truck threatened to topple into an irrigation ditch. Tugging on his badge to make sure Vin was intimidated, and bouncing his billy club in his hand, the deputy started asking the line of questions that meant Vin was not suspected of whatever crime was supposed to have happened, he was just being warned. Vin was tired, and tired of being warned by deputies whose insolent, insinuating voices told him that he had to reply to their meaningless questions even though he would be disbelieved, that they knew they were talking to a criminal and a liar, that it was only a matter of time until he trapped himself and fell into the power of the law, at which time the deputies would finally thoroughly enjoy themselves at his expense. The deputy poked the billy club in his chest when he got to the part about smart-guy Okies and the way they all eventually made a mis-step, then knocked Vin's hat off his head by backhanding the brim where it was pushed high above his forehead. Thinking about it afterwards and trying to explain it to the judge, Vin supposed the thing that had made him come out

119

of the cab fighting was that the club missed his nose by only a hair, and that it was obvious that the deputy's finesse with the club was the result of long practice on people like Vin. It was no defense, and for an Okie to plead provocation by a deputy sheriff was to buy a ticket to jail with no chance of passing Go. Vin said, "Just sentence me," which the judge did, passing the sort of severe sentence which fails to warn others and is guaranteed to make an underground hero out of the convicted criminal.

Vin had been sent to prison up north near Sacramento rather than nearer where he had committed the crime in the south of the valley. The location, which was also supposed to be a deterrent by being seen to be a kind of isolation, on the contrary made it convenient for his mother to visit him, and she brought his brothers to see him. He hadn't had any brothers, or sisters either, and the men who came were those who were trying to put together a self-defense movement among the migrant workers, especially those with Okie in their background. It wasn't long before one of Cappy Petrillo's organizers had recruited Vin. He behaved himself and after serving just under two years he was released from prison, hitchhiking his way north to Sonoma County, to a place where some cabins in a redwood forest were the setting for a small school paid for and run by Harry Bridges' Teamsters Union. The San Francisco papers, which regularly condemned Bridges for anything they could get their typewriters into on the reasonable grounds that he was a Communist apologist, said the school was supported by money from the Communist Party. The publicity forced it to be closed shortly after Vin was indoctrinated and trained. With a new name and a rewritten past history, he wove himself into the migrant population that worked the farms of the west side of the central valley. When Cappy needed someone who had not yet worked as far north as Red Branch, Vinnie Duffy, also known as Irish Duffy, was his man.

*

Lee Roy Stagg knew none of this, aside from seeing the pattern that was emerging. A union man, unacknowledged but to all intents official, had been planted at Las Cruces. Someone knew the area well, knowing that Sam Tolin was a weak employer and would be first away from the start when the picking began. Probably, if Red Branch was the target as the rumor said, there was an organizer in every camp and it would be useless to try to sidetrack Sam's negotiations by going to another camp for non-union labor.

"Let me ask you this question, Sam," Lee Roy said. "How'd you ever expect to make any money? What they were asking as the rate for a pound was too high for you or anybody else to pay, and you know it."

Sam was contrite but firm. "I knew the co-op would play along, Lee Roy. They'd give me a rate the pickers would never know about. What they didn't know couldn't hurt 'em."

"Yeah, but supposing they have people in the co-op, or maybe they poke around until they see a piece of paper that says what you're really getting," Lee Roy answered. "Sam, what I'm trying to get through to you is this: You are not dealing with a bunch of stumblebum pickers trying to put enough money together so they can go back to skid row and their wine bottles. You've got an organization against you. And it's against all of us."

The reality frightened Sam. It was what he didn't want to hear. When he didn't reply, Lee Roy continued the process of taking power out of Sam's hands. "We've got the makings of what's called workers' demands here. They come in with a high price package that they never expect to get. They want us to negotiate pay and what they call working conditions. That means things like rest days. And that eight hour day, Sam, how in the name of all things holy could you let that go by? No, I'm sorry, I shouldn't have said that. You missed that one, though, you really missed a big one there, because what comes next is overtime, and if you say Sunday is a rest day and you have to work Sundays to get the crop in, then you pay extra again. Factories pay double

121

the rate. Where's your profit gone, Sam? This grading business now, that's a foot in the door. If they decided to grade for first quality and the packers didn't agree with their grading, who's right? Instead of the boss, you're in the middle. Sam, you're the man ought to be paying the piper, calling the tune. But where are you? You're standing watching the union man get his orders on the telephone, probably your own phone, and pass on the orders to you. You're the banker for Cappy Petrillo, that's what you are, and nothing more."

Lee Roy stopped speaking abruptly, as though there was more to be said but he thought it wise to keep it to himself. It was just the technique to use on Sam, who pleaded with his eyes to Lee Roy to spare him any more of the horrors.

"What do we do, Lee Roy?" Sam asked. "The bank owns so much of me that I can't let this crop go bad. I just can't."

Lee Roy looked away and frowned, making up his mind about something important. When he turned to Sam again, it was the face of a deeply concerned man. "Sam, you've hit on the real trouble there, but I don't think you or any of the others have any idea of it. I don't want you to think I've gone crazy or I'm imagining things. I just want you to listen and do some thinking and see if I don't make sense."

Sam nodded, emboldened by being taken into Lee Roy's confidence in this way. Lee Roy framed his preamble with great care. "I don't want you to get all upset or in a panic, now, you understand, don't you?" Sam nodded again. "Sam," Lee Roy continued, "the idea behind all this is to bust you, make you go bankrupt. It's not about workers and their pay and their rights, not now. That comes later. They want to break you, and then they want to break more of us farmers."

Sam struggled for a rational rejoinder. "That don't make good sense, Lee Roy, there's no money in it for them if I'm in the poorhouse. The bank will sell me up, they won't work my land and hire people to do it."

Lee Roy intensified the pressure of his eyes. "Let's say

just for the purposes of trying to understand this business that these people make you pay out so much that you can't meet your notes with the bank," Lee Roy said.

"I'd know that I was paying out too much before it got that far, Lee Roy, I know how to keep my books," Sam said.

"This is just a 'for instance', Sam," Lee Roy explained. "Let's say it happened the way I say. And let's say the same thing happens to Pete King over to the east of you, because he's about the next to pick his fruit. And then Schumacher along by the river. Whitmore's pretty safe, he's got money, they probably couldn't get him, but then they might go for Andy Allen, he spends a lot of time at the bank these days."

"How about the Indian, Proudfoot?" Sam said. "He's no better off than I am, maybe even worse if you believe what he says."

"All right," Lee Roy said, encouraged by Sam's under-standing of this script for regional disaster, "there you are. Who's the bank for all of you? Bank of America. What happens at the end of the month? You all default, can't pay, you're all up for foreclosure. What does the bank do? They can't sell you all up. They can't collect their money. They have to pay you to stay in business, they give you new loans, something you can afford, which means less money for the bank and less for you. Next time you have a crop ready this summer, same thing happens. The bank is deeper in the red, and the same thing happens with all the farmers one right after the other. The farmers are gonna lose, sure, Sam, and you know all time that somebody can come along and buy you out for next to nothing just so the bank can get some money out of it. It's bad for you, no doubt about it, but who's it really bad for?"

Sam had understood. "They got plenty of money some-where, Lee Roy, my loan ain't gonna break the Bank of America if it don't get paid, now is it?"

"We're not talking just about you, Sam," Lee Roy insisted.

Sam breathed deeply. "You reckon they could break the bank that way? Lordy, Lordy. Why?"

Lee Roy flinched at this near miss with blasphemy but stuck to the point. "Do that up and down the valley and it'd all be over bar the singing of *The Internationale*. That's the fight song of the Communists, Sam, and that is what we are up against. I'm convinced of it."

Sam was awed by the spectacle that had come into view. "You reckon we oughta tell the government, Lee Roy?"

Lee Roy had thought about this already. "We'll let the newspapers do that for us. They're pretty good at it. We got to get a few other people behind us that will make Red Branch too hot for Mr Petrillo and his boys."

Sam said, "You've already got this figured out, haven't you, Lee Roy? How come you done that?"

"I've seen this coming for months now," Lee Roy said, "if I do say so myself. I don't want to brag, but I guess I'm the sort of person who can see when someone is coming up at me for a reason I don't like. I could almost smell this one coming."

"Have you got a plan?" Sam asked.

"I have," Lee Roy said with satisfaction. "You're the key to it, Sam, you're the one to make it work. It'll take guts to do it, I warn you."

"I've got a lot to lose, Lee Roy," Sam answered.

"What we have to do is get those pickers to strike," Lee Roy said.

Appalled and astonished, Sam could hardly form the words to reply. "Now hold on, that's just what I don't want, no sir, that's just what I want to keep from happening. It'll ruin me, Lee Roy, you know that."

Lee Roy tried to soothe him. "Hold on now, Sam, just hold on for a minute. What we're going to do right now, you and me, we're going to find Roger Preece."

Sam said, "The bank manager? It's Saturday afternoon, he don't work but banker's hours."

"We're going to his house," Lee Roy insisted, "and we're

going to get him to open up his office at the bank and we're going to tell him all about it. When he sees the picture of what's in store for him, there won't be any foreclosing. He'll stand behind you, and he'll promise that, or we don't do a thing to stop his bank from being ruined by these union people. We won't force them to strike unless the bank is behind us, Sam, that's a promise. Okay? Then we're going to tell Mr Halbkeller so he can get it in the papers, and the Commander of the American Legion, whoever that is this year."

"Jimmy Sturmer," Sam offered.

"Jimmy Sturmer," Lee Roy repeated, "he can get to the ear of the State Representative. Between us you and me are going to make sure the Rotary Club gets to know before tonight's out, and the Lions, and the Twenties and Thirties, and who's a Mason we can tell? Never mind, bank managers are always Masons, aren't they? And the preachers, they'll get things going, this will be a good one for them."

"You've lost me," Sam said. "I'm way behind."

"We're making history, Sam," Lee Roy said. Grim still, but now in a triumphal mood, Lee Roy had his mind's eye on a new and grand perspective. "We're fighting a Communist conspiracy, Sam, that's what it is. Cappy Petrillo and his Russian buddies aren't going to get away with it. No, sir. He's after our kind of capitalism, Sam, and that's what makes us tick. By the time the big city newspapers get a hold of this, Red Branch will be fighting for the American way of life. This is going to be a good one, Sam. Yes, sir."

Before the flood control project put a dam on the Placid River and throttled down the flow in the Red Branch of the Placid, the people who liked a little more privacy than was afforded by Greenfield Avenue, and who didn't mind the light of their wealth being obscured by the bushel of living on a side street, built expensive houses on Bridge Street. The bridge was narrow and inclined to be rickety, made so by each winter's floods. It collapsed about every third year, with the consequent closure of the street for six or eight months while it was tested, strengthened and repaired. It made for a nice, quiet street. Roger Preece lived in a two-storey house with long, slightly curving rooflines and gabled dormer windows, which was an architect's idea of an English country house. The architect was the wife of the former owner of the *Red Branch Herald* newspaper, who had never been to England but had seen bigger versions of this house style when she visited Hollywood. The house was still sufficiently impressive that it made a strange picture when the amalgam of Sam's trucks pulled up at the curb, followed by Lee Roy's black Chrysler. The two men were kept waiting in the front hall with the door left open while Roger was found, and then admitted only to his den. Mrs Preece was a great guardian of her husband's private life, so that she was all the more astonished when Roger left the house with the men, saying he was going back to the bank and would phone her from there about their dinner date that evening. Preece's maroon Oldsmobile led the short cavalcade to the bank, all three of them parking on East Park Street to avoid giving the people at the Rex Hotel a reason to think that something was up. Up, however, it was. When Roger phoned his wife at a quarter past seven that evening to say that they couldn't get to Baldino's Restaurant before eight-thirty, a trap had been set for Vinnie Duffy which would bring violence to Red Branch once again.

The Angel's Wing
and the Voice of God

Lee Roy Stagg came to Red Branch from Kansas when he was already a grown man with a wife and a mission. He had also already beaten the wife into submission, not with his fists but with his principles. She kept out of the way, stayed indoors, cooked his meals and washed his clothes, let him lead the way at the grocery store on Saturdays – and pay the bill, since he controlled the family purse – didn't gossip, didn't talk with other women over the phone, did in essence everything right except bear children. Around Lee Roy that was the great unmentionable.

What was overwhelmingly mentionable was God. He had come to the town with his religious convictions wrapped around him skin tight. He cast his eyes at the available churches and settled for the Presbyterian Church. The building suited him perfectly. It was a dull gray, dour, depressing building of stucco standing high up atop a half basement. The steps were steep and long, making the sinner reach his pew with the blood beating in his ears sufficient to make him aware of mortality even before the first prayer. The preacher was also ideal for Lee Roy's concept of religion. He drummed away in a nasal baritone at peculiarly private sins, the sins of the conscience that are revealed by God to His believers and are cured only by withdrawal from temptation, the tempters being people not of your persuasion. Sin existed only if you dealt with the irreligious in a way that assumed they were equal to you in the eyes of God. Grind the heathen down, and hasten the ways of the Lord. If there wasn't a direct line of descent from the first Scottish Calvinist who preached there down to the incumbent, Reverend Ward, it wasn't for want of ironclad assurance that God's elect were here and only here in the Red Branch Presbyterian Church. The gospel had been changed from "Be still and know that I am Lord" to "Be still and know that you are chosen", and a more selfish, benighted collection of God-fearing hypocrites had not yet been found that far west of Aberdeen.

Then there was the choir. Lee Roy remarked often on the bliss of the moment when he first heard the choir. It was, he said, a real old-fashioned choir; people sang because they loved God so much they just had to sing about it. Mr Cook, for instance, the assistant district attorney, might be said to sing a little flat, or else his undecorated tenor was possibly pushed above his natural register. It was, however, an honest voice, and the transparent purity of his motives for singing in the choir seemed to relieve him of criticism both for some failure in technique and for the way that his virulent halitosis cleared the ends of the pews directly in front of the choir's benches. But Lee Roy said, while his wife nodded in agreement, that if he had been inclined to be critical, he would have forgiven anything for the soprano glory of Mrs Wilson. A tall woman, full chested, her glossy hair suspiciously black for a woman of about fifty, she had sung every solo for thirty years in a singleminded dedication of her talent to her Lord that allowed no other choir member to be even mentioned in the same breath as the word solo. Her voice soared in a rich tremolo that, combined with Mrs Cook's work on the organ, flattened the competition from the choir. She won hands down every Sunday of her life.

Another joy for Lee Roy was Mr Halbkeller, who weekdays was the deputy editor of the town's only newspaper but whose real calling in life was the position of deacon he had first been elected to fill in 1923. To mark his gratefulness to his Lord for honoring him with this call, he had begun that day to grow the nail of the little finger of his left hand, without let or hindrance. It now curved like a miniature scimitar toward the palm of his hand, and shone with the best lacquer of which the Red Branch Drugstore was possessed. When the dark walnut collection plate was borne round by Mr Halbkeller, its circle of green baize inviting the congregation to cover it with something similarly green but made of paper, the oddly sinister fingernail, held high up out of danger, seemed almost to smirk as if it was its owner's pet. It was that kind of private devotion, inexplicable but inspired, that Lee Roy Stagg felt called to, and he joined the church like a man possessed of all the attributes of sainthood required of any devotional cult worthy of the name. In no time at all he was invited to reorganize the Sunday School. What better job for a childless man who didn't particularly like people?

Lee Roy emerged to everyone's surprise as a master of membership campaigns. He was a natural as a salesman for God. He built the Sunday School in three galloping years into an organization that knew its product and sold it with inspiration. The highlight of the Sunday School year changed from Christmas, with its pageant and carols and Christmas play, to the spring "mission" that he devised. Each year the mission was something different. The most talked about was the year of the Ark. Each Sunday for six weeks the children earned the right to load a pair of animals on board their individual arks, first by simply attending, then by knowing the week's Bible passage by heart and saying it out loud in front of the assembled parents before Sunday School proper began. They also earned the right to load single animals by being on time, being clean, singing the hymns by heart, and so forth. Little extras earned the right to load a female animal, while the more important ones loaded a male. The big extra was to bring a stranger to Sunday School, which

129

gave the prospective Noah loading rights on two pairs of animals of his choice. The large Sunday School room was divided into arks constructed of cardboard boxes. Around the edges of the arks were cards with line drawings of the animals successfully loaded. In the prow of the arks sat each competing, prospective Noah, with behind him his wife, his three sons and their wives. It was up to each aspirant Noah to nag, bully and cajole his "family" to support his efforts to if necessary sink the ark with the sheer weight of animals before the deadline. The boy who became Noah that year went on to become a very successful warden of a reformatory for young criminals.

The year of Lee Roy's fourth mission was the year of the voyages of Saint Paul. It was agreed among the Presbyters that, though Paul had made a few errors along the road to Damascus, he was a suitable subject lesson for the children. Lee Roy scoured the county for row boats, hauled them to the Sunday School room and propped them up so they wouldn't rock too precariously, and prepared a chart of the voyage from Asia Minor to Athens. Every boat had its log, and every task of the Sunday School successfully completed earned an entry in the log that propelled the boat along. The bonus of sailing through a terrible storm was earned by bringing a strange child, something difficult to earn since every child in the town seemed to have been dragooned into Sunday School during one mission or another, and it didn't count if the stranger was a Catholic attending out of curiosity. The competition to be a real saint was fierce. Some of the faithful had worried at first that it might be sacrilegious, but after Lee Roy pointed out that Paul was a flawed saint the opposition disappeared.

The actual lessons at Sunday School were taught in classes that met in small rooms throughout the church building wherever they could be found. The Mission of Saint Paul to the Athenians, as the big sign labeled it on the exterior of the church, had attracted so much attention that the spaces to accommodate the children had become hard to find. By the fourth Sunday of the mission the twelve-year-old boys – the classes never mixed the sexes – had to meet in a storage room. In it were the costumes and paraphernalia of last year's Christmas pageant. The diminished status of that event was evident in the condition of the things being stored. The angel wings, in particular, had seen much heavenlier days. Their fringed tissue paper, in imitation of white, celestial feathers, was now sadly limp and grubby. In the class was Ledyard Job. That day Ledyard, who was making an effort to be Paul for his mother's sake, had brought a boy new to the town. Whispers said his parents had been Okies, and it was true that his best suit of clothes was a new pair of denim overalls with copper buckles. However, Billy's dad was a hard worker in a local garage, and except for blowing his nose on his fingers in public had adopted the ways of his betters.

Billy sat attentively in Ledyard's boat as the preliminary events of Sunday School proceeded, even seeming to know some of the hymns and songs that were played. It was plain from his face when the time came to go into the class that he had some reservations about the school part of Sunday School, however. He whispered fiercely to Ledyard when they got to the little storeroom and had to be shushed so the opening prayer could be said. The usual teacher was unable to be there because his wife had morning sickness, so the class was being taught by Mr Halbkeller. Billy caught sight of the famous Halbkeller fingernail, which kept him interested for a while, watching how it was protected in the gestures that its owner had adopted. He had chosen to sit in the corner up against the pile of angel wings. Finding nothing else to do, he tore off a piece of white tissue paper and, using the pencil intended for the end-of-class quiz, wrote to Ledyard, "When are you going to pay me off?" He passed this by way of several hands to Ledyard, who read it and ignored it without even looking toward Billy. Billy consequently smouldered and glared, and Mr Halbkeller decided this was a heathen who was not worthy of communication in

131

his present state. Shortly afterwards, the first white spitwad hit Ledyard. After two or three of these, Ledyard flicked one back when the teacher had glanced away and, having accepted the challenge, was locked into retaliation. The white missiles flew silently and annoyingly past Mr Halbkeller, who was attempting to convince himself that the whole episode was not happening. He was about to say the closing prayer a bit early and get the boys back to their boats when Ledyard miscalculated and flicked a return in full view of Mr Halbkeller. Caught up in the spirit of conflict, balked in his spiritual duty, the teacher in him grasped the challenge as a way out of his frustration.

"Ledyard," he shouted, "I've a mind to take you by the ear and make you apologize on your knees for your sinful behavior!" He paused, almost out of breath with anger. "What would you think to that?"

Always quicker than he should have been with his retorts, Ledyard answered, "I'd guess I'd have to find out if you can see without your glasses. I'd take them off and see if you could still find my ear."

Mr Halbkeller grabbed for Ledyard's ear and twisted it as if it was detachable, pulling the boy forward and pushing him onto his knees at the same time. Ledyard defied the pain of moving against the twist, reached up and pulled the glasses off Halbkeller's nose. When Mr Halbkeller didn't let up the pressure, Ledyard snapped the tortoiseshell frame of the glasses and let the lenses fall to the floor where, in his exertions, Mr Halbkeller stepped on one of them and smashed it. Finally he had Ledyard on his knees.

"Apologize!" he shouted.

"Go to hell!" Ledyard answered – a directive, in the context of the Presbyterian Church, that had never before been given to the deacon.

The loud voices had brought Lee Roy into action. He opened the door onto the spectacle of a boy apparently being punished for breaking Mr Halbkeller's glasses. Stagg got the boys out of the room and into their boats, Ledyard sobbing and holding a crimson ear, then led the almost blind Mr Halbkeller into the Sunday School room and away from the scene of the crime in order to discuss their best course of action. Lee Roy said the best thing was to let everyone calm down, discuss it quietly, get the whole story, and let the incident be settled between the boy's parents and Mr Halbkeller. The Deacon would not hear of it, demanding that Ledyard be publicly drummed out of Sunday School post haste and his own dignity restored by a parental apology before the whole adult congregation in the course of the church service. In response to Lee Roy's advice to temper his wrath, Mr Halbkeller exhibited the concrete evidence of the boy's iniquity – the famous fingernail, the symbol of devotion to God's favor, had been shorn of at least two of its former three inches.

Playing to the audience of Sunday School children, he lifted up the maimed member for all to see, pointing with his right hand at Ledyard sniveling in his boat. "This is the Devil's work!" he pronounced.

Momentarily lapsing into the sensible belief that rational thinking and fair play were required, Lee Roy said, "Oh, now, come on, Mr Halbkeller. I'm sure he didn't mean to do that. He's not that bad, really."

In the list of innocent statements that look idiotic when examined in retrospect, Lee Roy's character reference for Ledyard comes somewhere near the top. As happened with a frequency and certainty that was accepted with an outward shrug but an inner terror, there came at that moment what Red Branch refers to as a roller. The earth under the church rose and fell and seemed to turn slightly as it heaved. The Athens-bound boats toppled from their props, and the three-globed chandelier on its ten foot chain swung in an arc that seemed to cross the whole ceiling of the Sunday School room. The children screamed and ran for the door, while Lee Roy and Mr Halbkeller, shaken to their knees, waited to see if it was going to be succeeded by a major, destructive

133

VI

Sunday

2

At twenty minutes to nine Mr Halbkeller left his house
around the corner from Greenfield Avenue on Second Street
and walked briskly east on the avenue until he got to the
Courthouse square. Instead of the diagonal walk that would
have taken him to the side of the jail, he chose the sidewalk
that ran parallel to the canal as far as Park Street. Passing a
spot about a third of the way along, he had vague feelings of
displeasure but suppressed them. If he had allowed the
memory to surface, he would have recalled that this was the
place Mrs Koenig had stepped off the sidewalk to smell a
particularly beautiful rose one year and dropped dead as she
did so. It was a day too full of potential pleasure to be
marred by memories, however. He arrived at the First
Presbyterian Church at exactly ten minutes to nine, as he
did every Sunday. Mr and Mrs Butler were on duty already,
waiting to supervise the orderly entry into Sunday School of
the expected children. Mr Halbkeller nodded to them and
went through the Sunday School room to the rear of the
church, into what used to be the choir room. Here he
rearranged the chairs unnecessarily, since they were all in
perfect order, for the adult Bible study class for parents who
brought their children to Sunday school and stayed to take
them home. He and the minister would both have preferred

the parents to stay on for the morning service. Bible study shouldn't be looked on as second best, he knew, but it seemed a shame that the minister's sermon wasn't seen as in its way equally vital to their lives. Still, people made choices, and only God could bring them to the right one in the end. That didn't mean you shouldn't help with good advice when you knew God's mind on the subject.

At ten minutes after nine Lee Roy Stagg came into the room to find Mr Halbkeller sitting with his eyes closed at the desk at the front of the room, smiling contentedly. It was his characteristic appearance when he was praying. Aware that his attention was wanted, he sighed, continued in his pose for a few moments, then opened his eyes slowly.

"Good morning, Mr Stagg," he said.

"Good morning, Mr Halbkeller," said Lee Roy. "Sorry to bother you. I wanted to be sure I saw you before the service."

"It's all right, don't worry about it," Mr Halbkeller answered. "I can always go back to my prayers. I try to pray through the entire day, you know." He examined his fingernail and buffed it briefly on his leg.

Recognizing that Mr Halbkeller was deliberately leaving him to make the running with their conversation, Lee Roy hesitated. For all his sanctity, the Deacon sometimes showed the wiles of a very mortal man indeed and Lee Roy was unsure what the game was. He ploughed on. "I talked with Reverend Ward last night, and I wanted to make sure you had an idea of what it was all about before you hear from somebody else," he said.

Mr Halbkeller smiled his most frank and open smile. "The only 'somebody' I would be likely to hear from would be the minister himself, Mr Stagg, now wouldn't it?" he said. After a brief pause he added, "Which I did, of course, last night, by telephone." He paused again. "I gave him the benefit of what advice I could."

"Would you mind telling me what that was?" Lee Roy asked.

Mr Halbkeller pursed his lips. "Ooooo, nooooo," he squeezed out, "I couldn't do that. You'll have to wait for the sermon like everyone else. But I think you'll approve." He was pleased with his comment, making him *éminence grise* and consequently a cut above everyone else in one short sentence. "In fact I know you'll approve, Mr Stagg, you can count on that."

3

Calvin Whitmore left his truck parked outside the train depot, convenient for picking up the package that he expected would come in on the ten-o-eight. He walked up the avenue past the Mariposa Hotel, the shoeshine stand, Gump's, Orville's Menswear, Ladies Only Lingerie, the Cigar Store, Red Branch Drugstore and Soda Fountain, and the Oddfellows Professional Building. The hot sun seemed to be channelled down the avenue straight into him, and it felt good to be picked out as one out of one by something as important as the sun. He turned off the empty street into the staircase that led to the second floor offices of the Professional Building, went up to the dentist's reception landing, through the second door to the left and up those stairs to Louella's door, where he knocked.

"Who is it?" she called from inside. "The door's locked." He heard her slippers flop toward the door and her voice close to the door jamb as she said, "The thing's stuck. The key won't turn." The door shook violently as she tugged on it.

"Take the key out of the lock and slide it under the door," Calvin said. "It's me."

After some fumbling, the key appeared under the door, being pushed to where Calvin could get his fingers on it and tease it out. Pulling up on the doorknob with one hand, he used the other to turn the key with some difficulty, and then opened the door. Louella was standing in a pink and black kimono held in place with her arm. "The door's sagged and the lock needs oiling," he said. "You got any oil?"

Louella shook her head and yawned behind her free hand. The challenge of thinking where oil might be found was too much this early on a Sunday. Calvin went over to the refrigerator where he found, as he had expected, a small can of Crisco. He stuck the key into the white grease and turned it around several times.

"What are you doing?" Louella wailed. "I eat that stuff."

"Not uncooked, you don't," Calvin answered, carrying the key back to the door. He stuck it in the lock and twisted it a few times, working the cooking fat into the mechanism. As it progressively freed, the grinding noise was replaced with a squeal that made Louella cover both her ears, momentarily allowing the kimono to fall open. Calvin had a quick look before she recovered her modesty.

"You did that on purpose," she said.

"Works every time," he answered.

"What'd you come for?" Louella asked.

"I have to meet the ten-o-eight to get a package coming in from Stockton. Parts for the tractor. So I thought I'd come cook us breakfast, unless you want to do it." He waited for her to say no and tell him to go away, but instead she gestured toward the former broom cupboard that served as a Pullman kitchen.

"Go ahead," she said. "I only want toast and orange juice."

"No coffee?" he asked.

"Of course coffee," she said. "Turn around so I can get dressed."

He got the coffee started, then sliced bread while the motel-size gas oven warmed up for the toast. He started to get the butter and honey out of the refrigerator, remembering too late that this meant facing her, as a consequence getting full frontal Louella's shouted "Turn around!"

"I'm sorry, I'm sorry. Jesus, you'd think I'd never seen you naked," he complained.

"Don't swear on a Sunday," was her only answer.

He put some bread under the gas flame, and when one side was toasted he turned it and then slid in beside it an enamel plate with two eggs on it.

"You can turn around now," she said. A few minutes more and they were sitting down to breakfast at her card table.

Afterwards, over cigarettes, Louella said, "Okay, now what did you really come around for?"

"It was a nice morning," Calvin said. "I've got to fix the tractor when I get those parts, so I thought I'd like to do something nice on what's gonna be left of my day off. So I thought of you."

"That's nice," said Louella. She waited for the rest of it.

"How about a picnic supper?" he said. "About six o'clock." He looked at her and grinned. "Up the River Road."

"Thought you'd like to do something nice, huh?" Louella teased. "Okay," she said, "I'll get some food from Old Gomez. You bring the beer."

He leaned over to kiss her, but she was exhaling cigarette smoke and turned her head. He took her ear lobe in his lips and tongued it for a moment. Then he stood up and went to meet the train.

4

Irish Duffy and his six head pickers took a long time to find Sam Tolin's farm. When they finally found it, one of the pickers realized that it had belonged to a man named Adams before Tolin bought it and that he had worked at the farm before, though not in the new orchards on the west side of the farm. The road to the house had to pass the packing sheds and some other barn looking buildings. For a Sunday with no picking going on, there seemed to be a lot of people at work. At the house Mrs Tolin said she was just leaving to go to church and her husband would be somewhere near the drying sheds working on the racks. Irish followed the smell of sulfer to the end of a line of open sheds, finding Sam emptying bags of the yellow sticks into a wooden bin.

Sam was on the attack from the moment he saw Duffy. "I don't know who I'm talkin' to. What's your name?"

"Vinnie Duffy," came the answer. "The boys here call me Irish but that ain't my name."

"I guess you wonder why I didn't come and pick you up this morning," Sam said.

"Sure do," was the curt reply.

"Well," said Sam, "I don't rightly know any more if I'm going to hire you, any of you. I got to figuring out my costs and I reckon you boys has priced yourselves right out of my market."

"You found something cheaper?" Irish asked. He couldn't erase the shadow of a sneer in his voice.

Sam was up to him. "If I had, I wouldn't turn it down, but I wouldn't tell you if I did."

"You got to tell me something," Irish said. "You got to say if we work or not. And I don't think you're going to find pickers this side of the Colorado River that'll work for what you been payin' year after year. That's over with, I'll tell you that for nothin'."

"You're out of your territory, Mr Irish Duffy," Sam said. "The Colorado's down south. This here's the valley, and we make our own rules. And I own this farm, and I run it my way. Git off my land."

"We had a contract," Irish insisted.

"I don't make contracts with migrant workers," Sam said. The brutality was emphasized with a spit into the dirt at their feet. "I offered you a job. You're too expensive. That's it. Git off my land."

"We got us a union now, Mr Farmer Tolin," Irish said. "You ain't going to get away with this. If you want your fruit picked, you're going to have to meet union terms. Next year you'll be dealing with the union direct. This year's just a taste of what's comin' your way."

"Speakin' of taste, Mr Union Man, you better get your high and mighty union to figure out how you're going to feed your raggle-taggle babies when no farmer in the valley'll give you work." Sam threw the challenge at Irish like a rock.

"You just let us worry about that," Irish said, and he looked behind him at the men he was leading. They were not standing so close to him as they had been before. "Wouldn't be the first time the farmers tried to starve us out, would it, boys?" The pickers nodded and murmured agreement and moved back closer to their leader.

Sam smiled. "It wasn't no farmers that starved you, boy," he said. "It was the banks threw you Okies offa their land."

Irish blew up. "Our land!" he shouted. "Ours, not theirs!"

"That ain't the way it worked out," said Sam. "Anyhow, git."

"You're lockin' us out, is that it?" said Irish.

"I ain't got a key," said Sam, "but it come to the same thing in the end. If you can find a door, go through it." He turned and walked back into the drying shed, then through a double barn door at the back out into the orchard.

"Whatta we do, Irish?" an older man said.

As their leader, he had only one way to go. Irish stomped toward their truck. "Let's get outta here," he said.

Two of the older men crowded into the front with Irish, and the others climbed up into the back and sat down. Irish started to drive away the way he had come, then on an impulse nosed the truck around one of the barn buildings and found himself facing the long aisles of the apricot orchard itself. About twenty men were picking from trees four or five down from the end of the row, and filled boxes were stacked on the ground waiting to be collected.

"I'll be God damned!" Irish breathed. As if he hadn't heard himself, he repeated it, "I'll be God damned!" He stopped the truck and stared.

One of the older men said, "Who are they, Irish?"

"Blacklegs," said Irish. "Non-union. Where the hell did he find 'em?"

"Ain't many on 'em," the old man said, "not enough to git in a crop in a hurry."

"Enough to break a strike," Irish said. He pushed the truck into gear and labored off back to Las Cruces.

5

The Reverend Everett Ward was not a commanding presence in himself. He was short, inclined to be round, with the plump man's roll in his walk. His light-brown hair was becoming sparse, an effect which he tried to disguise by combing the hair from the left side of his head over the pink dome of his skull. The hair, not approving of this arrangement, sprang up soon after it was combed, forcing Reverend Ward to spend a great part of his time calling attention to his baldness by patting and smoothing the hair back to where he thought it should be. In the same way, aware of his expanding stomach, he cinched his trousers high up above his hips and held them there with a combination of suspenders and belt, camouflaging the extent of the protuberance further with an unusually wide necktie. The belly nevertheless jiggled unmistakably, causing him to pull up the trousers, check on the belt and braces, and smooth down the necktie in the way that other people adjust their glasses in a routine manner, thereby calling attention to his anxiety. The unedifying spectacle of a man patting his hair with one hand and his belly with the other in asynchronous rhythm was a gift made in heaven for those who wished to mock the good man.

In uniform, as it were, ready for his weekly appearance at

the head of his flock, Reverend Ward was another person altogether. He wore the ancient cap and gown of his theological college, which was the University of Aberdeen, Scotland. In flowing black robe and rectangular headgear, with the bright colors of his university draped over his neck like an elaborate Boy Scout neckerchief, he cut a defiant, slightly sinister figure who clearly enjoyed his dominance over his audiences. His Nova Scotian parents had sent him back to the old country for his divinity training as a genuine Scottish Presbyterian, after which he took the same road as so many of his Canadian-Scottish neighbors, south into the United States and west to a better prospect. He had come to the foothill communities east of Red Branch at first, to preach and found churches among the granite workers, Scottish or Cornish without exception. They quarried stone for the public buildings that lumbered their way onto the skyline in the first great flush of burgeoning civic pride in towns and cities throughout the state, and which now sat gray and glum turning away from the sun in defiant nostalgia. When Deacon Halbkeller led a search for a new minister for the Red Branch church, this man had all the right credentials and was still young enough to be molded to the ways of a conservative, demanding congregation. It was a union of great satisfaction to all concerned with the Red Branch First Presbyterian Church.

At exactly half past ten Mrs Cook sounded a chord for his entrance and Reverend Ward came onto the rostrum from an oak door in the back wall, a darker shadow appearing from the shadows. He sat in a carved chair to pray briefly, and then took his place at the pulpit, his glasses catching the sun and flashing as he moved his head from side to side to greet the congregation unsmilingly. As he did every Sunday, he led the way through the elements of the service by impulsion, as if up a gradient, surefooted in the buildup to the sermon. The same philosophy was detectable behind the sermons themselves, with Reverend Ward's delivery and phrasing almost theatrical in his concern to emphasize what was to him important, and to place in the minds of his hearers the importance of his message. No one slept through his sermons, and no one missed the point. At precisely five minutes after eleven the members of the congregation settled themselves as Reverend Ward prayed briefly for enlightenment, placed his hands one on top of the other on the Bible before him, and began his sermon.

"My dear friends: Until last evening I had intended to take as the text of my sermon a passage from the Bible lesson which is appointed for this day, the one which you have just heard. One of our brethren came to see me at the manse last night just as I was, in fact, working with my notes for today's sermon. What he had to tell me has disturbed me so much that I have done something which must be explained and apologized for. You will find that I have chosen a text which is unconnected to the Bible lesson, for the reason that we have in our community a crisis that will test us to the full. Satan has come among us. Our turn in the fiery furnace is not to come. It is here."

The members of the congregation sat bewildered, disoriented. This was not a preamble; it was a warning. Reverend Ward set himself more squarely behind his pulpit, physically gathering himself for a great effort. He moved his jaw without speaking, then, breathing noisily and deeply, like a showman about to do a feat of great strength and agility he swept the congregation slowly with a troubled, commanding stare. As he began his sermon, his phrases flowed in a deep river of passionate belief.

"'For inasmuch as ye do this unto one of the least of these my brethren, ye do it unto me.' This text which I have chosen is one of the cornerstones of our faith and of our religious denomination. We Presbyterians live by this text every day of our lives. We are the Lord's brethren, the very people our Lord Jesus Christ was speaking of when he said those words, locked together in the face of Mammon, standing firm as true believers in God's grace and righteousness. We rejoice in the fruits of God's grace that are shown to any one of us, knowing that the gift is given to all of us, not only to one. We sorrow for the evil day that lights upon any one of us, for we know it is retribution for violation of God's laws, and we know that each and every reminder of man's sin and frailty is meant for us all. We are joined together, yoked and chained and driven, in this passage through the valley of the shadow of death, fearful of the evil that may befall any one of us because the evil is the property of us all. Why do we do this? Why are we not individuals separated from each other by our personal needs and desires? Because we know that in the joy to come, the everlasting joy of God's presence, we will be one with God, and the mortality we share in this life will be transmuted into the immortality of God's eternal presence. We are chosen – mysteriously, magnificently, incontrovertibly, unalterably chosen. It is a burden in this world, we know that. God's blessing on us, the elect, is a burden, I repeat. It is a burden that we thank God for, in our certainty of bliss to come, even as we groan under its weight. And we have reason to groan. Because, my brethren, there are times when God has work that we must do, work that can strike terror in our hearts even while it sparks joy in our souls."

His hands, which had been hidden within the black shape of him, now appeared out of the wide sleeves of his gown and gripped the edge of the pulpit. He leaned far over it, looking down upon his brethren in a plea for their shared strength so that he could tell them of the horror he saw.

"Satan has come among us in our community. That is the terror of it. And my brothers and sisters, it is indeed frightening even to think of. It is Satan at his wiliest. Wearing the disguises of humanity and equality, he is among us. Let me explain. The power that gives us speech and breath and thought is God's. Likewise the power that directs those gifts toward an ideal is God's. Why does God give us notions in our heads that by coming together we can create a better life for all men here on earth? It is because we are learning on earth the lessons of heaven. We are children

150

learning our ABCs, the rudiments of immortal life. We are learning that there is something called happiness that is a gift of God, and only in God's power to give. We are learning that this gift is given to God's chosen people. We are learning that to deserve this gift we must know and keep the word of God, the laws that are for our benefit even though we may not always understand them. We are learning that the sinful world must be resisted in order that our souls may be kept clean and perfect, which is the only state which is acceptable in God's sight. In order to help us to do all these things, we have established here on earth imitations of God's rule. We come together in towns like this one where we live and choose ways in which right governance will be established for all sorts and conditions of men. We combine those towns into larger units of governance, which must serve the right needs of God's people, and so it goes on up to the highest forms of government that we will allow under God. At the same time, we establish codes of law which are taken from the understanding within our souls of the needs of God for His people, not the needs of a state or any other form of governance which has been allowed. Our laws, our courts, even our executioners do God's work. When the state flag flies over our jail, it is God's flag flying there. What has a just, merciful God to do with jails? The mystery of justice will be solved in heaven, not on earth."

Calmer now, his voice deepening to a more philosophical tone, Reverend Ward stepped back from the danger zone that lay before his eyes.

"Poverty, my brethren, is part of that mystery of justice. Why should one man have more and another less? Why indeed should some men have less than they need to sustain life? We do not know, and we never will know. It is God's will, therefore it is just. We have one clue as to God's intent, however. He sent us His Son, our Lord Jesus Christ, to teach us in the words of our text for today, to the least we must be generous. Our Lord Jesus Christ did not say that to be generous we must also be poor. Oh no. And those who

151

say that poverty is the basic requirement of the true Christian are reading the lesson from the wrong end of the passage."

With barely a change of face or voice, he became the Scottish dominie, the teacher and moral guardian, the some-thing-more-than-man with the biblical power to bind and unbind. To these people who were now transmuted to children, he taught a lesson while accepting that it would have to be taught and retaught to the end of a sinful world.

"How do we know that? Because our text does not say only that something done for – done for – a man is done for God. It says that something done to a man – done to a man – is also done to God. And here we come to the unfathom-able nature of justice. Yes, turn the other cheek when the insult is offered to the godly by the ungodly. Yes, be charitable even to the unworthy because charity reflects God's pity. Yes, even pardon the sinner among us when repentance has been learned."

Here he paused, remaining silent for so long that the members of the congregation studied every sign in his face for its cause. Slowly he raised his arm and pointed out the great west window, following its direction with his body until once more he leaned over his pulpit, so far, now, that the black pall of his gown spread over and concealed his open Bible.

"But, my brethren, what do we do when God's state is threatened, the model of God's heaven is attacked, the means by which we are learning and preparing ourselves to live in heaven in the light of God's countenance are being destroyed around us? We do not turn the other cheek to Satan. No, we do not. When God tells us that a deed done to the least of our brethren is a deed done against his divine order, we fight back in the name of God. Yes, that is what we do. There is a time to fight for God, and it has come upon us now, today, in our own seemingly unworthy community."

He was shouting now, his face pallid and sweaty as candle wax, his body jerking in time to the body blows of his words.

If there had been any doubt, there was none left. This was a champion for God, fighting against Satan himself.

"There is a conspiracy against divine justice abroad in the world. It is named Communism, but it is in reality named Satan's Rule. Satan has taken hold of the simple, unschooled people of an alien land, who have made converts among other simple, unschooled people in our own land. The Communists have taken advantage of ignorance and have used the sin of envy to spread the doctrines of satanic equality. Not God's equality, but satanic equality. What is satanic about equality? you ask. Let me ask you this: Why did Satan fall from heaven? Because of pride, because of envy, because that monstrous perversion of God's brightest angel wished to be equal to the Son of God. And how did he propose to gain that equality? By taking it from God himself. We have among us Communists who say they act in order to gain equality for the poor people who have flooded our land of plenty. How do they propose to gain their equality? By destroying God's state which we, God's people, have labored so hard and so long to construct."

Pleading with his people, dragging them in his wake, Reverend Ward threw all his voice and body into his oratory, triumph and pain in equal measure in the unearthly, inexplicable compound of his vision.

"Do you not see, my brethren, how under the guise of charity we are being led by Satan to turn our faces from our God? Which is the more monstrous perversion? The revolt in heaven by Satan himself, or the destruction of God's people here on earth? There is no difference, my brothers and sisters in God. Why did Satan choose earth as his battleground for the continuing struggle against God? Because we are the creatures created closest to God's image, His chosen ones, His last and greatest experiment in sharing His ineffable glory. We, my brethren, here in Red Branch, here in this fine church, we are the target of Satan's insidious evil. Are we, God's elect, His chosen few, going to give Satan our Godfearing, God-inspired, God-patterned lives in

153

exchange for a community that knows only the justice of Mammon, that which is injustice in the eyes of God?"

He threw his arms wide, his hands contorted into fists of strength, his chest heaving.

"Resist it, my brothers. Resist it, my sisters. For God's sake, enlist and fight on the side of God."

The black band of his mortarboard was soaked, and he fumbled with his fingers behind his glasses, pushing the sweat from his eyes.

"Let us pray: Oh God, give to the tongues among us the gift of your wisdom, so that we may see the way we must go. Give to the ears among us the gift of hearing the righteous cause instead of the siren song of the most profound evil. Give to our eyes the gift to recognize our true leaders, to our hearts the courage to stand with them, to our arms if necessary the strength to resist and to fight in your just cause. Oh God, be Thou this day and always our strength. Amen."

The energy that Reverend Ward had put into his extraordinary sermon had exhausted him. He backed away from the pulpit and sat down in his thronelike chair, forgetting to announce the number of the closing hymn. The combination of his omission and the message he had delivered reduced the congregation to sitting numbed, frightened and unable to conduct business as usual and get on with the singing. They sat not even looking at each other, waiting for the revelation. Mrs Cook looked into the mirror at the choir director, trying to get his attention without success. Corkscrewing herself around on the organ bench and leaning forward perilously, she roused him with a loudly whispered, "One hundred and seventy-eight." This wasn't the number of the intended hymn, and the choir director looked even more lost. Looking over her shoulder at the minister, Mrs Cook set off with a great chord into "Onward, Christian Soldiers", turning back at the end of several bars to pick up the choir, who had found the page by then and understood the way things were going. Mrs Wilson led the choir into the hymn, head high, chest expanded, jaw firm. She sang to the God of battle. It was not a hymn that day, more an explosion of support for wherever the minister was taking his people, to whatever confrontation might be required. Reverend Ward stood, sang and wept, removing his glasses and letting the tears roll unchecked.

At the end of the hymn he looked for a moment to be about to raise his arm in a very un-Presbyterian form of blessing before remembering and restraining himself. He stepped forward then as if to give the benediction, his head bowed like all the heads before him. Instead, he said, "Will all those so inclined please stay here after the end of the service to hear an explanation of the crisis we are facing. Thank you."

He raised his face and his voice soared. "The Lord bless you and keep you, the Lord make His face to shine upon you, the Lord lift up His countenance upon you and give you – strength."

The alteration of the last word went through the congregation like an electric shock. Not peace: strength. Reverend Ward vanished through the rear door.

6

After Reverend Ward had left, Mr Halbkeller abandoned his usual task of taking the collection plates into the vestry to count the day's offerings. He went to the front of the church and then turned to the choir. "Would you like to join us, please. We'll wait for you to take off your robes."

The members of the choir filed away, keeping their eyes fixed on Mr Halbkeller both in bemused attention and out of fear of missing anything. Mrs Cook sat expectantly on her organ bench, viewing the church as always through her mirror. Mr Halbkeller found her eyes on him and said, "We won't be needing the organ any more, thank you, Mrs Cook." She filed after the last choir member. One or two children, accustomed to meeting their parents after church as they shook hands with the minister, looked through the doors at the rear, one of them whispering loudly, "Why aren't they coming?" Before Mr Halbkeller's glare they disappeared.

With everyone assembled, the deacon turned sharply and said, "Mr Stagg." It was another Halbkeller, the business-man Walter Halbkeller, and his tone caught at and further confused the seated people. Lee Roy Stagg felt this and put on his most reassuring manner. He smiled the way an uncle does just before trying to explain why fathers feel the need to whip their sons.

"We don't want to go and get too alarmed about this, friends," he said. "As long as we know what we're doing and work together, we'll be all right. Now, let me tell you what's been going on."

Several people glanced at Mr Halbkeller, as if to get the deacon's endorsement that Lee Roy was an approved informant. The deacon turned his stern eyes on Lee Roy and all wavering eyes followed his. The floor was Lee Roy's.

"Yesterday morning we found out that Mr Sam Tolin, I'm sure most of you know him, was being held to ransom by his apricot pickers." Two or three ladies gasped, and Lee Roy realized upon what tender ground they all stood. "I don't mean literally held to ransom, I mean that the way the saying goes. He was being told that he had to ruin himself to get the cooperation of the people who came here to get in his crops. Instead of the union, this new so-called union of farm workers, coming out and saying that there was going to have to be a contract and talking about it, what they've done is get the pickers to demand pay and so forth that no working farmer can agree to."

Mr Halbkeller harrumphed, attempting to let Lee Roy know there was no need for this kind of detail. Lee Roy looked toward him, puzzled. Unaccustomed to ecclesiastical power, he failed to see there was no need to convince anyone. He continued with his argument, trying to put aside Mr Halbkeller's fidgets.

"With the crops about to rot on the trees, they figured the farmers would pay up in the end. They probably would. And then in about four–five months, the farmers would be broke. The money they spend in the town would dry up. The bills they owed wouldn't be paid. They'd either be sold up by the banks for whatever the market could get, or they'd just have to clear out lock, stock and barrel and find a place to start over again. It doesn't take much to see what the effect on Red Branch would be. We'd be back in the worst days of

157

the Depression. And worse. We'd be swamped by the migrants," he added sarcastically, "who were Okies just a few years ago, coming camping on us and drawing their welfare out of whatever we could pay in taxes."

With this thrust, he had his audience. Their black nightmare, and its (to their minds) cause, chilled their hearts.

"Now there's two ways of looking at this. Either we have people here who are too dumb to see that they can go but just so far before they kill off the people who give them their living, or else this is what they want to do – kill us off. Or maybe we have both of these things – dumb people so dumb they don't know that they're doing the dirty work of the people who want to kill us off any way they can. Either way, our town and our people are the targets, not just the farmers. Now, Mr Halbkeller has something more to tell you," Lee Roy added, handing over to a grim, unsmiling Deacon Halbkeller.

He glanced around at his listeners, who met his eyes with stricken stares. A few hands stroked shaven chins, not in wise debate but plain consternation. Mr Halbkeller knew no mercy. "We have two banks in our town. One of them has mostly farmers for its depositors and borrowers, and the other one has most of the businesses in the town. If you think about it a minute, you can see that there isn't going to be much difference between the effect on the Bank of America and the First National if the pickers get their way. The Bank of America will feel it first, because more money will have to come in from somewhere to get the higher wages paid, and when the checks come in from the buyers they won't be going up to reimburse the farmers. They will not. The buyers will be after the lowest prices they can get, as usual." His harsh voice, unmusical at the best of times, scraped at his throat in his sarcasm. "When all those checks are in and there aren't any more to come, and the expenses of the winter start to come through, where does the money come from? From the bank, if things happen the way they always have done. So how long will that go on, when the

158

bank sees the farmers are already broke and next year won't be any better? I think Mr Stagg is being generous; I'd give the farmers three more months of solvency before they are bankrupt. And that would put the Bank of America out of business. The rest of us, now, we depend on the money from agriculture to run our town. How long will our bank, the First National, keep us going if they see what happens to the farmers? How long will they keep their doors open if they see the Bank of America shut down? We can figure out what happens next. The town is out of business. Period."

Mr Halbkeller glared at an enemy that invisibly fenced him off from his place in the sun. He had been striking one hand into the other palm in his intensity. Remembering his fingernail, he gripped the right hand over the other as if to protect it. He saw the hordes at the gates, and his audience saw his eyes.

"What good would that do to anyone, you say? What did our minister tell us? Who benefits if our lives fall apart? There is only one winner, and it's the power of evil. Pull it all down, destroy what we have, disgrace everything that has been done in the name of good government, and what do you have? You have wiped away the works of God on earth, and heaven itself is threatened. Anarchy! This is the work of the devil. Everything we have ever known and feared about Communism is confirmed. Friends, we are already under attack."

His voice had sunk to a low, threatening, frightening growl. "How are we going to fight back? Mr Stagg." The crisp, hard, forceful Halbkeller, so unlike their endearingly saintly Deacon, handed a tamed audience back to Lee Roy.

"Well, we've made a start this morning," he said. "We're trying to help Sam Tolin keep going without the union pickers, trying to bring some of them anyway to their senses, bring them out of union control. When they see the crop being picked, maybe they'll see reason. Depends on how hungry they are, of course." He paused briefly, expecting their resistance to this weapon. "No, we've thought about it, nobody will starve, but a few hungry women and kids might have a lot do do with how their husbands vote. This is a fight, my friends, it isn't a love feast." He hurried on, "And if that isn't enough or it doesn't work quick enough, then we expect the union will come out into the open and we'll have a strike. They're out to bankrupt all of us."

What had been hinted at before was now made plain. The shock of this blunt warning dropped jaws, and quick tears started down the faces of some of the women in the audience. The men looked dazed or shook their heads, fumbling and reaching a hand over to pat their wives' hands and gain some reassurance in doing it. It was too sudden, they were not prepared to think about this. Their minds loped ahead, not into the realities of bankruptcy but to how they would protect themselves against it.

Mr Halbkeller's plan of action was perfectly prepared for. He said, "The information has gone to everyone who can help us, all the way up to the governor. There are special meetings being held today all over the state, not just here in Red Branch, to set up a combined response. Now, how can you help? Talk about it with your neighbors. Work out who can let other people know about what's going on, because things are moving very quickly. Keep your eyes open. Chief Thomas and Sheriff Atwater will need to know everything that is going on. When you're needed for more than this, you'll be told."

The rest of what he and Lee Roy said was a jumble of unrelated bits of advice. No one asked any questions because, say what you would about a community, the questions being asked in every mind were about how the events would affect them as individuals. The parents with waiting children began to leave, and women had to get back to see how the Sunday roast was doing. Outside on the high, broad steps a few men exchanged wry words about the unexpected things you learned by going to church. It was Henry Abbott, a first generation American of Scots parentage, who mentioned that he was going to be waiting for the doors of the bank to open tomorrow, and he would be taking out every penny of his money. Two or three heard it, and others heard it from them, and phone calls passed it on when the men got home. The one certain thing that was going to happen on Monday morning was that there would be a run on the banks that would alert head offices to a crisis in Red Branch that could spread disastrously. This was exactly what Mr Halbkeller had planned. He had the editor's backing and had already begun to write out his front page article and his editorial, also to be printed on the front page, before he left for church that morning. The *Herald* was going to lead a crusade against the Communists who had come to Red Branch in the disguise of the United Farm Workers. He would get the editor to double the print run for this special Monday edition, and he must remember to ask Mrs Ganz to get copies of all the big newspapers, even some from out of state, for the library. He was confident that Red Branch was going to make the headlines.

7

The pickers were leaving him alone, Irish Duffy knew, he could feel it. When he looked up from his reading, eyes were in the process of being turned away. Small talk that didn't mean anything, spoken in overly loud voices, stopped any attempt he might have liked to have made to connect with someone, anyone. They did not yet distrust him. They didn't like sitting and waiting for events to take place, that was all. They had come here to work, they had been ready to work, and now they sat here with nothing to do. Their conduct said, "Irish, what are you going to do about it? You're the leader." He had no answer.

He wouldn't have any answer, either, if he was unable to get in touch with Cappy Petrillo. The agreement was that there would be no direct communication until there was a situation that couldn't be handled locally. Unless something went badly wrong, the union was not involved in the process at this stage. Irish knew that he should sit it out and wait to see if Sam Tolin had to change his mind and get some workers in. He would have to do that, Irish knew, in a matter of days if he wanted to save his crop. A few blacklegs couldn't do the job. They were there to show Irish and his pickers something, but it wasn't clear yet just what that was. Tolin's changed attitude worried him.

His pocket watch read eleven thirty-five. Time to go. He walked to his truck, pretending not to notice the obvious way that no one showed any interest in his leaving, and drove toward Red Branch. The Greyhound Bus Depot opened again at twelve. It was not the way to handle this thing, he knew that, but he had to get some instructions. He would phone Cappy's office in Sacramento, where there was always someone on duty.

He came into town on Greenfield Avenue and drove straight to the highway. The traffic lights were out, and traffic was being directed by a policeman. He was a long time giving Irish the road so he could turn left for the depot, staring at the truck so intently that Irish wondered if his headlights were jiggling or if a tire looked doubtful, warranting one of these little peptalks the drivers of old cars and trucks seemed to get all the time now. He parked his truck on the soft dirt beside the highway and crossed to the depot. A working man was there beside the door, looking inside at apparent signs of life. It was just twelve noon. In a few moments the depot manager, Harold Stoll, came to the door and let them in. The working man ahead of Irish said he'd come to use the phone, and Harold said he'd have to wait because the phone was ringing right then with someone trying to call in.

"That'll be my call, right as not," he said. "I'm expecting my friend to call at twelve sharp."

"This is a depot with a pay phone," Harold said, "not a hotel lounge. If you want to use the phone, pay for it."

"Keep your shirt on," the man said, "I'm fixin' to do that, and Mr Stagg told me if there was any trouble with you about it, you was to tell him when he come in later on."

"Oh," Harold said, "well, that's okay, then. Why didn't you say you was working with Lee Roy? Get that damn phone before it rings off the wall, go ahead. What can I do for you?" he said to Irish.

"I come to use the phone too," Irish answered.

163

"This is gonna be a big day for sales, I can see that," Harold said.

Irish said, "I'll take a candy bar, ain't had no lunch. Hershey with almonds, please." He pronounced almonds as if it was the name of a man called Al Munz, giving away to the depot man that Irish wasn't the sort who often had spare money for things like candy bars.

"Yeah, this is me all right," the working man said from the phone booth. He left the door open a few inches, trying to get some fresh air into it to counter the stink of old cigarette butts and Saturday night's urine, which would be there until the cleaning woman came tomorrow morning. "Here's the message. You ready?" He waited while someone on the other end got writing materials together. "Tell him this: The work's here. Full pay and a bonus, for the women too. They want as many as he can get, for first thing tomorrow. Tell him they have to know if he wants transport. They'll have trucks out to Santa Fe to bring 'em in, if they know." He was silent while the message was apparently repeated. "Yeah, that's right, now you get it to him, okay? If they want the trucks, they got to phone Mr Lee Roy Stagg – that's the number you already got." The caller asked him something, and he answered, "Apricots. Plenty of work. They'd prob'ly even hire you." He laughed and said goodbye and hung up.

Irish took his place in the booth but closed the door tightly. He dialled a number that he carried with him and a man's voice told him that this was the emergency number of a professional answering service. Was the call really important? Irish told him the call was a message for Cappy Petrillo, and it was about as urgent as you could get.

"Take this down," he said, "and don't mess it up. He can't call me back. Tell him it's from Duffy. Tell him we got strike breakers being signed up in Red Branch and we ain't even got a strike yet. He better get here just as quick as he can, because this thing's already too big for me and it ain't even started yet. That's enough message. Goodbye."

164

When he emerged from the booth, Harold was fussing around the counter keeping an eye on him. "I'll take another of them Hersheys, Mister," Irish said.

While Harold went around behind the counter, Irish asked him, "You know a town around here called Santa Fe?"

"No town with that name," Harold said. "People in Red Branch say that when they mean the old station house out on the Santa Fe tracks east of town. Used to be a depot, but the town didn't grow that way. One railroad was enough. That all you want? Tobacco?"

"No thanks," Irish said. "I don't smoke. I might need some matches though. Think I'm almost out."

"Two candy bars and a box of matches," Harold observed. "Don't spend all your money in one place, will you." He snorted and went out to the parcel room at the back.

Mort Thomas switched the traffic lights back into operation and, leaving his car in the Shell station, walked down to the bus depot. The sound of the front door called Harold in from the back.

"What are you doing on duty today, Mort?" he asked.

"Ran the traffic lights a while to keep an eye on things," he answered. "Just looking, like they say."

"Looking for anything special?" Harold asked.

"Anything different," Mort replied, "like that migrant worker who just came down here. What did he want?"

"Used the telephone," Harold replied, "and had a couple of candy bars for lunch. That's all."

"You didn't hear where he called, did you?" Mort asked.

"He shut the door," Harold said. "Other guy didn't though."

"I know who he is. He's all right," Mort said. "This other one's new to me."

"He's some kind of migrant worker," Harold said. "I think he's looking for work. He heard the other guy on the phone, same as I did, talkin' about jobs and hiring, and right

165

away he wanted to know where the town of Santa Fe is. I told him there wasn't any such place."

"What's Santa Fe got to do with anything?" Mort said. "You lost me, Harold."

"Beats hell outa me, Mort. Guy on the phone said there was trucks at Santa Fe. You tell me what that's supposed to mean. Sounds crazy to me." Harold flapped his hands like some kind of loony and showed signs of wanting to get back to his work in the parcel room.

"I don't know either," Mort said as he left. Outside he scratched his head and gave it up. It didn't make sense.

Irish Duffy started to return to Las Cruces and then thought better of it. He doubled back on himself and returned down Greenfield Avenue, driving straight through town going east. The avenue went through a part of town he had never seen. A small ice plant with a drive-in ice cream parlor beside it faced the town's public hospital. Small professional buildings housing insurance agents and lawyers and doctors were followed by a large garage advertising cheap tires and batteries. Beyond vacant lots was a school for the poorer kids. You knew it was for poorer kids because it was surrounded by a wire fence, either to keep the kids in or the vandals out, if there was a difference. The houses got smaller and meaner, the lawns disappeared, the trees became untidy and disfigured by ropes and tire swings where a few children played, and boys on rickety bicycles chased after each other over heaps of dirt that had been dumped on empty ground. Decaying wrecks of old cars, ice boxes and stoves slumped in the weeds of vacant lots. Everywhere there were faded, peeling, tilted signs advertising houses and lots for sale. It looked like what it was, the town's underbelly, on the wrong end of the town's main street. It surprised Irish to find that not all of Red Branch was fat, fed and foolish, in accordance with his picture of the people in the valley towns.

When the road cleared the town there was an attempt at an aisle of oleander trees flanking it, then heat and golden grain and nothing else but a few signs for Valvoline motor oil and the midget car races in Placid City, which was in the wrong direction altogether from the way he was going. Up ahead he saw the line of the Santa Fe tracks, set high up on an embankment that ran north–south as far as you could see in a dead straight line. A two-room depot composed of a waiting room and an office, both of them locked and abandoned, squatted beside a signal tower. One man sat in the tower in a shaded corner, sound asleep. He didn't see Irish stop his truck and look for sign of a settlement, then drive on along the main road. After a few miles of nothing but wheat fields without so much as an advertising sign to divert the eye, Irish turned around and drove back to the depot. The signalman, awake now, watched him as he turned south on the narrow, graveled road that ran beside the tracks.

Irish caught sight of a farm off to the left a mile or two away and had that so firmly in his sights as a possible "Santa Fe" that he almost missed the huddle of shacks and shanties that hid itself beside the tracks where the road twisted east into more wheat fields. He drove a couple of hundred yards beyond the turn, where he found a place that he could leave his truck more or less out of sight off the road, then walked back. He approached the shanty town cautiously, staying out of sight in the wheat growing in the field across from it. Lying down in the wheat, he watched what he could see of life that was going on behind a makeshift fence and the backs of shacks. There seemed to be no men there. Angular women in faded cotton dresses and children in next to nothing moved quietly about their business. He was reminded of the Okie camps that he had known only a few years ago, set up on sufferance when a farmer could be persuaded that there was no harm in the gesture of allowing a corner of land to these people, and how the camps were hushed and the people careful so as to prolong the stay as long as tolerance would permit. These people in this shanty town were pretending they weren't here, and he recognized

167

the phenomenon with both sympathy and anger. He watched for about fifteen minutes before a few glimpses convinced him that there were men here as well and that they were staying hidden.

An old, rusty car drove up from behind him, leaving a wake of dust as it came. A few of the barricades were removed from inside, and the car drove into the compound. Now the men revealed themselves as they crowded around the car. He could see that they were working men like himself. After they replaced the barricades, he moved to a spot close to where the car had gone in. He could no longer see but he could hear what was going on. The phrases and sentences told him what he needed to know. The man in the car was the courier who took the telephone call. This was Santa Fe, and these were the blacklegs.

Irish returned to his truck and got it out onto the road so that he could get away as quickly as it would go. He would have to drive east when he left and try to find a cross road that took him back to Red Branch. Leaving his truck he backtracked again, this time walking past the point where he had approached Santa Fe, so that he could get up on the railway embankment. Stepping on the cross ties, he walked toward the shanties, shoulders down and hands in his pockets as if he was a hobo, until he could see inside the rough oval of shelters and barricades where the car stood. He saw the people almost as soon as they saw him, and he watched them melt away as he came closer. The driver of the car had not been able to get away in time. He shrank back into the seat of the car and turned his head away. Irish continued to walk the railroad ties until he was directly above the car.

"Where you from?" he shouted.

No one moved or spoke. Not even a child's whimper broke the silence.

"I'm from Oklahoma. Where you from?" he repeated, louder this time, though he knew it was not the volume that would get them to hear.

He bent double and looked into the car, where the man sat as still as death and showed no interest in answering.

"I think, you in the car, you're from Mr Sam Tolin's," he shouted, "and I think the rest of you better go there right away. Go on, he's bought you, even if he ain't paid for you yet. I wouldn't wait for his trucks if I was you."

He took a few steps down the embankment, as low as he dared without sliding down into the ditch behind the compound. There he was almost at eye level with the man in the car, who was still turned away from him.

When Irish spoke again, he talked confidentially to the man in the car, with what sounded like a purr of satisfaction in his voice. "This place looks like it would burn like a box of matches. It don't rightly look safe to me. It might even burn tonight." He remembered the box of matches he had bought at the bus depot and took it out of his pants pocket, rattling it above his head like some Indian fetish as he slipped and rolled on the stones getting back up to the top of the railroad embankment.

The scramble up the bank meant that he had turned his back on the hidden people. Once on top again, he half turned, expecting to see some sign of resistance, ready to run if there was going to be a move against him. No one challenged him. He stood as tall as he could, inviting an attack, and gave one last message. "When we was all from Oklahoma, we didn't steal other fellas' jobs."

Again he waited for a reply that was not going to come. "You stink!" he shouted with all the power he could put into the words, with all the truth he felt in him.

He ran for his truck and drove east with no one pursuing him.

8

Louella walked up to the Rex Hotel at a quarter to one, when she thought sandwiches and cold plates for lunch would no longer be ordered. There were some ham sandwiches in the glass display case, and about a quarter of a meat loaf sat beside them on a bed of wilting lettuce leaves. Old Gomez looked hot and tired, and answered only "Help yourself" when she asked him for the leftovers for her supper. She went behind the counter and found a paper bag and some waxed paper, then wrapped the sandwiches and the sliced meat loaf and filled the bag with it. She fished out a bag of potato chips from the box of snacks behind the bar. "How much?" she asked Gomez, who merely repeated: "Help yourself." She put fifty cents on the counter near the display case and went around to the customers' side of the counter.

She offered Old Gomez a cigarette and asked him, "What's wrong?" When he merely shrugged, she insisted, "No, come on, what's going on?"

"I don't want to talk about it," he said. "They want a fight. When you have a fight, somebody gets hurt," he said. "They're forgetting that. Somebody gets hurt."

"You know more than I do," Louella said. "I don't know anything about a fight."

"Yes, you do," Old Gomez said. "You listen a little bit, you know in a hurry. You don't want to know, that's all. The whole town knows, but it don't want to know."

"You're not making good sense," Louella said.

"Don't be stupid with me, Louella. You're not a stupid girl." Old Gomez came very close to her and looked into her face. He looked at every part of it, as if he wanted to draw it. His concentration made her nervous.

"What are you doing?" she said. She sat farther away from him, pushing back on the bar stool.

"Don't get hurt," he said.

It was a hot, still afternoon. The town melted away in the face of the heat. No one stirred beyond a necessary errand conducted at a snail's pace. The light bleached the color and detail out of everything, so that what had been light and shade was reduced to whiteness and blackness. Inside shaded rooms, pursuing what coolness they could find, the people of Red Branch listened to the radio or read the paper or simply slept, waiting for the day to release its sweaty grip.

Calvin borrowed a cooler box from Mrs Rossi and put eight bottles of beer in it, an opener and two glasses. He went out in back of the grocery store and sat in the shade with the family, talking of nothing much, adding nothing to their bits of gossip about the troubles at Sam Tolin's. When the low western sun took their shade, he loaded a blanket and the cooler box in his truck, and threw in a towel and his swimming trunks. By the time he got to Louella's it was seven o'clock. She made him a cup of coffee when he got there, and they finished off a tub of ice cream that she wanted to get rid of. It was eight o'clock when they got in the truck and drove to Bridge Street, crossed the bridge, and headed out the River Road. Passing the Okie shacks, they continued until they came to a flood control road that bore to the right. They left the truck there and walked down the road toward the river bed, carrying their picnic things with them. Where the river had pushed down some young

171

cottonwood trees last winter, a sandy beach no more than twenty feet square had been formed behind the roots and debris. The beach faced the river, with what was left of the trees behind. It was a completely private, secluded place that probably would not be there after next winter's high water. They spread the blanket and stowed the food in the exposed roots so that it wouldn't attract ants, then took turns changing into their swimming suits behind the screen of the dead branches, their modesty and good manners impeccable while there was still enough light to see by. In her dark blue swimming suit, Louella was blonde all over with no hint of suntan, miraculously untouched by the valley sun. Calvin was brown around the neck and face, and his forearms were burned as dark as tree bark. Everywhere else his skin was almost unnaturally white. His black trunks looked as foreign on him as a necktie would have done.

They splashed in the shallow water, which was warm and slow moving, looking for a channel into the deeper water that would not be too muddy. Calvin found a narrow, sandy run of faster water that they followed around the mud flats. The deeper water when they reached it was only about four feet in depth by now, with the river dropping closer to its summer trickle every day that the sun beat down. Neither Calvin nor Louella was a good swimmer, the shallower water suiting them perfectly. There was some good natured water fighting, a reciprocal set of duckings, the odd taunt about which was the better swimmer. Behind it all was a decorum and tension, as if they were waiting for something.

They waded ashore and dried themselves with the towels. It was still very warm, with no evening breeze to relieve the feeling of exhaustion after a hot day. They drank a little beer and started on the sandwiches, then lay back and watched the light leave the sky. Being cloudless, the sky was unable to retain the sunlight, and from being daylight it passed to evening in a moment, with light purple shadows sweeping across the land even as you watched. Still they lay and watched. They ate and drank a bit more while darkness came. When everything seemed covered with light that was like dark dust, Calvin kissed Louella and untied the straps of her swimming suit from in back of her neck. Then he tugged her gently to her feet, and stripped it from her. He took off his trunks then, and the two of them stood face to face looking at each other without embarrassment, then touching and stroking. They lay down and continued their love play. Out here where there was no one to hear, away from dentists' offices and Mrs Rossi's rooms, Calvin became a small animal, yelping, whining, licking Louella in his pleasure. His noises rose to whoops of joy and gasps of astonishment, and Louella laughed loud and indulgently and tossed her head back as far as her neck would allow. They shouted like discoverers of a new land, until stricken tongue-tied and breathless by the release of love.

After they had rested they talked lightly and gently, then waded out into the river so that they could sit in the warm stream and feel the night come on around them. Back on the blanket they lay close to each other wrapped in the towels and drowsed wordlessly until it was time to dress and go back to the truck. It was after eleven when they got there.

Calvin was about to start the truck and reverse it back up the road when he stopped suddenly. He put a finger on Louella's lips to silence her and jumped back out of the cab as noiselessly as possible. He stood there in the dark until Louella joined him to look and listen with him. Something was behind them on the road. They heard the sound of a small truck starting up and pulling away, but there were no headlights or taillights.

"What's going on, Calvin?" Louella asked.

"That's your favorite question," he said, "and as usual I don't know the answer. Something's mighty funny, that's all I got to say."

"What is it?" she asked.

"I looked in the mirror, ready to pull out, and I seen this set of headlights bein' turned off back on the road." He paused before adding, "Thought for a minute it was someone gettin' ready to jump us."

"Oh, come on, Calvin," Louella said. "Who'd want to do that?"

"There's funny things goin' on today," was his only answer.

"Where've they gone now?" she asked.

Calvin gestured into the dark. "Up the road 'thout any lights," he said. "Crazy sons of guns."

Suddenly he laughed and pulled Louella back to the cab of the truck. "Get in," he said. "He ain't the only crazy son of a gun in the county. Let's follow him."

"Calvin, you're nuts," she said, and readily climbed in the truck. In a minute he had gained the road. It was a new adventure, driving with no lights after a mysterious vehicle with no lights. Louella got two beers out of the cooler box and took their caps off. Calvin said, "Here's to you," and Louella answered, "Here goes nothin'!" They took a drink and laughed together and crept on in the dark until they caught sight of a black shadow ahead of them on the road. They kept it in sight, giggling like conspirators. Just the other side of the Santa Fe tracks it turned south on the gravel road that parallels the railroad, and Calvin followed.

Irish Duffy strained his eyes into the darkness until he felt as if he was pushing them out of his head. At least the gravel road was lighter in the night than the blacktop road had been. He had lost the road completely back where the flood-control roads kept turning off toward the river and had had to stop and get out and get a better idea of how the road curved before he could continue without headlights. He'd had to come out here on his own, too, there was no one to help him by spotting the side of the road. Even in the Okie days you had somebody to ride shotgun for you. Not tonight. Several times he thought he was approaching the main road, where he would have to be especially cautious, finally spotting the old depot ahead on his right, with the signal tower just beyond it. He pulled up beside the steps up to the depot and stared at the signal tower. If there was a signal-man in there, he thought, there would be a light of some sort. In the profound dark he would even be able to see a cigarette glow or a match being lighted. There was nothing to be seen; the signal box was empty. He crept across the main road and, once past it, accelerated again, the sound of the gravel under his tires reassuring him.

He was not disappointed to see no sign of light or life at the shanty town. He expected it. They would go to bed with the chickens and rise before them, especially tonight with everyone turning out tomorrow morning to meet Sam Tolin's transportation back at the depot. He drove past the last of the shacks until he found the place where he had hidden the truck that morning, where he switched on his lights finally and turned around. He came back down the road until the tops of the shanties, the only thing that showed from the road, were in the light. He stopped the engine, leaving the lights on. Nothing moved or stirred in the compound that he could see or hear. He took a kerosene lantern from the floor beside him and got out, lighting it beside the truck. By its light he found the way up the embankment again and walked along the tracks until he looked down on the space where he had seen the car before. Holding the lantern high, and with the help of the truck headlights, he could see that the whole place was littered with the sort of things that get jettisoned at a time of quick departure. He recognized unwanted things that, in this light, could have been paper or cloth, anything from bedclothes to newspapers. He remembered well the nights he and his family had had to pack up and leave, and with every leaving the treasures and rubbish that a real house might accumulate had to be left behind.

He laughed aloud into the empty night. He had not expected this kind of success. He had meant tonight only to put on more pressure, to see if he could scare some of them into pulling out of their deal with Sam Tolin. He hadn't thought they were going to take his suggestion and run to

Tolin's to shelter from his threats. He put down the lantern and picked up handfuls of the granite chips that ballasted the tracks and cross ties at his feet. Throwing them onto the roofs of the shanties, he yiped and hooted like someone rounding up cattle, continuing this with handful after handful. Still nothing moved. He laughed again, in triumph and relief, then picked up the kerosene lantern and threw it onto the roof of the nearest shack. The glass chimney of the lantern shattered, and the tin fuel well rolled across the roof until it fell to the ground. The burning wick, like a yellow tongue, licked at the roof where it had fallen free in a pool of spilled kerosene. The fire teased briefly at the tarpaper and then took solid hold. The dry roofing paper was tinder waiting for a flame, any flame, and it ate up the fire hungrily. Irish felt a flush of alarm as the little settlement seized its fate and blazed into the darkness. Was anyone left there after all? He had a sudden vision of a woman with a child sheltering there, waiting for her man to come for her, and he ran along the embankment from one end of the shacks to the other, looking for anyone trapped in there. No sound or movement came through the roar and crackle of the fire, joined now with the sound of pieces of timber and board falling as the roofs collapsed and the sparks flew up in a shortlived cloud of what looked like blazing insects. It was done, finished. Santa Fe would be ashes in half an hour, not even that.

"Holy shit!" was all that Calvin could say when he finally was able to make sense of the light and movement they could see ahead of them.

"What's going on?" Louella asked for the fourth or fifth time.

Calvin didn't try to answer her. "That son of a gun is going to set fire to the wheat if he ain't careful. You suppose that's what he's trying to do?" It didn't seem a very sensible explanation to him, even as he said it.

176

"Calvin, come on, let's just get out of here," Louella pleaded. "I don't like this."

"He's got the road blocked," Calvin said.

"Then turn around," Louella demanded.

"No place to do it," he answered. "We'd get ourselves stuck."

"Well, we're not just going to sit here until he comes and finds us, are we?" Louella said. Calvin suddenly didn't strike her as a great general in a time of crisis.

"We'll run for it," he said. "Hold on to your hat."

He started the engine, switched on the lights, put the truck into gear and bore down on the accelerator in one smooth movement. The truck's headlights picked out the man at the side of the road.

"Take a good look at him," Calvin ordered Louella, "and try to get the license number of the car. Hell, it's a truck!" he said, "taking up the whole damn road."

Irish stumbled down the embankment and had almost reached the road when he heard the starter of an engine engage. Thinking at first it was his own truck he heard, he looked to his right where it stood silent with its headlights dim in the brightness of the burning shacks. Then an engine roared to his left and a truck came toward him revving with as much as it could give. It swerved past him and slid through a foot or two of wheat to get past Irish's own truck, blatting on into the dark beyond it, its lights and its noise retreating up the road.

Irish at first felt the panic that comes with exposure. He wasn't at heart a criminal or an arsonist. The pride he had been feeling in his work was the response of a child to an exciting bonfire. Himself a migrant, he attached no special value to a home, no matter how its humble nature might plead for the thwarted needs of its creator. Just as gypsies will break up a campsite if it begins to look at all permanent, Irish Duffy had thought he was doing the right thing in reminding the people of Santa Fe that they were poor,

177

migrant, exploited ex-Okies whose real job was to wrest from their employers, their overlords who treated them like dirty foreigners, an acknowledgment of the right to something much greater than a marginal existence.

With all that, he was also an ex-convict. Someone had seen him. Had they seen enough of him to be able to identify him? There was a license number on the truck. Had they seen that? He calmed down, examining his predicament rationally. Who knew him or his truck? He kept out of sight, had driven into town only once or twice before today, he was a stranger, a drifter. It was probably only some kids who had been out doing what they shouldn't, and they couldn't tell what they had seen without someone asking them what they were doing out there in the wheat fields in the middle of the night. Never mind, he told himself, it was a job that needed doing. They had taught him up there in Sonoma that in the pursuit of justice for working people, it was inevitable that working people would suffer themselves. That took care of his conscience. They had also taught him that martyrs don't always welcome martyrdom, and it's all right to be worried about some of the things you will be called on to do. He would allow himself a little worry about the strange truck and whoever was in it, but not much. He got into his own truck to drive back to Las Cruces.

Once past Irish's truck, Calvin got into top gear and drove as fast as the road would allow. At a crossroads he turned to the right and found himself approaching Telegraph Road, where he turned right again and came to the crossroads with the main highway at the beginning of the giant eucalyptus trees. He turned right again, toward the town. Still he kept his speed up, turning off finally at Park Street and going to the jail.

The night light was on as always, and the door stood open, the policy which Mort Thomas and Herb Atwater pursued when they didn't have anyone in the cells. Unusually for Red Branch, however, there was a deputy on duty. Al

Moser by day sold used cars in a lot near Nick's Diner where the old Giant Orange used to be. Now he jumped to his feet as Calvin and Louella came in, surprised at anyone having any business for him after midnight, and jumpy about the things that people said were happening or about to happen.

"Hi Calvin, Louella," he said, "what're you doing here, something going on?"

"We seen something funny, Al," Calvin answered, "don't rightly know what it's all about but I don't think it's good news. Can I talk to the sheriff?"

Slightly offended, Al said, "Won't I do?"

"Maybe," Calvin answered, in his confusion unaware of giving further offense. "We was up the River Road, near the check dam, and this truck come by with no lights and having trouble seein' the road, so we figured it was up to something. He ran out to that little road that follows the Santa Fe tracks and come to a shanty town over the other side of the main road. I didn't even know it was there."

"Me neither," Louella chipped in.

"So then what?" asked Al, not about to admit that the existence of a shanty town was unknown to a part time deputy sheriff.

"Then the son of a gun burned it down," Calvin said, still reflecting the bafflement he felt over what they had seen.

"He did, huh," Al said. "Did you get a look at him?"

"Pretty good," Calvin said. "He was so busy doin' his burnin' that he didn't see how close we got to him. Louella here saw him better when we drove past him. She got the number of his truck, too. An old Dodge sedan with the back cut away and a truck bed put on it."

"It was an out of state plate," Louella said, "but I couldn't make out the state. Twenty-two B two hundred and eighty-two. All two's but one, with a B and an eight, that's the way I remember it. I think I got the numbers in the right places." Calvin smiled approvingly at her.

Al wrote it down carefully and studied it. "I guess I better wake the sheriff up," he said.

179

"I thought you would," Calvin said. "If you get him on the phone, I'll give him the description. We'll get on home then." Calvin felt tired and he smelled a big day coming.

"Well, I don't know," Al said. "Sheriff Atwater might want to ask you some more questions."

"It won't be anything that can't wait," Calvin said. "You ain't gonna make sense of this tonight. And you sure as hell ain't gonna catch him tonight. Just get the sheriff on the phone and I'll talk to him, and then we'll go home. Okay?"

VII

Monday

1

Monday morning early, Sam Tolin led the way to the Santa
Fe depot rendezvous in his piebald truck, followed by Lee
Roy with a tractor and trailer and one of Sam's boys driving
another tractor and trailer. They were there at six, and they
were still there at seven. At half past seven they decided
that the message hadn't got through, and Sam's boy started
back empty. Lee Roy was about to follow when a rusty car
drove up and stopped beside Sam, its motor still running.
The driver said abruptly, "They ain't comin'. They're gone.
You'll have to get some different pickers. They ain't comin'
back." Ignoring Sam's questions, he drove off.

Sam turned a bleak face to Lee Roy.

"Now come on, Sam, just take it easy," Lee Roy said.
"We knew this was one way it could turn out. Let's get back
and take a look at things on the farm."

Sam made better time than Lee Roy. When he pulled his
truck in behind the packing shed, Sheriff Atwater's black
and white County Sheriff's Department car was there, with
Herb sitting patiently waiting.

When it came to being patient, the sheriff was master. He
had started his adult life as a gospel singer in Tennessee.
Hoping to receive the call, he studied to be a preacher and
was almost there, when he got a different call. An elderly

relative of his, Nettie Atwater, had tracked him down. She was gathering in her relations to share her bounty, as she put it. Her husband had sold about half the county to a big Italian winegrower from up north and promptly dropped dead. She was rich, and she was lonely. Herb picked up himself and his family and moved to Red Branch. Herb, his wife Suzanne and their two young sons soon made up the Atwater Gospel Quartet, singing a circuit of Methodist churches at first, then finding that people all over the valley had a taste for their close harmony. Possibly one of its virtues was that the harmony was so close that you never knew if they were in tune or not, leaving you free to relax and enjoy it. Herb Atwater was so transparently a good man, uncomplicated and incorruptible, and the singing had made him such a star in the restricted Red Branch firmament, that when he ran for sheriff he was a shoo-in. It was annoying that he was never able to drop his preachy way of talking and speaking in public. However, it was unique in a sheriff, which was worth a few votes as well.

"Would you like to come and get in the car, Sam," he called. It was a command, not an invitation, no matter how it sounded, and Sam heeded it. As soon as the door thumped shut, the sheriff turned to Sam. "You're not really under suspicion, now, Sam, you know that, but you got to give me some answers before you're clear. Not of suspicion, you know, just clear."

Sam goggled at him. "Clear of what?" he asked.

The sheriff said, "You ever been out beyond the Santa Fe tracks, you know, just taking a ride out there, and seen a shanty town, past the old Santa Fe depot?"

Sam answered, "I know there's one out there somewhere, 'cause I was supposed to get my labor from there. I went out to the depot to get 'em but they wasn't there. That's all I know. The shanties must be around there somewhere, but I don't know where. There's a man that does, but he didn't turn up this morning any more than the pickers did." He would like to have kept quiet about Albert Baines. A circle of involvement got started, and it just seemed to get wider. Sam sighed deeply.

"This man now, Sam, the one that didn't turn up. What's he like?" the sheriff asked.

"Short, red hair, walks forwards like his arms is too long," Sam answered.

"Now this man with the unfortunate arms, Sam, would this be the same man that you sent to the bus depot yesterday morning, the one who used the phone?" He paused. "You and Lee Roy?"

In his exasperating, longwinded, courteous way of asking questions, Sam reflected, the sheriff had a way of sounding a little too damn dangerous.

"That's him," Sam said. "He was hiring for me, to keep me going without havin' to cave in to the migrants up to Las Cruces. Lee Roy told you about it?"

"That's right, he did," the sheriff said. He chewed on his finger a bit, then said, "Thank you, Sam, thank you very much. He's in the clear, thanks to you and Lee Roy; it wasn't him." He chewed off the offending flesh and picked it off his lip and dropped it out the car window, then asked, "Do you suppose I could possibly use your phone?"

"Sure, Sheriff, help yourself," Sam said. "You going to tell me about this?"

"When I come back, I'll tell you all about it, that's a promise," the sheriff said. "Your phone up at the house? You wouldn't happen to have another one down here, would you?"

"Up at the house," Sam said. He got out of the car and watched as Sheriff Atwater drove around the sheds and past the barns toward the house. From the far end of the farm road he could hear Lee Roy's tractor approaching. Before it got to the sheds, it stopped. Sam went to see why Lee Roy had stopped and found that the tall young man from Las Cruces, Vinnie Duffy, had caught up to Lee Roy in his old truck. He stood in the road waiting, knowing he was on

185

enemy territory. Lee Roy waited for Sam so they could approach the union man together.

"What you here for, Mr Duffy?" Sam asked.

"My pickers want me to talk with you again, see if we can work something out," Irish answered. "We want to work. At the right wages."

"I'll hire your boys the same way they been hired for years. I'll pay what I can, and I'll post the rate up at the end of the shed every morning. If you want more money, you stay and work longer. I work six-thirty in the morning till eight at night, you can do the same if you want. I work seven days a week. I won't hire anyone who won't do the same, and if somebody don't turn up 'cause they're sick or tired, I'll find somebody else who's healthy. That clear enough?" Sam made his pronouncement with his eyes flickering to Lee Roy, who nodded approval of both the terms and the performance.

"You want the same old paid slavery, then," Irish said. "I thought you might have come around to seein' that you was dealin' with people, not animals. All right, if you won't deal with us like we're human, you'll have to deal with the union. I'll talk with you by the rules of organized labor, Mr Tolin."

"You're running a little bit too fast for yourself there," Lee Roy interjected.

"I was about to ask who you were, mister," Irish said.

"Lee Roy Stagg, President of the Farmers' Cooperative that covers this district. I got my own union," he added. "Now where's yours?"

"I got my local at Las Cruces, and there's a lot more comin'," Irish answered.

"Prove it," Lee Roy demanded. "Let's see you make it legal. Let's cut this big talk and see what you're made of. You're an agitator, Mr Duffy, Mr Irish Duffy. Oh yeah, I've done my investigatin', I know who you are. You're a union man tryin' to put a union behind you, but you haven't got one yet. You figure you'll have a union aplenty if you can beat more money out of Sam here and the rest of the growers. That's what you promised your pickers. You might have a few signed up, just a few, but you're not the mister mighty we have to deal with yet, not by a long way. We'll hire you people, sure we will, same as always. They turn up, they see what we'll pay, they say yes or they go away. Take it or leave it."

They had Irish, and he knew it. He had counted all along on simple greed. Employers' greed, that was his strong card. If they wanted their money for their crops, they wanted his workers. Once he had won from one farmer, the rest would come along. He would have wages where they ought to be, and he would have his union. Once he had that, he would screw them till they screamed and he'd have them where they hurt the most, he and his people would put their fingers around the throats of every rotten capitalist that got in their way, they would with their bare hands pull to pieces the structure that had sent him, his family and all the rest of the Okies through hell and still kept most of the migrant workers there.

He exploded in his impotence. "You can talk like that because you've bought blacklegs," he shouted, "traitors, I know all about them. People that ain't fit to spit on!" Thinking of nothing worse, he repeated, "Traitors!"

Sam said, "If they want to come back and work for me, they're welcome, them traitors, as you call 'em. I'll hire 'em, same as you."

Lee Roy pushed Sam back with his arm, facing Irish himself, but he couldn't seem to think of anything to say that would undo the damage.

"Wait a minute," Irish said, beginning to smile. He stepped away to look at the empty tractor and trailer, and he listened to the silent orchards, then looked back at the two men who now realized that the cat was out of the bag and rampaging around their acres.

"You went to get 'em," Irish said. "They didn't come here last night at all, you went to get 'em. You ain't got any blacklegs. They're gone, and me and my pickers is all you

187

got." He smiled broadly and put his hat on, master of the masters. "Well I'll be damned," he crooned.

To match his croon the purr of the sheriff's car approached them from behind the tractor and trailer. When he saw the three men, Sheriff Atwater speeded up and swung the car into an avenue of trees to bypass the obstruction, driving on past them and their vehicles before he pulled back onto the road. When he got out of his car, the men all watched him approach. He smiled pleasantly, all the time looking hard at Irish and his truck, then walked up to them until he stood close to Irish, staring at him with a friendly, puzzled look on his face.

"Now let's see if I got this right. Is this the union man from Las Cruces?" he asked.

Sam answered, "This is him. Name's Duffy."

"Of course you are!" he exclaimed, as if he was delighted to be let in on the news. "You're the same one went to the bus depot yesterday," he said. "You and Harold heard everything that peckerhead said about pickin' up those people at Santa Fe this morning." He was smiling broadly in delighted recognition. "Is that your truck?"

Irish said, "Sure it's mine. I paid for it."

"Nevada plates," the sheriff said. "You've been traveling some."

"Arizona," Irish said.

"Is that right? What's its number, its license number?" the sheriff asked.

"You already know it," Irish said.

"Now I may have got it wrong. You tell me anyway," the sheriff said.

"You arresting me?" Irish asked.

"Well, I've got a problem if I don't, if you see what I mean. You fit the description of the man who burned down a shanty town out past Santa Fe last night, and your truck was seen there," the sheriff said. "What do you think I ought to do in these unfortunate circumstances? I don't see that I have much choice."

"Who complained?" Irish said. "I burned down a shanty town. It was empty. Nobody and nothing there. What's the law that says you can arrest me for that?"

"Well, there's a fine for careless fires," the sheriff said, "but I guess you'd raise the money for that, wouldn't you?"

Irish rummaged in his pockets and produced some paper money. "I guess it'd be about five dollars, wouldn't it?" He offered the money to the sheriff, counting out five one dollar bills.

"Tell you what," the sheriff said, "I'll take the money from you down at the jail. I'll be taking all your valuables off you. You're under arrest, I'm afraid. Don't you worry none about your truck, I'll get somebody to bring your truck, long as you give me the key."

"There wasn't somebody in those shacks, was there?" Irish asked. His nightmare vision of innocent victims passed again over his mind.

"No, you're very fortunate there. You're under arrest for trying to set those wheat fields on fire," the sheriff said.

"What are you talkin' about?" Irish said. "You got to prove something like that."

Sheriff Atwater smiled at him with a very unhumorous smile, the kind of smile that says there's only a short way to go before there's danger ahead. "You burned the shacks, now, you admitted it. You're a union man, they tell me." Lee Roy and Sam nodded. "That means you're a Communist," the sheriff said in his gentlest voice, "and you're here to stir up trouble and try to wreck the whole Red Branch area, town and county and all." Irish tried to protest, but the sheriff bore down on him, smooth and insistent, face to face. "I know why you tried to burn those wheat fields, Mr Irish Duffy. Same thing you're trying to do to Sam, and to all the other growers. You're trying to ruin all these good people around here, all the time saying what you want is jobs for your union people. Well, what you don't know is that they're not going to stand still for you to do what you want, and that causes me twice as much trouble."

189

"Just what the hell do you mean by that?" Irish demanded.

"I'm arresting you for attempted arson, as much to stop things from going farther as to put you where you belong," the sheriff said. He turned to Sam and Lee Roy. "And you boys, both of you, now I'm telling you in front of this man here, stay within the law. That's a warning, I'm afraid, and I expect you to listen to it. This whole thing's building up, and somebody's bound to get hurt. Now, like they say, that somebody is not going to be me." He smiled his most charming smile and touched the bill of his cap with a finger. "I hope you understand," he said, and courteously opened the door of the car for Irish.

2

Mr Halbkeller didn't have all that many chances to let rip with a good editorial, and few of those had warranted being run on the front page of the *Red Branch Herald*. The sheer joy of being let loose on a topic that offered every element dear to the heart of a newspaperman shone through his prose that Monday morning, and he was a happy man when he saw his handiwork looking back at him from the paper that Jubilee gave him to read while he had his shoes shined.

"Sorry, that's the only paper I got," Jubilee said. "Guess you done seen everything in it."

"It looks different when it's set in type," Mr Halbkeller said. "Sometimes it looks better, sometimes not quite so good. I like this," he said sincerely.

The editorial was set in a box at the top of the page just under the name of the paper. It had an unusually bold headline on it, heavy, black, portentous, TIME TO SPEAK AND ACT. The headline and the setting were the work of the editor-publisher, Doyle Thompson, who had been in touch with Roger Preece several times while putting the edition together. The power of the press and the power of the bank, Mr Halbkeller mused, maybe the union people hadn't realized what they were doing when they took on Red Branch. The town wasn't a weak, meek collection of

191

nobodies, not a bit of it. The article surrounding the editorial, about the union moves and the victimization of Mr Sam Tolin, was almost pushed into secondary importance by the look of its rival. Was it a bit too much? In some circumstances, yes, it would have been. But not this time, not with this to say. He read it once again, letting the sentences roll through his mind in a stately procession.

"A declaration of war or a cataclysmic natural disaster could not affect Red Branch more than the attack which has been unleashed against our community. Let us be perfectly clear about that. What might appear to be a little local difficulty between a fruit grower and his workers is no less significant than the assassination of a member of the Austrian ruling family by a misguided fanatic. That last act began a conflict that claimed the lives of husbands and sons of Red Branch. Their sacrifice was given willingly for ideals and principles that were as dear to them as their lives, and are still as dear to all of us. Now they are under threat again.

"We have learned with rising indignation of the tactics and intentions of the Communist International. In pursuit of domination the agents of this conspiracy have convinced people in many nations to work from within to undermine democracy and economic stability, to bring them down, so that out of the wreckage and chaos the Communists could present themselves to the people as the only ones with a solution to unrest and privation. After that, in the name of equality, the state would abolish private property, conduct business, indoctrinate children, break the sanctity of marriage, outlaw religion, and create a secret political police force to subjugate the very people who had put such a regime into power. This is the kind of tyranny against which the patriots fought to give us the country and the way of life that today we prize and enjoy.

"Now we learn to our horror that this faraway, foreign menace is here, not merely on our doorsteps but in our houses, attacking us. The means to attack us is the envy felt

192

for our community by a class of people who come here for a few weeks of the year, take wages, welfare payments and charity from us, and give nothing in return. The old saying 'The poor are always with us' is wrong. These poor, who are poor because they choose to be, because it is easier to be poor than to work hard and long, live morally and frugally, and build a secure future, are fortunately with us only part of each year. In that time, however, they intend to destroy us.

"Their plan is simple. They will bankrupt our farmers, which in turn will bankrupt our businesses, which in its turn will ruin our banks. With them will go our savings and our property.

"Who will be the winners?

"What is left after the passage of a plague of locusts?

"The evil face of Communism has come among us. Red Branch has been chosen to defeat it. In the name of our country, our God, our future generations, yes even in the name of our pride, we must join together to defeat it."

"Have you read this?" Mr Halbkeller asked Jubilee.

"Yessir, I have," said Jubilee, "as much as I could get of it. Some of it I didn't understand though."

"What part was that?" Mr Halbkeller asked. Maybe his prose was too dense, he thought. He hadn't written it with people like Jubilee Hubbard in mind.

"The part about bein' poor," Jubilee said. "I'm poor, no one can't say I ain't, but I ain't no Commoniss."

"It doesn't say that," Mr Halbkeller said.

"It comes as near as almost," Jubilee argued. "I'd like to be rich as you, but that don't make me no Commoniss. I feels sorry for poor people, likely 'cause I feels sorry for myself, even if some of 'em is white people. I know I ain't supposed to feel sorry for white people, they's better off than me, but I do. But I got Jesus, Mr Halbkeller, you know I have, and ain't no Commoniss got Jesus."

Mr Halbkeller smiled at the thought that God's mysterious

ways were so pervasive. "Jubilee, I know you aren't a Communist. No one who knows you could think you're a Communist." He tried a little joke. "You're not a Red, you couldn't be." Jubilee either didn't understand or didn't think it was funny, and Mr Halbkeller pressed on quickly. "You're a Godfearing man who loves his Lord. Maybe you don't know enough about your Lord to see that you shouldn't envy me, and maybe you could look a little more closely at who likes being poor and who doesn't like it. You're maybe not clear in your thinking, but you are definitely not a Communist. Don't worry about that."

"That's good," Jubilee said, and finished off the polishing with a slap of the cloth across the gleaming toe of each shoe. He stood up and prepared to hold out his hand for his twenty-five cents, straightening his back with a bit more dignity than he usually allowed himself to show.

"Ain't nobody likes being poor, Mr Halbkeller," he said. "You got it wrong there."

"I haven't the time to explain," was the answer given over his shoulder as Mr Halbkeller hurried off. It was unfortunate that he did not recognize that for the second time in only a few moments God's mysterious ways had been revealed. If he had, at least some of the wonders that He was about to perform might not have been so unexpected.

3

After Lee Roy left, and after somebody came from the sheriff's office to pick up Irish Duffy's truck, Sam Tolin struck again. He had had time to walk through his empty orchards, almost feeling the apricots ripening around him as the morning heat built up to a scorching noon, and all he could see was money, hanging on the tree and going bad. He couldn't stand it. He got his truck out again and drove to Las Cruces. The old man who had met with him before came to meet him, while other people kept their distance.

"He ain't here," the old man said.

"You mean Irish?" Sam answered. "You bet he ain't. He's in jail. Likely to stay there for a while, too."

The old man looked at him in amazement, then turned and went to the nearest tent and told the people there the news. There followed a scurrying between tents that would have done justice to a relay race, the news being picked up and carried to the next tent or shack or shelter as soon as the words were out of the teller's mouth. The old man came back to Sam.

"Is that what you come for?" he asked.

"No," Sam confessed, "I thought you'd know about Duffy already. No, I came to offer you jobs, if you work on my

195

terms. It'd be back to the old way of doing things. You know what that is."

The old man flared up. "I know all right, back to you holdin' all the cards and couldn't give a crap about us!"

"What do you know about me?" Sam demanded. "When did you ever work for me?"

"I don't have to know about a boss to know what it's like to work for a boss. I been around too long for that." The bitterness in the old man's voice cut at Sam like a blade.

"Well, maybe everybody don't feel that way," Sam said.

"Oh yes they do," the old man said. "Just that they need the work so bad they have to hide it. Maybe you oughta know that."

"I'm hirin' tomorrow morning. Come if you like." Sam said this loud enough so that others would hear, and turned toward his truck to leave. The old man followed him.

"What's happenin' to Irish then?" he asked.

Sam thought there was no harm in their knowing what their hero was going through on their behalf. It was worth their knowing in case someone else tried to step out of line.

"There's a special hearing this afternoon at the Courthouse to hear the charges," he said. "He won't be coming back, he won't get bail," he added. "He'll be held in jail for trial."

The boy who broke up the pasteboard boxes out back of the Safeway store was the first to know something was up. He went back to his task after a short lunch break to find a group of men, evidently migrant workers, standing waiting for him.

"We need some of these here boxes," one of them said.

"Do you buy here at the Safeway?" the boy asked. "Are you our customers?"

"When we got the money," the man said. "What's it to you?"

"I'll go ask the manager," the boy said. "He might let you have some if you're customers of ours."

He went through the back of the store and found the manager in his office. "There's some pickers out back who say they need some of the boxes," he reported. "Should I let them have them?"

"What do they want them for?" the manager said.

"I didn't ask them," the boy said.

"Not for carrying groceries anyway, huh?" the manager said.

"No. Not for that," the boy replied.

"Cottonpickin' people come in here, try to beg things off us all the time," the manager said. "Don't they know we sell that stuff for scrap?" Answering his own question he added, "They don't even think about that."

The boy waited. "What have you got this morning?" the manager asked the boy.

"We got in a shipment of Kotex," he said. "The supervisor said to start breaking the boxes up so they wouldn't get put in the store for carrying groceries. That's what you wanted, wasn't it?"

"Oh Christ yes," the manager said; "don't leave them hanging around. People don't like to know about things like that. They buy their Kotex all right, but they don't want other people to think they know anything about it."

The boy said, "There's nothing else out there yet today."

The manager was tired of the conversation. "Well, we haven't got anything else anyway. Let them have as many Kotex boxes as they want. It won't matter if they're going out to one of those Okie camps. It's not like the Okies are going to get fussy about it."

What was going on inside the Courthouse was meant to be routine, even if the circumstances were anything but that.

The hearing was being held at the front of the big, square courtroom. Since no case had been listed for hearing that day, the windows had been left closed with the blinds raised, so that now with the room pressed suddenly into service the pitiful breeze that played with the attorneys' papers was

197

hardly enough to relieve the breathtaking heat. Judge Dix had put on his black gown over his fishing clothes, having been called back to duty just as he was preparing to leave for the rest of the day. He was not happy about this, and the blue workshirt that poked its collar above the neck of his gown underlined his impatience.

Irish was led in to the courtroom in handcuffs. The charge was attempted arson. The attorney handling the case, Mr Cook, said it was a difficult case from the point of view of proof of intent, he accepted that. However, the defendant had admitted setting fire to some abandoned squatter shacks and refused to give his reason for doing so. Whatever his real motive, which the judge could be assured would emerge in the course of further investigations, it wasn't of any interest or concern to the defendant, he had made it plain, if the wheat field had gone up with the shacks. The short of Mr Cook's long story was that the misdemeanor charge of fire raising was sufficient to detain the defendant in jail while the police and sheriff's deputies found out more about a possible felony arson case.

The judge agreed. He would be held in custody.

There was some noise outside, something unseemly for the normally hushed space outside this court of law, singing or something close to it. A group of people singing outside the Courthouse on a hot Monday at lunchtime? The clerk of the court had placed himself near a window to get some air and was now trying hard to avoid looking out to see what the commotion was, thinking it would annoy the already irritated judge further.

"Mr Clerk," Judge Dix said, "look out that window and see what the dickens is going on out there, would you? This is supposed to be a court of law, not some kind of circus."

Doing as he was bid, the clerk went to the window, looked, then started back from it after the briefest glimpse. "Judge!" he called. "Your honor!"

Everyone except Irish and the deputy guarding him crowded to the windows to see what had excited the clerk.

198

It was quite a sight. Around the Courthouse was strung a solid line of pickets, both men and women. They were quiet for the most part, although a few of the women had begun to sing. Sprinkled along the line of the pickets were a few men bearing handwritten signs saying "Duffy is innocent", "Free Irish Duffy" and so forth, as well as one which said "Jail the police". When the pickets saw they had an audience, the singing grew in volume and the column slowed down so that everyone could appreciate that the protest had produced a reaction.

The judge snapped an order to the deputy: "Bring your prisoner over here." When Duffy got to the window, the people down below saw him and immediately called the others to gather below the window, until there was a crowd of over a hundred shouting encouragement to Irish as well as suggesting that the police and the judge could do some pretty disgusting things to themselves.

When the first wave of shouting had spent itself, Judge Dix ordered Irish, "Now tell them to disperse."

"What do you mean?" asked Irish. "They're my friends. They come here to see I got a fair hearing. Why should I tell them to go away?"

"Because that's contempt of court," he said. He spoke quietly but he was fighting to control his anger.

Mr Cook intervened, telling Irish, "What they're doing is trying to influence the judge. It's called attempted coercion. They're trying to get you special treatment."

"Maybe that's the way they feel," Irish said.

"Do you refuse to tell them to disperse?" Judge Dix said.

Irish refused even to answer the question, clamping his jaw elaborately so that the judge couldn't miss the message of his silence.

The judge went back to the bench and slammed down his gavel at the same time that he sat down. "Contempt of court," he said. "No question of bail, he's in contempt. When we get around to sentencing him, there'll be some time to add for this offense. Hold him in jail."

He got up to leave the courtroom, stopping short when the clerk called again.

"Judge," he said, "come look at this."

The judge walked to the window and looked out. As he did so there was a jeering, whooping sound from the pickets. Those who carried signs had turned them around and now were waving them the printed side toward the window, making it clear that they meant their message for the judge. Looking down at them, he was being greeted by sixteen advertisements for Kotex written in large blue letters diagonally across what had been the sides of cardboard boxes.

"So that's what they think of our kind of justice, huh?" he said. "That's what you think of us, is it, Mr Duffy?" Irish didn't know what had happened, only that whatever it was had hit home. He smiled and said nothing. "Lock him up and throw away the key," Judge Dix said to the deputy. "I mean it!"

The schools in Red Branch were under pressure to keep going as long as they could in order to cut down the summer vacation a little bit for the sake of the harassed parents. This meant in practice that a week past Memorial Day was about the limit, because the rooms heated up to such an intolerable temperature that no learning could take place in any case. It was however not a matter of mass juvenile idleness after the schools finally closed their doors. The church-going kids went to summer camp up in the mountains for a week. The Boy Scouts, Girls Scouts and Campfire Girls went to rival establishments, one of which was only across a small lake from the church camp. The older boys and most of the older girls started summer jobs right away, some of the girls working as helpers in day camps to entertain the younger kids who had to stay in the town. High school boys who could wangle it postponed the start of their summer jobs until after the Fourth of July holiday, on the grounds that it wasn't sensible to begin a new job and then take a break just about the time they were getting the hang of it.

A few youngsters, only a very few, were footloose. For them, and for all the kids when they could steal the time, the town swimming pool was their oasis, as long as they were white. The rule wasn't as rednecked as it seemed, however, since there were no negro children in the town until a year or two later, and the Mexican children had to help their family incomes with what work could be found for them, or else they had to go along with the family when the others went into the fields to work. The older boys had a variation to the routine use of the swimming pool. When the heat was enough to melt the roads and make bicycling through the black goo into too much hard work, they diverted to the pool hall next to the Aragon Theater and sheltered in its shady gloom. Here they played pool for as long as their money held out, shredded the reputations of the girls of their acquaintance, and bragged about their emerging sexuality as if it was a new wonder for the world to take note of. The younger boys gathered on their fringe, drinking root beer and marveling at each utterance of an obscenity.

Mort Thomas's son Richie had been working at home on an airplane model won by a boy down the block at an amateur show at the Aragon Theater last Saturday matinée. The child sang a torch song written for a badly used kept woman. Somehow it touched the hearts of the kiddies' matinée audience, and the consequent applause earned him an unwanted airplane model kit. When he offered it to Richie, who was known among the youngsters as an expert on these things, Ritchie got to work on it without any ado just in case there was a change of mind. He spent the morning working on the fuselage, cutting the pieces from balsam sheets and gluing them, pinning these to a drawing board to let them set. He begged some money from his mother for a sandwich and started for the swimming pool shortly after twelve. By the time he had struggled to Fourth Street, the sticky tar made him decide to give up. He returned home to pry some change out of a piggy bank with one of his mother's best silverplate knives, and resumed his ride, this time by way of Greenfield Avenue, to go to the pool hall and hang around the older boys. As a result he was the first person to see the events at the Courthouse.

Beyond a collection of migrant workers marching around the building to show they were mad about something, he didn't understand what was going on. By the time he got to the pool hall and had settled on the story he had to tell, he was certain that he had witnessed one of the great events in the town's history, gleefully rubbing it into the other boys. Games stopped and drinks were abandoned, and a flight of bicycles swarmed down the avenue. The lunchtime crowd in the Rex Hotel saw the boys, one of the men extracting a garbled explanation from the cyclists about things going on down at the Courthouse. Calvin Whitmore was parked just outside and was young enough to behave as if he belonged to the pool hall brigade. By the time he had his truck started, he had two passengers in the front with him, and more men were clambering over the side boards to ride in the back. He spun a U-turn in front of the Rex and raced to the Courthouse.

At the same time, the deputy who had escorted Irish Duffy back to the jail and lodged him in a cell was trying to get in touch with Sheriff Atwater. He phoned the bus depot, giving Harold the message that hellzapoppin down at the jail and the sheriff was needed pronto. The same message went to the cigar store. Harold carried his message to the barber shop, only to find it closed for lunch. He phoned Nick's Diner and passed the word along there. Tom Potter repeated what he had been told to the men reading papers and smoking, emptying the cigar store quicker than a fire alarm would have done. One of them went across to the Bank of America to tell his brother, who gave up his place in line only two away from the cashier in order to go see what the fuss was all about. The cars and trucks that converged on the Courthouse square were a spectacle in themselves, so much so that a luncheon meeting at the BPW Club was disturbed. The ladies, thinking it was a fire or something

202

worse, asked the speaker to excuse them if they were a little late back for her speech, scheduled to be given when lunch was over at about one o'clock, and walked across as a group to see for themselves what was causing the uncivil goings-on at their civic center.

It was the presence of this group of respected wives, mothers and maiden aunts that did the greatest damage to the pro-Duffy demonstrators. Having watched Irish being taken to jail, following the deputy and shouting at him all the way, the pickets had moved to the diagonal sidewalk that ran between the Courthouse and the jail. Here they put on a show of solidarity, strutting up and down, waving their signs and singing something more or less in unison, looking uneasily defiant as the crowd from uptown gathered. The boys did what boys do, picking up on the hostility that was being generated. They started to play chicken with the pickets, riding their bikes at them and turning away at the last minute, so that it was only a matter of time before someone would miscalculate and there would be a more complicated situation than there was already. The Red Branch men were for the most part trying to keep the boys out of possible trouble rather than provoking them to be antagonists. They were also trying to find out what on earth was going on. The deputy had slammed the jail door and was saying nothing until the sheriff arrived, and Irish's hearing had taken place so peremptorily that gossip had not yet caught up with events. In the confusion some honest consideration was given to the theory that the marchers were advertising Kotex, as well as trying to get someone out of jail by public pressure tactics.

The ladies, unable to see any of this activity taking place at the rear of the Courthouse, walked in a chattering group along the sidewalk to the front of the Courthouse and then along its west side, turning the corner of the building just where the pickets turned around for the return trip to the jail. What they saw confronting them was the blue trade name of the leading brand of women's sanitary napkins, held

203

up in their faces in full public view. The ladies were shocked and incensed, taking it as a personal insult. Why they should have thought the insult was being offered to the ladies of Red Branch is not clear, but they did. They registered the degree of offense they had taken by instructing the marching men to take their signs down immediately. The men ignored them and continued marching. This was too much for the growing crowd of Red Branch men, which by now outnumbered the sign carriers. Though few or none of the men were anything directly to do with the specific women there, the offense to Red Branch women had to be answered. In a rush that began as a single assault and grew into a general attack, the men went for the signs. If a picket didn't release his sign when it was seized, he was knocked to the ground and the sign taken from him. If others came to defend him, they were struck with the stake to which the sign had been nailed, the sign being by now torn off and trampled. More men joined in, men in overalls, jeans, business suits, a pharmacist's white coat. They were a small army defending their home territory, shouting outrages at the invaders and encouragement to each other.

The picketing women made a halfhearted attempt to defend their sign carriers and then ran for safety. The bulk of their men followed them, a few fighting a rearguard action defending their honor more than their comrades, fleeing into the thickets and gloom of Garfield Park. The Red Branch men pursued them to the edge of the park, stopping on the service road that ran to the back of the jail. There they stood in a group, amazed at the turn of events that had altered a normal, hot, Monday noon into a battle with people they had not seen before. The boys on their bikes, now bold and savage when the day had been won, shouted at the unseen enemy and rode into the edge of the park, pretending to be in hot pursuit. The men told them to stop being a damn nuisance and go home.

From the sounds that could be heard from beyond the park it was clear that the pickets had run through the park to their vehicles and were now retreating. The Red Branch men were content to stand their ground, which is where Sheriff Atwater found them when he arrived, siren screaming, from wherever it was he had finally been located.

The sheriff's Tennessee origins were always well to the fore when he was under stress. "Okay, boys," he said, "okay now, you boys done a mighty fine job, yessirree Bob. And I thank you. I really do. Now I want everyone to go away, the situation is nicely under control. Yes sir."

The men were ready to go. They turned it over to the Sheriff without any dissent, still baffled by what they had wandered into. He stood on the far side of the service road with his back to the park, waving them away like you would a flock of only marginally controllable chickens.

His behavior annoyed Roger Preece. "What are you doing that for, Sheriff?" he asked. "There's no need to do that. We're not a mob, God damn it, we were only doing your job for you if you come down to it."

Sheriff Atwater stopped his flapping immediately. "That's right, Roger, sorry." He cleared his throat as if to speak. The men paused in their egress and turned the sheriff's way. He had never been able to resist a gathering, as preacher, singer, politician or now as sheriff.

"I want to thank you men," he said, "sincerely thank you all, for defending my deputy. I'm not saying the jail was under threat exactly, but my deputy needed friends, and he rightly found them in you gentlemen. We 'preciate it. Comes a time we need help again, I know where to go. I thank you all."

In spite of what Roger Preece said, it had been in truth a mob action. An issue of justice had been settled by force which was undirected and out of control. The sheriff approved of it, therefore in the minds and spirits of the men of Red Branch it had been a noble mob, a just mob, almost an official mob. It was a mob that set a precedent for what was to come.

4

Cappy Petrillo for once in his life had been slow to react. He had decided to do a bit of staff work on Irish Duffy's message. He contacted everyone he could think of who would be able to shed some light on what had prompted Irish's plea for intervention from head office. At eight o'clock that morning, no one had much to say about it. Nothing, as far as they knew, was happening. At nine o'clock it was the same. At ten o'clock it was very different. A little bit of genuine information and a lot of rumor had altered the picture Cappy got to one of confrontation between leaderless forces. That might be a situation that union leaders liked, leading to some productive fishing in muddy waters, but when the muddying had been to a certain extent the work of the union man on the ground, it was disastrous. Cappy swore at himself and the world, called for his car and a driver, and set off for Red Branch. He had four hours in which to regret his failure to trust Irish Duffy.

A map of the central valley highway shows a spot about ten miles north of Red Branch labeled Manzanita. Because of its location drivers don't often approach it except when they are busy going somewhere else. Its one gas station and the truck stop cafe next door are buttressed by some six or seven houses that crouch against the flat landscape at the best of times, and seem to be actively burrowing into the ground when the heatwaves perform their unsettling dance. From a distance the Standard Oil sign on a steel pole is all that can be seen, and is all that could attract anyone to the place.

Cappy and his driver needed a rest stop and the car needed gas. The station manager let them leave the car in the little bit of shade afforded by the flat canopy while they went to the cafe. Grace Grund said she made the best tuna sandwich you could eat and recommended it with slices of red Bermuda onion. Cappy said he had forsworn onions. They had their sandwiches and followed it with banana cake, freshly made. The coffee was rich and black, also freshly made.

It wasn't often a customer came in who could afford the luxury of a driver. Grace was curious anyway about her customers, and this one made a nice puzzle to unravel on a dull day. She studied Cappy as he sat over his second cup of coffee. He for his part wasn't looking forward to walking into the Red Branch situation knowing so little of what was going on. The second cup was strictly a delaying tactic. It suited them both to enjoy a little bout of conversational fencing.

Mrs Grund opened it. "Should I know your face, from the newspapers or someplace?" she asked.

"You might," he conceded; "not around here though."

"You're from the city, then, up north," she said.

"That's right," he said. Anticipating her next question he said, "Just down here on business."

The driver knew when he was excluded. He got down from his revolving stool and sat in a corner booth and closed his eyes. "Got a headache," he said. He put back on the Army Air Corps style cap and sunglasses that he had taken off when they entered, tilting the cap down to cover his eyes.

Cappy was dressed in a linen jacket and trousers, with a white shirt and a silk tie gleaming under the buttoned up

207

jacket. His shoes were brown and white, to go with the beige suit. The sun had picked up the thinning parts of his brown hair and turned them gold, shading in the grey at his temples. The effect was of a theatrical impresario on his way to Palm Beach where he expects a difficult encounter with the leading lady. Mrs Grund fell for it.

"Of course," she scoffed at her foolish old self, "I recognize you now," she lied. "Well, welcome to my humble abode."

"Thank you," Cappy replied. He would have said more but she cut him off in order to keep him from discovering that her ignorance of his identity was still total.

"I ask all my celebrities to sign my autograph book," she said. "Would you mind?"

She got out a blue padded leather book with Autographs written diagonally across the lower right corner, opening it to the section with pink pages and placing the blue ribbon marker in the page. Pink was for the people who were possibly important ones to have in your autograph book. The yellow and light blue pages were for the truck drivers who wanted to say nice things about the food.

She slid it across the counter to him, pretending to look for her fountain pen as she did so.

"It's all right," he said, "I'll use my own pen. Matter of fact, I prefer it. My signature doesn't look right if I write with another person's pen." He laughed an unnecessary laugh and held down the page against the blast from the big fan that circulated the tepid air.

"Lorraine Finch, the famous movie star, now, when she wrote she said how much she liked my devil's food cake," Mrs Grund said. "I haven't got any of that today."

Cappy was about to return the book with "Sincerely, Cappy Petrillo" written in it. Prompted by Mrs Grund, however, he added above the signature "Delighted to find such comfort" and put parentheses around the Petrillo to make it look like he and Grace Grund were first name friends. He added a squiggle after his name just to finish off the page.

Her joy at the effusive compliment was tempered by realization that Cappy Petrillo, the famous Communist, had been her mystery celebrity. She wasn't sure that was altogether a good thing to advertise. She smiled broadly and shook hands as he got up to leave.

"Let's go!" he called to the driver, who woke with a casual lifting of the cap and adjustment of the glasses. Cappy left saying more thank-you's, and the driver said his and started to follow. He turned back to take a toothpick from a small glass cup and put it between his teeth, tilting back his aviator's hat to show a quiff of black hair that, with a bit of teasing, could be made to tumble out under the cap onto his forehead like Clark Gable's. He touched the cap with a finger in salute to Mrs Grund and made a second attempt to leave.

He turned back once more, however, asking, "Is there a back road to Las Cruces that doesn't go through Red Branch?"

Mrs Grund assured him there was and drew a rough map with the driver's repeating pencil on a paper napkin. Take the next road that turns right off the highway, go about three or four miles on a straight road, turn left where the sign at the crossroads says you go right to come back here to Manzanita, then right in a mile or so to the Las Cruces Slough.

"He's not going fishing in those clothes, is he?" she asked the driver.

"Mr Petrillo?" the driver said. "Nah, he's going out to the camp there. He's got union business there."

Through her window she watched the car on its way, then lunged to the telephone and bounced the receiver rest until the Red Branch operator answered. "Eunice, dear, can you get me my sister, please; she's working lunches at Nick's Diner. Thanks, dear, we'll talk later."

Hazel Klinghofer wasn't a natural for Nick's clientele.

Tall, stringy, past her best, she had a denture smile, augmented blonde hair and black glasses to correct myopia. Aside from Grace Grund for a sister, she had as her assets a sister-in-law who worked at a very expensive restaurant this side of Placid City and eavesdropped on that city's celebrities without qualms, and a husband who as clerk to the sheriff saw every piece of correspondence that crossed the law man's desk including the wanted bulletins before they had even been posted. She was good for business.

When she took Grace's call she knew she had the scoop of her career before the receiver was back in its place. "Nick!" she called through the serving window. He came running when she called like that. "Cappy Petrillo is on his way to Las Cruces. Boy, are we in for it now!" She repeated the news word for word from one end of the counter to the other. Nick went for the phone but she got there first. "I'll call my husband," she said, which is how the sheriff knew in time to send a car to intercept Cappy, which he didn't do. Nick phoned the bus depot to get Harold to give the message to his brother Mike in the barber shop, just in case there were customers there who needed to know. One of Nick's customers diverted from his intended route in order to give the news to the holdovers from the mob that had been at the jail, who were still drinking at the Rex Hotel. Calvin Whitmore, nursing a bruise under his ribs, heard it and walked to the cigar store immediately. He got Tom Potter to phone Lee Roy again, this time brooking no nonsense from Mrs Stagg and ordering her to get her husband to the telephone. Whining, she obeyed.

"Lee Roy?" Calvin said, omitting the polite address he had always used before. "This is Calvin Whitmore, and I'm one of the farmers you're s'posed to be protecting against this here union. What the hell are you doing for us, Lee Roy? Cappy Petrillo is out to Las Cruces planning things for us, and you're hiding out on your farm. I bet you don't even know what happened at the jail a half hour ago." Calvin cut off the comment from the other end. "Lee Roy, I suggest you get your ass into town and stay here till this thing's over. We're gettin' mad." He hung up the receiver and stalked out, forgetting to leave money for the call. Tom Potter let him go without a challenge.

At almost the same moment Cappy Petrillo arrived at Las Cruces to find the pickers still limping back one truck at a time from the confrontation at the jail. He heard their version of what had happened to Irish and concluded that he had been caught dead to rights doing the union's business. Irish had burned out the blacklegs to keep the picking from going ahead, the farmers knew it, and Irish was being victimized in order to intimidate the union pickers. He applied his rational brain to what should be done next and came to the solution that would suggest itself to any union leader under these or similar circumstances.

"We strike," he said.

The rest of the afternoon he sent men from Las Cruces to the other camps to activate the union agitators who had been placed there. On pieces of paper headed Destroy After Reading he gave his instructions. Every grower without exception who could be expected to employ fruit pickers was to be shut down. He didn't care that this was an illegal strike, this was the way it was going to be. At dawn tomorrow he wanted every farm road blocked with people and trucks. Anyone entering or leaving was to be intimidated. No delivery trucks, no packing trucks, nothing of any commercial importance was to be allowed in or out. The strike would be total and too big for the local law people to handle. There would be no leadup to strike action, no discussions, no negotiations. He was going to show muscle and people. He was going to show power.

He left Las Cruces and drove into town just in time to get to the Parks and Recreation Department before it closed. He asked the girl for an application to use a public facility and reserved the Garfield Park band shell for all day Tuesday. Purpose of reservation: To hold a mass meeting of the United Farm Workers Union. She read the application

211

and quoted to Cappy the ordinances that said the good behavior of the crowd had to be guaranteed and that the police had to be informed if the gathering concerned more than fifty people. Cappy told her he expected it would be at least ten times that and would leave it to her to tell the police. As he went through the door she was already reaching for the phone that connected her to the Courthouse switchboard. The message went out to find Police Chief Thomas quickly. The switchboard operator, accustomed to keeping overheard secrets genuinely secret, did not pass on the news of the mass meeting, and the girl in Parks and Recreation forgot to say what he had come for when she told her parents she had taken care of business with Mr Cappy Petrillo, who, she said, didn't look anything like a Communist but more like one of those people who owned big hotels and married movie starlets. Cappy then went to the Red Branch Printing Company, where he placed and paid for an order with a check that two hours later allowed Oscar Jelling, the printer, to pay his bill at the liquor store that was six months overdue. He ordered signs that demanded the freeing of Irish Duffy, an end to victimization of union workers, fair wages for a fair day's work, and all the rest of the slogans that applied. He also ordered the printing of a thousand union cards and an equal number of receipts for membership dues, in case the question of union representation for non-union labor were to come up. He sent his driver to reserve and pay for a room for two at the Mariposa Hotel, and to get some sandwiches and beer sent up to the room at ten o'clock. The drug store was still open as he walked, unidentified, down Greenfield Avenue. He bought a copy of the *Red Branch Herald* to read in the hotel, glancing only briefly at the front page editorial. He had seen worse.

Louella passed Cappy Petrillo without knowing it as she went to the Rex Hotel for her sundowner, a Coke with lots of ice. Calvin was there on the edge of a tense knot of men, with someone at the center she didn't recognize at first.

When she did, there was no great pleasure in the recognition. It was Mr Stagg, whom she had known briefly at Sunday School a few years ago. That short acquaintance was enough to tell her that when she went her own way, when she began to live her own life, he would be one of those who would condemn. He and the rest of the men were hardeyed, smiling if at all in a way that was not humorous. Instead of pulling at their drinks contemplatively at the end of a hot day, tipping their heads back and letting the cool flow do its work, they bit at the alcohol with their lips and forced it down with the backs of their tongues. They were excited. Louella had seen men drink that way when they wanted to sleep with her and felt they were on the verge of getting her to say yes.

She gestured to Calvin to come over to her. He looked no better than the rest, taut and flushed, roughened by the excitement the men shared.

"What's going on?" she asked.

"Lee Roy's taken charge," Calvin said. "This is it. We ain't sittin' still for no workers. This is where we show who's the boss around here."

"What's happened?" She had thought the incident at the jail pretty well settled the question of who was in charge.

"Cappy Petrillo's come to Las Cruces. He's come out in the open with his union. This Irish fella was just a stooge." Calvin was properly scornful of the bungling Duffy who had let himself be caught in the act.

"Is this Cappy meeting with Lee Roy, then?" Louella asked.

"We ain't meeting with nobody," said Calvin. "They do it our way or they get run out of the county. That's it."

Louella looked at this near stranger. A man had burned down a shanty town where people might have been sleeping. Ordinary workers had started a fight over his arrest. Sam Tolin was in trouble over his apricot picking. Adding the three together didn't equal in her mind the mood of dangerous violence that she sensed in Calvin.

213

"We're gonna fight 'em," Calvin said, "all the way."

"Calvin, come on," she pleaded, "use your head. Somebody's going to get hurt. This thing's got all out of hand."

While they had been talking, Lee Roy had moved nearer the couple at the bar, needing his lieutenant at his side. In his new alliance with the ungodly he distrusted all his allies except Calvin, who had the quality of decisive, innocent, youthful savagery that defines the true pagan and who therefore should have been anathema to the likes of Lee Roy. Now, hearing this last comment from Louella, he moved toward Calvin, standing with him, coming just short of putting his hand on Calvin's shoulder to show their interdependence in the face of a challenge.

"Somebody's got to do what's right," Lee Roy said. His voice shifted gear and dropped into a richer register as he moved from the moralistic to the sententious. "That's not too hard to do, you might think." He looked hard at this rival who represented what he despised. "Maybe the hard part is telling what's good from what's bad. When you're not used to doing that, it's not easy."

"I don't rightly understand that," Calvin said.

Louella did. She finished her watery Coke and walked out. Outside in the still, hot evening she thought maybe she would take in the movie. The Aragon was air conditioned now; she'd walk up there and see what was playing.

Lee Roy excused himself and said he had to run out home for a while. He would be back to spend the night at the hotel, he said. One of the men started to make a highly flavored comment about why he needed to visit home and wife and was cut off in mid-ribaldry by a shot from Lee Roy's eyes that was as deadly as a ray from a Buck Rogers gun. Calvin said he was going to find something to eat, thought he'd try the chophouse south of town.

It took the switchboard girl more than an hour to speak to Mort Thomas. He got her message to return the call when he came in to tell his wife he wouldn't be home for supper,

214

and to change out of his sweatstained shirt. He was meeting a few people, he said, from Placid City. He phoned the switchboard number and got a peevish report that his failure to keep other people informed of his whereabouts had meant she had had to sit there and wait for him for an hour and a half. He promised her a box of chocolates, apologized and asked for the message. She was only partially mollified.

"I was to inform you, when and if you bothered to return my telephone calls, that a Mr Petrillo has reserved Garfield Park for a mass meeting tomorrow," she said.

"Son of a bitch," Mort mumbled under his breath.

The girl said sharply, "What did you say, please!"

"He's not wasting any time," Mort said. "Do you know where the sheriff is?"

"Mr Klinghofer is taking his calls," the girl answered.

"I don't want Mr Klinghofer," Mort said and hung up.

He went to the bathroom, where he splashed water in his armpits, arching his back in pleasure as the cold hit his tender spots, towelled down, put on his clean shirt and went out to his car. He was halfway down the street when he remembered he hadn't said goodbye to his wife. If Kling was taking Sheriff Atwater's calls, that meant the sheriff was out in his car. Mort drove to the now closed Shell station and parked in the forecourt where the tires were usually stacked up in what passed for a display, facing the intersection of Greenfield and the highway. To pass the time he kept tabs on the number of petty violations that he could have stopped cars for, reckoning he could justify a deputy if he sat down and made out an official report of them. The idea of a deputy didn't appeal, however. The young men coming into the police force these days didn't inspire his confidence. The good ones were joining the Army or the Navy, and the really good prospects were trying to get into the Marines. If he had it to do over again, he might have joined the Marines himself. The combination of discipline and meanness was about as good as you could get. On the whole, though, he thought it was a pretty good idea that he didn't have it to do

215

all over again. He was tired and wanted to go to sleep, but he couldn't take a chance of missing the sheriff. After a wait of almost two hours, the sheriff's car came along the highway from the south and pulled in to the service station beside his. A very worried-looking Atwater put his head out of the window. "We got some talking to do," he said. "Leave your car here and come ride with me."

Calvin had finished his pork chops and mashed potatoes, leaving the carrots on his plate. He couldn't stand root vegetables, they made him feel like a pig. He was drinking off the last of his coffee when, looking over the rim of the mug, he saw Chief Thomas and Sheriff Atwater come in and take a table in the far corner. He was glad to see them come in, because being the last one to leave a cafe always made him feel he had to hurry in order to shorten the agony for the waitress. They waved to Calvin, talked between themselves for a few moments, then beckoned to him to come over. He picked up his check and joined them.

"How's your daddy?" Sheriff Atwater asked him as Calvin sat down in the offered chair.

"Oh for Christ's sake," Mort Thomas said. He wiped one of his large hands across his face.

"He's fine," Calvin said. What did they want? He waited patiently; he was the one who had been summoned.

"Calvin," Mort said, "you did a good job on that business with Irish Duffy."

"Thanks, Mr Thomas," Calvin answered. He told himself he had all night, and he was a very patient young man, but he didn't like this pussyfooting around.

"How do you feel about this trouble with the pickers?" Mort went on.

"I hope we get it over with before our own fruit is ready," Calvin said. He paused and then added, "Of course I hope the other farmers don't get hurt bad or nothin' like that. Us Whitmores can take care of ourselves, when it comes to pickin' and shippin' the fruit. The others ain't in such good shape. I worry for 'em."

216

Sheriff Atwater cleared his throat. "Does that mean that you think somethin' oughta be done to bring things to a head, sort of?" he asked.

"I think that might be best," Calvin said. "I know Lee Roy feels that way, and I'd go along with him."

"Could you do something to help the cause, you might say, without Lee Roy to say it was the right thing to do?" As he asked his question, the sheriff leaned back and looked into the distance, as if he was asking a completely theoretical question that only barely touched the subject at issue.

"Don't need Lee Roy to hold my hand," Calvin bristled. "He ain't my daddy. One's bad enough." He lowered his voice, leaned forward over the table and said, "Why don't you guys cut the crap and tell me what the hell you want?"

Mort snorted. "You won't help us much if you can't keep your temper, Calvin. You also are going to keep your mouth shut tight, even from your girlfriend. We'll take a gamble on you, but only if you can take orders and shut the hell up. Are you in or out?"

Calvin knew that at another time, when he was not as curious nor as excited by the circumstances, he would feel enough anger that he could stage a minor blowup and a to-hell-with-you walkout. Right now he very much wanted in, on whatever terms were being offered.

"What are you lookin' for me to do?" he asked.

"Huh-uh," Mort said. "In, or out?"

"God damn it, Mr Thomas, in!" Calvin said.

"That's good, son, that's fine, now just calm down," the sheriff said.

Mort smiled. "What we want is for you to take a run down the highway a few miles. We're meeting some people from Placid City who are going to give us a hand."

The sheriff added, "We would like for you to meet them too, Calvin, and to give them any little help they might need, sort of assistance, if they need it."

"Okay," Calvin answered, "I can do that, sure. When do you have in mind?"

"Right now," Sheriff Atwater said, getting to his feet.

"Yeah, that's okay," Calvin said. "I ain't got any plans."

Mort put a hand on his arm. "We'll go in your truck, Calvin. Okay? Bring it around to the side, away from the neon sign. The sheriff will be out in a minute or two. Don't start the engine or turn on the lights after you get it moved. Just sit there and wait. I'll be out after the sheriff."

Calvin was impressed with the secrecy. He was also stunned by it, so much so that he stood and looked at Mort with his mouth open all set to catch flies.

"We don't want to be seen going to this meeting, Calvin," Mort said. "Somebody sees you, well, it won't matter too much."

"You go move your truck, Calvin, and we'll be along right soon," the sheriff said. As if a thought had just struck him, he scratched his ear and frowned over the idea. "Tell you what," he said, "when you get out there, have a look around you, stop and light a cigarette, something like that. Then get in your truck and turn on the lights. If another car does the same thing, especially a big sedan that looks like it's a city slicker's car, drive away into town and forget about us. We'll come find you if we still need you. The car will follow you, but don't get worried."

"I wasn't worried before, but I kind of am now," Calvin said. He tried a laugh but it didn't come out right. "You're makin' it sound downright dangerous, Sheriff," he said.

"Oh, it is, Calvin," the sheriff said, "it is."

Calvin went outside to his truck and got in. He put a cigarette in his mouth and lit a match, holding it as long as he could before dropping it to the floor. He lit another, and this time touched his cigarette with it. He turned on the ignition, pulled on the starter, and when the engine caught switched on the lights. He moved slowly to the side of the cafe, waiting to see if anything or anyone seemed to respond to his movements. No one was watching. He turned off the lights and the engine and waited. Beyond the arrival of the two policemen, he couldn't guess what he was waiting for.

He laughed aloud and struck the steering wheel with the palm of his hand. Life was getting exciting, and he liked it.

Calvin drove the three of them south to an unused agricultural inspection station just beyond the Placid River Bridge. There waiting for them was an officer in a black car. All four of the men went into the single small room of the station, where the officer was introduced to Calvin as the man in charge of a squad of riot police. Thirty minutes later, after he and the lawmen had finished their meeting, Calvin wasn't so sure he still liked the excitement. He was, however, in, as he had wanted to be. Nothing could change that now.

VIII

Tuesday

1

The migrants in the camps liked to give the impression that they went to bed with the chickens and woke with them too, the old expression being one of their own favorite ways of describing themselves. It was one of the subtler ways they had of encouraging outsiders to leave them alone. There were seldom any lights in the camps at night, but not for lack of activity. When a guitar player sat himself outside a tent or a shack and a few people gathered around to hear him and sometimes sing with him, there was no need of light. The same reticence or simplicity applied to their conversations. They spoke quietly in small knots away from the dwellings, squatting on their haunches and picking at pieces of weed and grass, the groups taking on new people and shedding others as if some process of organic growth was going on. The subjects of these gentle conversations, being the simple utterances of uncomplicated people, should have risen out of the natural philosophy of people who are in tune with a natural life. In a way they were, since the subjects usually got round to the need for violence, the threat of violence, the consuming envy that produces violence. The two sides of man's nature, which everyone from the deepest philosopher to the Chinese herbalist tries to bring into balance, more for his own need of a quiet mind than man's demonstrated need for balance in his life, were as disharmonious in these migratory tribes as it is possible to imagine. Creatures sketched in watercolor paints that melted into shadows or distances, they seemed sometimes to be the reflection of people rather than the people themselves. Push against this pale, bleached out, transient reflection, however, and rock lay behind it.

Two or three men had kept watch all through the night, the identity of the watchers changing from hour to hour, but the darkness had been unbroken inside and outside the camps. At first flush of false dawn the watchmen moved through the camp waking everyone up. By dawn itself the trucks and cars were moving from every camp on the west side, each going according to a plan agreed among the union agitators to a particular farm road. As each one arrived, the driver drove it into contact with the next one bumper to bumper, and one or two men bounced the springs of the car or truck until the bumpers were interlocked. By sun-up not one farm road remained unbarricaded.

Farmhouses in the valley were by design always set back among the orchards, to take advantage of the cooling effects of the trees and the irrigation. Wherever possible they were a good distance from the working buildings too, as if a discreet separation might squeeze something in the way of gentility and comfort out of what was a hard way to make a living. It happened to be Calvin Whitmore's father who was the first farmer who went down his road that morning. He intended to leave letters in the mailbox and put the little metal flag up, telling the postman to collect even if there weren't letters to deliver. Mr Whitmore, by virtue of having worked later than usual getting his correspondence caught up, was therefore the first person to know that his farm was under siege. Acting under Lee Roy Stagg's emergency plan, he phoned the alarm in to the Rex Hotel. As the news spread and each farmer warily explored the state of things on his own farm, the extent of the strike became clear and panic descended. Everyone tried to phone Lee Roy, jamming the Rex Hotel telephone. Before eight o'clock Old Gomez had had enough. They would have to find somewhere else. The Farmers Cooperative offices were too far out of town, too far away from what Lee Roy saw as the center of the tangle, Irish Duffy in a cell in the jail. Calvin was rousted out of bed and called to duty. He went to Lake Street to Tom Potter's house and brought him back to open up the cigar store.

In this manner Lee Roy entered another den of iniquity, his crusade forcing him once more to compromise with lesser evil in order to pursue the greater good. He walked to his new center of operations down the street, staring into the show window at the display of pipes and cigar boxes, trying without craning his neck too obviously to see through the thin blue curtain at the back of the show window into the room beyond, finally opening the door and going in like a schoolboy entering a shower room naked for the first time. He stared at the brass spittoons and the buttoned leather chairs, the square table with its selection of newspapers and magazines, the humidor boxes behind the counter each labelled with its brand of cigar. It took a while, but gradually the wrinkle around his nose produced by the cigar smoke relaxed, and he found himself to his surprise leaning his elbows on the mahogany counter and talking with Tom as if the latter were not the purveyor of the devil's weed that Lee Roy himself, in imitation of Mr Halbkeller, had condemned more than once.

Cappy Petrillo rose early and had a light breakfast sent up to his room at the Mariposa Hotel. The driver, Clancy Spargo, chose to eat a substantial breakfast downstairs. As a result he was the one who learned that the first carload of reporters and photographers from the big newspapers had been sighted. Expecting Cappy to travel first class as usual, they had laid siege to the Regency Hotel, refusing to believe that he wasn't the guest in the top-floor suite who insisted on absolute privacy. When Clancy brought this news

225

upstairs, Cappy told him to take the car to the printing works and load up everything that had been printed so far, then come for him at the service entrance behind Gump's grocery store so that there would be no need for him to go into the lobby and risk being seen.

Clancy, a simple man whose deceptions were practiced on himself alone, was alarmed by the need for secrecy. "What's the deal, Mr Petrillo?" he asked. "They don't have guns, do they, whoever's after you?"

"They'll have a court order as soon as they can get the judge to sign it," Cappy answered.

"Oh," Clancy responded. He knew nothing of such things.

"They'll try to serve me with a court order pretty soon," Cappy explained. "They'll order me to stop the strike because it's illegal. It is. In a town like this the guy trying to serve the subpoena will probably be wearing a uniform, a deputy sheriff or something like that. I don't want him to get near me."

"Okay," Clancy said.

"If I'm in the car, keep driving. If I'm not, try to get a crowd around me," Cappy instructed while the driver nodded. He took a quick tour of the room and came back to Clancy. "No," he said, "that's risky. Tell you what, get the stuff from the printing works and then go to the S.P. station. Meet the train that comes in about eight forty-five from the south. There'll be two goons on it. Pick them up, and then come back here for me, at the back like I said, and tip me off on the house phone."

"Two goons?" Clancy asked.

"Bodyguards," Cappy said.

"It's gonna get rough, huh?" Clancy said.

"Maybe," Cappy said. "If they can keep away subpoena servers, they'll earn their money."

"Who do I look for?" Clancy asked him.

"If you watch the people getting off that train, and you don't see two thugs that you'd prefer to stay away from, just

226

come on back and forget about it. I don't want them if they don't scare the pants off the yokels." Cappy wasn't joking.

Lee Roy drove himself to Mr Cook's house on Divisidero Street. Being fellow Presbyterians, he felt, would be a great advantage, helping him cover for the fact that he was out of his depth in legal matters. He had outlined the situation to Mr Cook over the phone a few minutes before and now found him ready with his briefcase, waiting in the open doorway. He was grave as he shook Lee Roy's hand and took a legal folder from him, looking him in the eye as men do when they share a burdensome and worrying task. The task before them was to defeat Cappy Petrillo, and the worry was whether the law which they deployed would be enough for a man like Cappy, who knew more law than most lawyers and had been in as many courtrooms as Perry Mason. They drove in Lee Roy's sober black car, at a sedate pace conducive to constructive thought, to the Courthouse.

Once the word had gone around that all the farm roads were blocked, delivery trucks and other commercial vehicles had been pulled off the roads. Except for the men who buzzed along the roads in their flivvers carrying messages between barricades, the roads out to the west were practically empty and the migrants settled down for a tight strike. The farmers, who ran a gauntlet of jeering, obscenely filthy suggestions in order to get their cars and trucks past the barricades and out onto the roads, drove past other farms to see what it was like for the rest. Everywhere they found the same situation and the same atmosphere. The predictable code of business and personal relationships between employers and employees had ceased to exist, blown sky high in a conflict that most of the farmers had not thought was anything much to do with them. The old order no longer existed. One by one the farmers drove on into the town to see if anyone there could make sense of it, and to see if from Red Branch there was a way to foretell what was to happen next. They were confused, their pride was deeply wounded, their normal farmer's refuge of preparing for reverses by pretending to anticipate disaster now taken away from them by the reality of disaster itself.

Judge Dix received Lee Roy and Mr Cook in his room behind the courtroom. The beige curtains of lightweight velvet hung gallant but tired, the American flag seemed pulled into folds by its own overwhelming weight, the desk pressed its brown bulk into the dusty oatmeal carpet. The room was dispirited and without hope, infested with cigar smoke and boredom. The visitors explained why they had come, why the strike was illegal and why an injunction was the legal tool they needed.

"In my legal training, Mr Cook, my professors always used to say that I had to ask myself what I was trying to achieve," Judge Dix said. His manner was challenging and not very respectful. "Just what are you trying to achieve?"

"Well, we want the strike confined to the dispute between Mr Tolin and the Las Cruces workers," Mr Cook said.

"That means between Tolin and this Duffy fella," the judge said, "and the Duffy guy is the union man. He can call in Mr Petrillo any time he wants to."

"That's correct," Mr Cook said. "If he does that, Mr Stagg here will want proof that the union is representing the workers who are in dispute. He will want a ballot of the Las Cruces workers to see if they want the union to represent them and if they're prepared to join to get representation."

"I see where you're headed, Lee Roy," Judge Dix said.

Never one to fail to dot an i, Mr Cook ploughed on. "If Mr Petrillo represents the workers in talks with the farmers, he will have to call off the strike against Mr Tolin before they can talk, because he'll have to ballot them legally in order to represent them."

Judge Dix thought about it a few moments and then smiled at Lee Roy. "The old three-pronged offensive. You want Duffy to rot in jail. You want a court order to make

Petrillo call off the strike against the whole lot of farmers, or else he's in contempt. And then you want Petrillo to call off the strike against Tolin until he gets union representation legally, or else he's in contempt again. Good thinking there, Lee Roy."

Mr Cook smiled and waited for his compliment. He wasn't going to get one, however, because the judge delighted in withholding little prizes from this man whose halitosis made life a misery for him in every courtroom conference.

"Okay," the judge said. "Duffy won't be getting out soon. I won't bail him even on a habeas corpus, and he's got contempt to purge, which for that young man is going to be something close to swabbing out the jailhouse latrines. You can have your court order to try to force Petrillo to call off the strike. Let me have the papers as soon as you have them ready, and I'll sign them in here. Phone the sheriff to get a server to stand by for the subpoena. We'll see how far that gets things settled."

"Thank you very much, Judge," Mr Cook said. He was unable to restrain a little bow as he picked up his briefcase.

Judge Dix looked up at Lee Roy and suddenly saw in the man's face something a shade too smug. "You can prove it's Cappy Petrillo's strike, can't you?" he asked. "If it comes to a hearing, you'll have to prove that."

Lee Roy deferred to his partner. "Mr Cook," he said.

Mr Cook chuckled and opened the buckles of his briefcase, taking out a folder closed on its three open sides with a whole handful of paper clips, the same folder Lee Roy had given him earlier. Unclipping one side, he peered inside and located the paper it contained, then held the folder chest high and shook it up and down. At last a single piece of paper dropped out onto the judge's desk. Above a printed heading that read Destroy After Reading was the name of a man followed by Dry Lake Camp. Below that a list of directives was written and finally the signature Cappy, followed by a flourish.

"Evidence," Lee Roy said, "in his own handwriting."

229

"I won't ask you how you got it," the judge said, "and maybe you better not let me know."

Lee Roy smiled again. It occurred to Judge Dix that the moral righteousness that judges are paid to feel was being taken away from him by people who didn't know that such certainty was a very rickety platform from which to be superior to the common man.

Once outside and on the way to his own office, Mr Cook almost ran to get the order ready for the judge. He stopped suddenly and looked both ways along the corridor before asking, "Is there anything that could crop up later about the way you got hold of that memorandum, Mr Stagg?"

"Dry Lake Camp is the closest one to me," Lee Roy replied. "My workers come from there. The union man in the camp leaned on them a little too hard. I just leaned back the other way, and one of them brought this and gave it to my wife last night."

"Last night," Mr Cook repeated. He felt suddenly as if his calendar had shifted out of control. The strike had started this morning, he was certain of it. He looked in some confusion at his fellow churchman, whom he had thought he knew very well.

"That's strictly between us, Mr Cook. Not a word to anybody."

"Yes," Mr Cook said, "yes, not a word."

"I could explain why I did it," Lee Roy said, "but some of my farmers might not understand. They might not agree. All right, I kept quiet when I knew the strike was going to happen, I'll admit it to you." He added after a pause, "There's not much chance I could have stopped it, anyway."

"No," Mr Cook said, "I suppose not." He looked on the bright side. "Still, we'll never know, will we."

Mr Halbkeller's article in that morning's *Red Branch Herald* about the pickets at the Courthouse and the jail was a masterpiece of evasion. The central issue, "the obscene provocation", as he put it, was never explained. Anyone

230

reading the article would think the migrants were using finger gestures or dropping their pants at the judge. As to what they did to the ladies to insult them so terribly that they had to be defended by the mob from the Rex Hotel, minds boggled and tongues wagged, with more obscenity in the speculation than there was in the commission of the offense. Young Ledyard Job, he of the evil tongue, observed that it couldn't have been much of an obscene gesture, because you can't get out of denim overalls without five minutes' warning beforehand.

Thinking about it afterwards, the men in the mob couldn't accept that they had reacted with violence to a trade name printed in blue on the side of a cardboard box. There was more to it than that. The phrase "They were asking for it", with "they" referring to the pickets and "it" being response to provocation, covered the event in the minds of the men. The women were silent on the subject, merely allowing word to filter out that they were grateful to their defenders.

Accompanied now by his two bodyguards, Cappy Petrillo made his escape from Red Branch undetected and headed west. Using a rough map drawn up for him the day before, he toured the barricades in order, leaving posters to be propped up on the vehicles. By lucky coincidence that had involved a tipoff, photographers found him at one of the farms and ensured that, by the wonders of modern photography, his personal involvement in the fate of Irish Duffy would make the papers the next day. Cappy's personal involvement didn't extend to doing anything very soon, however, since he had decided that Irish would continue to languish in jail, being of more value to the cause as an imprisoned martyr than as a union agitator who had still to explain his foray into arson. When the pictures had been taken and the questions of the reporters had been answered with slogans, Cappy was driven off with his bodyguards standing on the runningboards of the car as if it was an escape by Clyde Barrow with gunmen hanging onto the car ready to shoot anyone who followed the boss.

Finally, after all the strike barricades had been visited, Clancy the driver was directed to find a place where they could get a sandwich. He promptly reversed Mrs Grund's map and found his way to Manzanita, where today's specials were devilled egg sandwiches with anchovies and Boston cream pie. The thugs pushed two tables together in the corner of the cafe. Cappy however declined to join the others, sitting at the counter on his own, sometimes in his concentration swinging the revolving stool rhythmically to the sound of a dance band on the radio back in the kitchen. When he had eaten and was enjoying a slow cup of coffee, he began to drum his fingers as if he was making the sound of a galloping horse. Faster and faster he drummed, until suddenly he broke it off and called to Mrs Grund where she was washing dishes out back.

"Mind if I use your phone?" he said. 'I'll pay for it."

"Go right ahead," she called back.

"Do you have a directory?" he asked.

"Behind the counter, right in front of the telephone," came the reply.

He looked up a number in the book and asked the operator to get it for him. The girl in the Parks and Recreation Office remembered him, yes, the application had been approved, yes, it was reserved for him all day today.

"Do you get the public address system, or do I have to get that for myself?" he asked her.

"We can do it," she answered. "I can get a microphone and a loud speaker for you, if that's enough."

"That'd be fine," he said. "I'll need it for three o'clock this afternoon. I'll need it until about five."

"Do you want it there in Garfield Park?" she asked.

He couldn't think where else he might want it. "Yes, sure," he said, "in Garfield Park, up on the stage, you know, in the band shell, at three o'clock. Who do I pay?"

232

"You come by my office and give me a check," she said. "I'll see that it gets to the PA man."

Grace Grund was still crouching in hiding behind the kitchen door, where she had stationed herself in order to overhear the telephone call, when Mr Petrillo and party called their goodbyes and left.

Nick answered the phone this time and called to Hazel that it was for her. "Sounded like Grace."

It was indeed Grace. "Hazel, you know that mass meeting you told me about last night, the one in the park?"

Hazel was all ears. "Did you find out anything?" she asked.

Grace said, "He was just here, that Cappy Petrillo, again."

"Must like your sandwiches," a jealous Hazel said.

"He used the phone," Grace said, "and I could hear everything he said. Do you think I ought to tell?"

"You can tell me," Hazel answered. "After all, dear, my husband's in the sheriff's office."

This kind of point-scoring at her expense was one of Hazel's worst characteristics, Grace thought, and it occurred to her to keep her news to herself. Out of civic duty, though, as much as anything, she felt compelled to tell.

"It's at three o'clock, that meeting," Grace said, "and it's going to be big because he has a PA system coming."

"Wow!" Hazel said. "You hang up, Grace, and I'll call my husband right now."

Alerted by her tone of voice, Nick heard her message as she phoned her husband. He followed Hazel to the phone and asked the operator to connect him to the cigar store.

Clancy Spargo delivered Cappy to the service entrance of the Mariposa Hotel at a quarter to twelve. Cappy got upstairs without being seen, retired to his room and stayed away from windows, having taken with him one of the bodyguards to screen all phone calls and answer any taps at the door. He was going to lie low until the mass meeting.

233

Accompanied by the other bodyguard, Clancy the driver began a second tour of the strike barricades, this time carrying a message from Cappy. Written by hand on a full sheet of paper, it was addressed:

To all the strikers of the Red Branch area of the United Farm Workers Union.

My fellow workers:

Our oppressors know we mean business.

Congratulations! The strike is a great success. Now we must make sure that the pressure is continued.

We must show our solidarity. We must demand the release of the victimized Irish Duffy. We must repeat the conditions that the employers have to agree to before we will rescue their crops for them.

Therefore, we will meet today at 3 o'clock in Garfield Park. This does not mean the strike is off. The barricades will come down for this meeting only. Bring as many vehicles as you can. Fill them with people, and display the signs. Everyone come to the mass meeting, women and children too. If you can get to Red Branch before 3, drive your cars around, let them know your strength and your resolution.

Comrades, our time has come! Together let us cut these little capitalists down to size!

The telephone rang at the cigar store with the stridency that indicated that Eunice, the operator, was trying to connect what she considered an important call. Tom Potter answered it. It was Klinghofer, the deputy in the sheriff's office. He asked for Lee Roy, who was at that moment catching a bite to eat in the soda fountain next door.

"Will you hold the line while I get him for you, or do you want him to call you back?" Tom asked.

"Don't bother to call me," the deputy said. "Give him this message, Tom. The sheriff is on his way up there right now, and he's got Chief Thomas with him. This is big, Tom."

234

"I'll go tell him myself, Kling," Potter said.

He walked out of his own door, took the few paces to the door of the drugstore, and leaned in at the doorway. "Lee Roy!" he shouted, and retreated.

When Lee Roy came in at Tom's door seconds later, he got the message verbatim. "Find Calvin," was his response.

A phone call to the Rex Hotel brought Calvin at the same time that Sheriff Atwater and Chief Thomas arrived. Tom Potter opened the door to the back room and gestured for the men to go in. Mort Thomas was the only person in the group to have been in that sanctum before, having been called once to dispose of a poker player who was drunk or suffering from a heart attack and in either case making a nuisance of himself. The sheriff took a firm step into the back room as a matter of duty; Calvin strode in eager to satisfy his curiosity about this fabled place. Lee Roy lingered on the threshold before crossing into the third den of iniquity he had entered in the last twenty-four hours. Mort Thomas closed the door, giving Tom Potter a signal that they were not to be disturbed.

The first of the strikers' vehicles got to town shortly before two o'clock. It was a truck with a tilted bed to it, a rear spring so recently broken that the only mechanical assistance applied thus far was to have the crowd of people standing in the back group themselves so as to balance it. The truck drove down the avenue to Divisidero and stopped there, looking as though it might come terminally to rest by buckling at the middle. After some discussion with the passengers, the driver turned it around and drove back up the avenue. He stopped this time near Mrs Rossi's, to be joined within minutes by another truck coming in from the west. With a companion for support, the first truck boldly drove back down the avenue, now displaying the printed signs, followed by the other doing the same. At first hesitantly, then stronger but still without real conviction, the passengers shouted things about Irish Duffy and wages and

235

victimization, going silent when there was any danger of being clearly heard by a pedestrian or a passing car. Another truck joined them, then another and another, until by two-fifteen the avenue looked like a parade of junk trucks and boiling cars, proceeding in an unbroken oval between the highway and the western end of Greenfield Avenue, sprouting signs and crowded with people shouting slogans and giving rebel yells. Faced with this sort of provocation, the citizens of Red Branch went indoors and disappeared. Except for the boys on their bikes looping around and between the vehicles and laughing at the spectacle, the town turned its back on the strikers.

Across the highway, uptown in the cigar store, the meeting went on behind the closed door. Chief Thomas was the one who came out from time to time and used the telephone in the closed booth. At about two-thirty Klinghofer came in, asking Tom to let the sheriff know he was there. Tom did, knocking deferentially on the door to the back room and then showing the deputy in. No one shut the door, so Tom heard Klinghofer report very briefly, saying that as far as he could tell everything was going to be in place by three o'clock, but he needed to know from the sheriff and the police chief who he was supposed to be working with. They had to coordinate things before they went down to the park, he said. Potter moved away as far as he could get, pretending to be checking on the display in his window, trying not to hear what he wasn't supposed to hear but couldn't help listening to. Soon after Klinghofer left, Sheriff Atwater came out into the store to ask Tom for a glass of water. He drank it down, standing by the counter and staring out into the street. Then he called back to the men in the back room, "That's it. Can't think of anythin' else. Let's go."

At three o'clock the string of battered vehicles stretched from the highway end of Garfield Park to the cross street three blocks past the canal, on both sides of Greenfield Avenue. The doctors at the sanitarium put oxygen cylinders out in the avenue to keep their emergency entrance free, and the toilets in the library, the Shell station and the Courthouse were all locked against people who by reputation didn't know how to use or treat indoor plumbing. Townspeople persisted in staying off the streets, instead darting into the Courthouse and the library, where they peered from the windows from time to time in an overly casual manner, determined both to see what was going on and not to be seen to care about what they saw. In the park the strikers crowded into the benches and seats in front of the band shell, enjoying the great occasion and socializing with friends and acquaintances, even though the gloom under the trees did little to break the heat which in its fierce intensity seemed to be resisting any attempt by any breeze to relieve it.

The convoy of boys who had been harassing the train of old vehicles made their way to the service yard behind the Memorial Hall, where they hid their bikes among the garbage cans and old boxes. Led by Richie Thomas, the leader by virtue of his father's position, they crossed Park Street one or two at a time, trying not to be seen so that no one could tell them it was no place for kids. Having gathered behind the jail, they made a run for the park the way they did when they played Boy Scout games, running in a crouch, shouting and laughing, then snaking through the shrubbery until they fringed the left side of the crowd, faces peering from the undergrowth like a waiting party of Indian raiders. The few strikers who saw them chose to ignore their presence.

Up on the stage a succession of guitar players of varying talent, none outstanding, played and sang a few of the old Okie songs. The crowd liked them, especially when they played the Woody Guthrie songs which they all knew and sang along with. The singers in their determination to be heard crowded the microphone, so that the PA system alternately boomed with overload or screeched with feed-back, and the adolescent girls in the crowd shrieked in mock agony and clutched their ears. Large numbers of children wandered from parent to sibling to friend, clambering over laps and limbs to do so, and babies cried from one part of the crowd or another without ceasing. Jubilee Hubbard had been finishing a garbage run south of Park Street when he heard all the excitement, and now he joined the crowd at the back. A few people muttered things in his direction about him being at the wrong party, then moved away from him as many steps as they could to show that poor whites are a cut above poor blacks at least.

At last it was time for the speakers. When the first of the agitators got up to speak, the grown-ups in the crowd shouted "Tell 'em! Tell 'em!" and the process of slander and vindication began. Even moral certainty and righteous anger can pall, however, and some of the steam had gone out of the rally when, at four o'clock on the stroke of the Court-house clock, Cappy Petrillo walked from behind the band shell and took the stage. In the standing, yelling crowd there were few who had ever seen him before, and even fewer who cared that he was the sort of leader who had to have two bodyguards, who came on stage on either side of him and then went to sit on either end of a row of folding wooden chairs.

Cappy stood in the center of the stage holding his hands up, turning slowly from side to side and smiling his broadest smile, giving the whole crowd, every single one of them, the benefit of his protection and power. The ovation waved up and down in volume as he turned again and again, giving a personal blessing that flowed back to him six-hundredfold. As the cheering began finally to wane, he turned away and took off his suit coat, giving it to one of the bodyguards. The man of the people, standing in his shirtsleeves before them in the hour of their test, overwhelmed the crowd again, and the ovation rekindled. Finally, pleadingly, winningly, he begged them to give him a chance to speak.

"Can you hear me out there?" he asked while making bumping sounds as he tried to adjust the microphone. A screech of feedback pushed him away from the mike as the crowd's "No!" thundered back at him. He tried several other phrases, which echoed loudly and indistinctly as if the sound was weaving its way around the trees. Eventually he pulled the loudspeaker to the center of the band shell, almost to his feet, and tried again. "Testing – one, two, three. Now can you hear me better?" he asked, and this time got a swelling "Yes!" He and the crowd were both ready for his message.

"Folks, it's a privilege to be here, I hope you know that. From the bottom of my heart I can say, I feel honored and humble to be here at the head of this great gathering. I feel like the most important man in the world [a shout of, "You are, Cappy!"] right here and now, the most powerful, important man in this state that's for sure [rebel yells]. And it's not fancy talk. It's fact. I'll tell you why. You know that old saying, 'Might makes right', the saying that people like farmers use when they want to rub the faces of the worker in the dust of their farms and say 'Do what I tell you, nigger, because I am the mighty one around here'. [an "Amen!"

239

from Jubliee Hubbard]. Yes, It's the same saying that a Hitler uses when he takes over another innocent country and puts a bayonet through another innocent mother, and kicks an innocent baby out of his way. There isn't that much difference between a farmer and a Hitler, when you come to it, is there? [roars of approval, especially from those who weren't sure who Hitler was] 'Might makes right' – a saying you could use anytime Mr Big wants to grind down Mr Little, to make Mr Big bigger and Mr Little littler, anytime the fat, rich pigs of this world want to swim a little bit higher in the sweat of the workers, the masses of this world. Yes, folks, lying on their backs floating in a sea of your sweat. That's a pretty picture for you, now, isn't it?

"Well, today it's my turn to be Mr Big, and it's not because I'm that bloated capitalist floating on anything. It's sweaty enough, I'll agree to that. [Big laugh.] No, it's because you've done something today to make me into what I am only as long as I stand up here in front of all you fine people. You've turned it around. You've taken that saying and you've turned it right around. It reads now: RIGHT MAKES MIGHT".

Cappy gestured like a magician producing three rabbits out of one small hat and stepped back as three girls came on the stage to his left carrying a sign each – RIGHT, MAKES and MIGHT. The girls were dressed in swimsuits and high heel shoes. They held the signs high up above their heads, shaved armpits and toothpaste smiles gleaming. Until it was explained, the crowd in general didn't understand the point being so dramatically made, but no one cared. It was a show, a grand show, staged for them by their Cappy Petrillo, and their warm hearts and blanked minds loved it. At a wave from the puppetmaster, the girls skipped and jumped offstage to even more shouting.

"Right makes might. [The bellow through the loudspeaker overwhelmed anything left of reason.] Who's right? My friends, YOU are! ["You bet!" "Amen!" "Tell 'em, Cappy!"] What are you right about? Well, just about everything, but right now here are a few things I can name right off the top of my head: YOU are the workers, the producers of wealth. You supply the shoulder that turns the wheel of progress, it's not that fancy, expensive new tractor. It is the sweat of your brow by which the earth lives. ["Amen" from Jubilee.] My friends, I don't need to tell you that it takes two things to make a crop grow. Fertilizer and water. We already know about the water, we know too much about it; look at my shirt and tell me about it – yes, sweat, the salt and smell of good, honest work that drains from all of us. You think the water from that big new dam, that was paid for and given to these farmers by the federal government, you think that water is enough to grow their apricots and peaches and cotton and potatoes and everything else that comes to fruition in this abundant land? It won't happen until you add the sweat, my friends, and our enemies, the farmers, know it and they know it good! [yells]

"Fertilizer. It takes that too, we all know it. God gave us the good rich earth ["Amen"], and that's enough if we use it for our needs. But it's not enough if we use it for our greed – the way your employers use it. Which is the same way as they use you. No, if you're going to be greedy with Mother Nature's gift of a bountiful earth, you're going to have to enrich the land; like it or not, you're going to have to put something back. I'll bet it hurts their black souls when these farmers have to put something back into what they thought was for free, don't you think that, folks? [Jeers] No, they can't get away from it, they have to enrich it, they have to use fertilizer. Now there's one kind of fertilizer we all know more about than we want to. It's the kind you get your faces rubbed in by the bosses that employ you. [Big laugh.] I won't give it its name, there's ladies and children present. No, matter of fact, I WILL name it. You know it by its look, which is disgusting, its feel, which is enough to make your flesh crawl like it had maggots, its smell, which makes you puke your guts out. You know it, and you know its name. It's called INJUSTICE. That's what they rub your faces in.

241

That's what you get thrown at you when you ask for enough money for your work to keep your wives and your babies alive. That's what stinks to high heaven over every farm and field in this blessed and beautiful land. INJUSTICE. That's what is spread on this land to enrich it so that the profit, the stinking, slimy, disgusting profit, can go to the bosses. [Leaping, ecstatic, hysterical cheers.]

"They think it doesn't show, it doesn't stick. They're wrong, folks, aren't they? You and I, friends, we can smell a farmer a mile off, can't we? [Prolonged cheers and yells.]

"And there's another kind of fertilizer. It comes out of the slaughter houses. It's made of blood, and ground up bones, and some of the flesh. It's what is left of an animal after it has had a useful life producing wealth for the farmer, or else it is what is left of a beast that has been killed in its prime because it is worth more dead than alive. That kind of fertilizer is produced in another way, you know. It doesn't all come out of slaughter houses. There's a kind of slavery that will do the same thing, and you don't even have to build a slaughter house to produce it. As a matter of fact, you don't build anything. You just use what you can get your hands on – or maybe I ought to say WHO you can get your hands on. You ever heard of wage slaves, comrades? You ever heard of people who struggle through life without enough time to know they ever lived life? You ever know any of those people? There aren't many of them around. No, not many at all, because they die early. They give their strength, and their blood, and their bones to the land they work on, they give it all they've got, because that's the only way they know to keep going, the only way they know to do something for their kiddies so life might be better for them, and then they die. Fertilizer. That's what they are. Bodies. Bodies that have enriched the land, the crops, the lives of who? Who, comrades, who is it who got rich off the bodies of your mamas and your daddies, who profited from their deaths, when death mercifully came to put an end to a life of grinding poverty, vicious exploitation, degrading injustice? Let's name the beasts that ate the hearts and muscles and souls of our dear ones, comrades, through whose foul, devilish plotting your mamas, your daddies, your sisters and your brothers were destroyed, the same way the beasts want to destroy you now. Let's name them, comrades. Let's give them the name that stinks in the face of heaven. CAPITALISTS!"

There was a roar from the crowd at this, but it was tinged with disappointment. They wanted to hear names named, they wanted to hear Tolin, Stagg, Adams, all the rest. They wanted to put a face to the beast that they could hate so that they could tear it apart when it came, as it would, into their hands.

On the east side of the band shell the giant sycamores thinned out and gave way to smaller evergreen trees and tall shrubs. This was the side of the park where shade could be pursued with less vigor than on the west where the blasting afternoon heat came from. All eyes now were on Cappy. Not a word or a grimace or a gesture could be lost without remorse by a member of that crowd. Screened by this perfect adoration, a dozen farmers had come to the edge of the crowd, where they sheltered behind a clump of laurel bushes on that east side. Calvin was at their head. The men behind him, steaming with indignation at the oratory they had heard branding them less than human, stared at Cappy like the rest of the crowd. Only Calvin looked across the restless surf of faces, scanning back and forth along the shrubbery that closed off the opposite side of the benches.

"You wanted me to name them, didn't you? I couldn't do that. For one reason, I don't know all their names. I expect you do, though. [Shouts of names cascaded from the crowd.] Besides that, you're forgetting a few, comrades. You're naming the people you have to deal with out there on the farms, the vicious capitalists who are only the forward battalions of this army of filth. How about the rest of the slavemasters, comrades? How about the people who sell you food for more than you can afford, just to make themselves

243

a profit, not because you are hungry? Give me the money, they say, and I'll give you food to save your lives. If you haven't got the money, go some place else to starve. Does that sound familiar? How about the doctors? Give me the money and I'll heal your sickness. You and the wife and the kids can stay sick until you give me the money. How about the banks? Give me your money and it's none of your business how I lose it for you. How about, comrades, how about the churches? Put money in the plate, and I'll see if I can fix things up for you with God. Capitalists, comrades, capitalists – leeches, bloodsuckers, Draculas. And listen to me, comrades, it is these swine, these gods of the earth who have sold their souls to the devil himself, that devil called Capitalism, who are pitted against you right now!"

There was a roar as from a generation of roused giants, with most of the men on their feet waving whatever was left of the signs they had brought with them, the washed out, sunburnt women screeching "We'll kill 'em!" and the children shouting and laughing at this circus like no other they would ever see again. In the laurels Calvin used his height to try to see across to the other side. Through a gap in the antic mob he saw the hidden boys suddenly pushed from their hiding place from behind. Trapped between whatever was behind them and the crowd in front of them, they pushed their way in the direction of the stage until they could fight their way back into the surrounding bushes. From the stage Cappy saw it too and in that instant lost the bearing of a majestic, prophetic Caesar that he had draped over himself so effectively.

Seeing this, Calvin shouted to the men behind him. They broke into the open and moved toward the stage, while Calvin pushed his way ahead and around the back of the band shell. The men forced their way to the apron of the stage, where they grabbed the loudspeaker and pulled it onto the ground, then, using it as a stool, began to clamber onto the stage. The two bodyguards, running from the rear, pushed them back but were two against a dozen. Finding the crowd bewildered by the attack and slow to react, Cappy tried to rouse them by a babble of shouts into the microphone, which had the effect of creating panic among the women. They scrambled to their feet, reaching for children, screaming and fighting to get away from the stage. Behind the band shell Calvin found the cord for the microphone and cut it with a fishing knife, then ran up the steps onto the stage and, pushing Cappy out of the way, picked up the microphone with its heavy, cast iron stand. The bodyguards, caught between the men below and Calvin on stage, were sitting targets for Calvin as he hit first one and then the other with the iron stand, swinging the weapon like a great sword, knocking the two off the stage down onto the ground, where the farmers fell on them.

The men in the crowd tried to push the screaming women and children out of their way in order to get to the fighting in front of the stage, sending bodies, women, children, themselves, sprawling over the concrete benches, clambering over the fallen, stepping on those in the way. Calvin looked up in time to see Cappy Petrillo coming for him with a folding wooden chair in his hands. Cappy brought it down intending it for Calvin's head, but Calvin heaved up his shoulder and an elbow to protect himself. The shattered fragments of the chair back hung around Calvin's arm as he sprang from crouching under the blow into an attack on Cappy. He hit Cappy in the chest with the same shoulder that had broken the chair, and the leader went down. Calvin pursued him, rolling and throwing him off the stage, then turned as the crowd of men fought their way toward him. He reached into his pocket and took out a red bandanna handkerchief that had already been knotted, slipping it over his head so that it covered his nose and mouth.

Instantly, from the left of the benches, where the boys had been pushed out of their hiding place in the bushes and shrubs, a file of men in tan uniforms charged into action, wearing the leather gaiters and Sam Browne belts of the State Highway Police. They carried stubby riot guns with brown canisters stuck in the muzzles, and on their faces they wore gas masks. The first can of tear gas hit the front of the stage and bounced near the men fighting there. Another followed it, each policeman firing as he came past the one who was reloading. The seething crowd in full panic fought to get away to the open grass at the rear of the benches, as far as possible from the stage and their unconscious leader. As they retreated the police followed, clouding the space being cleared with the choking, peppery, acid gas. The fighting men broke free as well as they could, some of them collapsing on the ground, where they lay vomiting, then heaving to get air into their lungs, their eyes bulging and fingers clawing at nothing. Calvin lay on the ground beside Cappy, guarding his still unconscious prisoner. He stayed on his face, finding untainted air close to the ground, while the screaming, rushing mob fled farther and farther away. When the air began slowly to clear, he raised his head to see one of the bodyguards and several other men, farmers or pickers, one or the other, lying sprawled on the ground, either unconscious or gasping for breath. Cappy Petrillo, lying by his side, was unmoving.

Out of the misty gloom came Lee Roy and Deputy Klinghofer with wet cloths tied over their lower faces.

"You all right, Calvin?" asked Lee Roy. "You hurt?"

"Not much," Calvin said. "Hurry up, before he comes to."

"You saw me serve the subpoena," Klinghofer said.

"Yeah, I did," Calvin answered. "Hurry up, I'm gonna puke."

The deputy stuck a document in Cappy's pocket. He lifted the unconscious man's shoulders and Lee Roy took his legs. One or two of the gassed comrades raised their heads to see their leader being carried away.

"Where you takin' him?" one of them said. "What do you think you're doin'?"

"It's legal," Klinghofer said.

"He's going to jail," Lee Roy said.

3

The smell of the tear gas and the screams of the women and children had brought the good people of Red Branch onto the streets. Blown into fragments by the hot wind, the sound came and went like good sense in a bad dream, while the wind drove the gas into a pervasive, light, sinister reminder that trouble, bad trouble, was only two blocks away. The people came from their houses into the business center of town to stand facing west, talking, worrying out loud, commenting when a whiff came more strongly or a single scream emerged clearly out of the general sound. They had done this before when there had been earthquakes, and another time when the foothills on the east side had been ablaze from one end of the valley to the other. Those were natural disasters. This time the disaster had been of man's making, exactly how and by whom still unknown.

The women and children from the park ran as far and as fast as they could, some slower than others because of the age of the children or the pregnancy of the women. The men overtook them before they had got far and tried to stop them and persuade them to go to the truck or car that had brought them. No one would listen. To get away, far away, was the only imperative they knew. Wide-eyed, crying, still screaming to no purpose from time to time, they ran and ran. The men manhandled a few stragglers into the trucks and cars that had drivers and drove west. At the end of the avenue where there was a large vacant lot with tumbled concrete columns, showing the place where a dreamer once had wanted to build his castle, they stopped their vehicles and formed a human barricade across the avenue and the sidewalks. As the women and children, still hysterical but now exhausted, ran to these men, they were caught and taken the few steps to the lot where they were unceremoniously laid on the ground. Those who would not stop crying or screaming were slapped until they subsided into more normal sobs. Then, not knowing if they were still being pursued by the police, the men called out the destination of each vehicle and filled it with the people from the camp it was bound for. A few whose senses were addled with the shock of the riot, and children lost from their mothers, were taken in hand by other women, to be removed to somewhere, anywhere, until they could be returned to their own camps. In an hour only the oil stains from leaky sumps marked where the trucks had stood, and flattened grass among the fallen columns was the only sign of what had been a refuge.

The heroes returned quietly to an uneasy welcome. Among themselves there was a sense of violence accurately aimed and efficiently delivered, like the proving of a good new gun. There were a few waves and shouts to them as they came back to the Rex Hotel, mainly from youngsters, but most other people were worried, weak smiles offering support with no word of encouragement to give the smiles meaning. A few other people, such as Louella in the dentist's waiting room, stood back from windows so that they could see what was going on but would not be identified. Heroes in the movies are greeted by people waving from upstairs windows, with a girl to smile and blow kisses when her special man comes back safe and miraculously matured by his experience. The action didn't follow the script in Red Branch.

There were a few wounds, black eyes, puffed up cheek bones, one broken arm. Nothing, however, to worry a real man, except that no one was happy with the victory.

Calvin went first to the cigar store, where he got word from Tom Potter that Cappy Petrillo had regained consciousness before he got to the jail, having been only winded and not really injured. As was expected, he had refused to call off the strike, so he was being held in jail in breach of the court order. When there was a hearing he would be judged in contempt. Calvin went into the back room and shut the door. It was cooler in there, the dark and cool of a secret place. He put his mind in neutral and tried not to think of the pain in his shoulder. The recollection came to him of the boys being driven out of their hiding place into the crowd that they feared, innocents driven into danger by men with guns and deathwatch masks. He shuddered and tried to put aside his own responsibility, knowing he had to come back to it, but at another time. He felt nausea come at him irregularly, in waves of sour sickness that coincided with a shaking in his hands and the feeling of emptiness in the bowels that comes after diarrhea. He reflected that it was the first time that he had been in a serious fight, and he thought now that fighting was overrated. The pain in his shoulder increased, throbbing for seconds at a time and then fading merely to a sort of red smear across his mind. He thought he had probably popped it out of joint, and from the feel of it when he turned the steering wheel of his truck, he wasn't sure it had gone back in. He needed to see people, to take him away from himself. He went out of the cigar store and walked up to the Rex Hotel, hoping to see Louella.

She saw him go, but she wasn't ready to meet him yet. She watched from her vantage point in the dentist's suite as he walked up the sidewalk, pulling himself together as he went, straightening his back until he looked young again, striding out until the swagger came back into the sway of his trunk, flexing his knees slightly to produce the provocative swing of his hips that was his trademark. No other man she knew could wear jeans like Calvin. Tonight, however, she distrusted him and decided to keep to her room.

The first ungarbled report of the events of Garfield Park that Red Branch received came in the six o'clock news bulletin from radio station KPLA in Placid City. The fragments of gossip and hearsay, the piecemeal stories of some participants, all fine and exciting in their way, gave way to the report of an eyewitness. "The trouble started," he said, "when Cappy Petrillo inflamed the crowd at the union mass meeting with slanderous accusations about the farmers, so much so that when a group of farmers tried to use the microphone to put their side of the dispute to the strikers, they were attacked, and a general mêlée ensued. A special force of the highway patrol, detailed to Garfield Park in case there was any trouble, had to intervene with tear gas in order to keep the situation from deteriorating into a riot. Several people were hurt, none seriously, and Mr Petrillo was taken to jail charged with failing to keep public order in breach of his undertaking when he scheduled the mass meeting. He is also to be charged with planning and organizing an illegal strike of agricultural workers in the Red Branch area."

Louella heard the report on her small, ivory, bakelite radio in her kitchenette. When it finished she waited for more, expecting to hear a commercial jingle followed by a return to the news. Instead, the station rejoined the network for "Cocktail music by Sammy Kaye and his orchestra from the world famous Coconut Grove of the Ambassador Hotel on Wilshire Boulevard in Los Angeles, California". She got up and took the radio in both hands, shaking it and squeezing it as if she could get the rest of the report out of it. It wasn't real: the report was unreal; the reality had been the screams, the drifting sounds of children's hysterical crying on the whiffs of tear gas that flowed from the park. Was this all? Were the screaming women so unimportant? Were they some kind of cattle to be herded away by tear gas when they got overexcited? Was there no way to restore those cattle to being people, with real terror and real screams? God damn it, she raged in her head, she had not imagined what she heard and smelled! A bitter tide, a lament for all the duped and ignored like herself, rose up in her and she put down her head on the little table and cried from the deepest part of herself, crying for all the frightened people who counted for nothing.

When Calvin knocked on the door and came in, she was smoking a cigarette seated in front of a pile of tear soaked Kleenex, hiccuping and dabbing at her face with tissues from the box in front of her, her eyes red and her hands still fists.

"Hey, look at you," said Calvin.

She turned to face him. "Bastard!" she shouted. "Bastard son-of-a-bitch killer! Dirty, lowdown –" Words failed her, and she sobbed again.

"Don't talk to me like that!" Calvin shouted back. "You ain't talkin' to no scum! Killer of what? Killer of who? Come on, Miss High-and-Mighty, what the shit are you talkin' about?"

"Get the hell out of here!" she returned. "Scum! You said it, Mister Scum! Get out, now, go!"

"You shut the hell up!" Calvin raged. He took her wrists in his hands as if by pinioning her he would quiet her.

Louella snatched her wrists away and, turning to the table, took a handful of the wet paper tissues. She tossed her cigarette into the sink so that she could use both hands. She threw the soggy mess at Calvin, then stooped to pick up what had fallen in order to continue to pelt him. He had had enough. This time when he took her wrists he held them in a grip like handcuffs. She struggled to her right, pulling him partially with her, then switched her movements to the left. As she did, Calvin had to take the strain of her pulling in his left shoulder. He released her wrists as if he had been knifed, grunted once loudly, and fell to the floor.

Louella watched him go, distrusting what she saw as another tactic. "Get up," she ordered. "I'm telling you, I want you to get out of here. I'm not fooling, Calvin, I can't take you. Get out!"

When he didn't answer she took him by the hair viciously, pulling back on it so that the skin of his forehead was stretched and his eyelids were pulled open. His eyes were empty, clouded, unseeing. Louella screamed and went to the sink where she soaked a dish towel. She squeezed it over Calvin, and when the cool water didn't produce a result she stuffed the towel down the back of his shirt at the neck. He moaned slightly and moved, then slumped back down again. She repeated the treatment until, moving one limb at a time with her help, he got across the few feet of floor to the bed, where he collapsed again into unconsciousness.

In some movie Louella had seen, the heroine revived the hero by rubbing his wrists. It was hers that hurt where he had held her, but nevertheless she rubbed Calvin's. He revived enough to say, "My shoulder." She unbuttoned his shirt and took if off him, to see the shoulder joint blue and distorted, the flesh bleached ashy gray by the trauma.

"Oh Christ, Calvin, what the hell have you done?" she moaned, and burst into tears again.

Later, his arm in a sling and his shirt drying on a coat hanger in the window, Calvin told Louella some of what had happened in the park. He was vague on why he was there, mum on what had transpired to put him, a riot squad and Lee Roy's legal weapon into such close coordination.

"I'll tell you what got me, Louella. You wanta know what got me?" he said. She didn't, really, but it was good for him to talk. She nodded.

"It was when Pertrillo started sayin' what he felt about us," Calvin said, "and all them people started cheerin' and shoutin' for him to lay it on us. Those are the people we been workin' with all my life, Louella, for Christ's sake, and I'm tellin' you they hate us, they hate us big."

"They had a strike to win," she said; "everybody talks big when they're out on strike."

"No, it was worse than that," he insisted. "It was all this communist crap. He made us out bloodsuckers, and even worse than that. The way he was goin', he wanted us all dead. Said we was all in it together, doctors, store owners, everybody."

"He's a Communist," she said; "they all say that. In high school we used to tell the football team to kill the other one. We didn't mean it, but maybe the coach did. That's what he's paid for." She added inconsequentially, "It never made any difference."

"What do you mean?" Calvin asked.

"We always lost," she said.

"Yeah, well them pickers lost too," he said.

"They're sure gonna love you now," she said. "If they hated you before, they're gonna have to think up a new word now."

"Yeah," he said. There was a long pause while they found their way around what they realized was a subject they were not going to agree on. "I never thought about women and children bein' there," he said. "I thought it was a meetin', none of this picnic stuff."

"Did you go after them, Calvin?" she said. "Did you hurt any of them? You tell me the truth."

"I went there to get Cappy Petrillo," he said. "That's what I did, honest."

"Well," she began, then was silent.

"Wonder what's gonna happen now," he said. "Wonder if we beat 'em so bad they'll call the strike off."

"Jesus, Calvin!" Louella exploded.

"What's wrong now?" he asked, genuinely bewildered.

"Who did you beat?" she shouted. "Their wives and kids, that's who, and that's how you win a strike? You know what it would take to win this strike now? You and the rest of you big shits would have to crawl out to those camps and eat dirt in front of them. You'd have to say you're sorry, and you're too big for that, so you won't win!"

She got up from where she had been sitting beside the bed and got her purse and cigarettes. "If you won't go, I will," she said, slamming the door as she left. Whatever was on at the movies, it was better than talking to Calvin.

4

At Las Cruces camp, the last of the trucks had returned from town and, allowing for a couple of the women who were missing but known to be at another camp, everybody was accounted for. The old man who had been one of Irish Duffy's councillors squatted near his truck, waiting for others to join him. They wandered across the dusty campsite, bare of grass and swept by the evening wind into flat plains cut by little rivers of sandy soil. Three men joined him, the youngest still coughing with a harsh rasp and wiping at his red eyes.

"You caught yourself a full dose, Billy," the old man said.

"Tried to throw one of them cans back," he said.

They waited a while longer, until the old man said, "Guess this is all that's comin'. Let's get it goin'."

Billy misunderstood. "Did you call a meetin'?" he asked.

"Nope," the old man said. "We got things to do that's got to be done tonight. Let's get it goin'."

One of the other men asked, "Are we packin' up and goin'? It's all right by me."

The old man said, "That's one thing we can do. Trouble is, that leaves Irish still in jail. Cappy too, but he can get hisself out, he's got lawyers."

The other man spit instead of swearing, but his attitude

254

was just as clear. "We ain't got no money for no lawyer for Irish! God damn it, we're here waitin' for work because we ain't got a dollar between us. What's this horse shit about a lawyer for Irish?"

"Be quiet," the old man ordered. "I didn't say nothin' about a lawyer. I said either we pack up and creep away like a bunch of whipped dogs, or we try to get Irish out of jail."

"How we gonna do that?" another man asked.

"I dunno," the old man said. "I'm goin' in there to that jail at ten o'clock tonight and I'm gonna see what I can do. Any of you boys wanta come with me?"

The idea was so audacious that they all stood up. "Just go in there and get him?" the man called Billy said.

"It won't be as easy as that," the old man said, "but in general that's about the idea, yeah."

"Christamighty!" Billy exclaimed. "Ten o'clock?" He smiled at the old man, the worry lines erasing as the smile spread across his face. "I'll go over to Dry Lake and tell Vern, see if he wants to count hisself in. He can pass the word."

"We'll do what we can," the old man said. "I ain't layin' down and playin' dead, that's all I know. Not yet."

The pickers had learned one lesson from the afternoon in the park: Leave vehicles where they can be used to get away. They drove to the west end of Greenfield Avenue and then circled to the right, behind the vacant lot they had used for their evacuation area earlier that day. Reversing into the lot from its southern side, their vehicles then faced south, so that they could leave by going around the old Atwater place rather than go straight west, just in case they were followed. The woman who lived across the avenue from Cass Dellon's old concrete columns, Mrs Cloda Poole, had been sitting on her unlighted porch as she usually did when the nights were hot. At about half past ten she noticed a row of taillights across at the far side of the lot. Thinking it was high school kids up to no good, she telephoned Chief Thomas at home.

255

Mrs Thomas took the message and said she would pass it on to her husband as soon as she talked to him. In a few minutes Mrs Poole phoned again, telling Mrs Thomas that the lights were gone and she must have made a silly mistake. Mrs Thomas believed her and made no effort to find her husband.

Mrs Poole was mistaken the second time; the lights hadn't gone, they had been turned off. The men were on foot now, going in small groups rather than in a solid force, walking in the dark along Park Street, out in the middle of the road. It was Dickie Hawser who discovered them. He lived four blocks down the avenue from the vacant lot. Being a big boy who did things pretty much as he wanted to, he decided to go for a bike ride in the warm, dark night. Riding no hands had got to be old stuff with him, so tonight he added no lights to the excitement. In this way his large, dark figure loomed up in unlighted Park Street and ploughed into a group of men. They cussed at him and he more than returned the favor by using some of his father's obscenities back at them. It was almost as much fun as it had been in the early afternoon when he and the other boys had harassed the pickers' trucks on the avenue. Later, in the park, it hadn't been much fun. It had frightened him, but he was a resilient boy and had recovered completely. He rode over to Richie Thomas's house now and told him about the men walking down the dark streets. Richie slipped out the back door while his mother was listening to the radio in the front room, and together they rode to Ledyard Job's house in the next block to get him to join them. The three then rode all the way out the avenue and then down Park Street from the very end, until they found the end of the straggle of men and followed them silently and unseen.

Through the residential areas there are no street lights on Park Street. A bond issue was supposed to cure the omission but lost out to more glamorous ways to spend municipal money. The walking men had got all the way to the canal before a car turned from a side street to go west on Park and picked up the figures in its headlights. It reversed back into

256

the side street and disappeared. The car was being driven by the morning desk clerk at the Mariposa Hotel. Like everyone else in Red Branch, he was jumpy after the day's events. When he saw what he took to be a crowd of men gathering in the region of the jail, he drove to the cigar store, only to find it locked and dark. Leaving his car in front of it, he ran the few yards to the Rex Hotel and burst into the bar.

"There's a mob on their way to the jail!" he shouted.

Old Gomez was the first to react. He picked up the phone and told Eunice to warn whoever was at the jail. He also asked for Lee Roy Stagg's number. Mrs Stagg told him that Lee Roy was on his way to spend the night in town and should be at the hotel – she couldn't bring herself to name the Rex as the hotel – any minute. The men who were there ran or drove to the Greenfield Avenue side of the park and, leaving their cars there, ran along the sidewalk to the jail. The first one who tried to go to the front of the jail to get in discovered that he was too late. The strikers were already gathering outside, and the big door had been slammed shut on them. As more of the farmers and their supporters arrived, they broke into two groups that flanked the jail in the darkness in order to prevent the strikers from surrounding it. The front of the jail they conceded to be lost to the mob already.

When Lee Roy arrived at the eerily empty Rex Hotel, Old Gomez told him what had happened.

"Was Calvin here?" Lee Roy asked.

Old Gomez answered that he hadn't seen Calvin all evening. He said he thought he was busy, and winked. Lee Roy understood the wink, and he knew where Louella lived, everybody did. He found the stairs and went up to her door on tiptoe. He put his ear to the door and listened for a minute or two. Hearing nothing that he might connect with sexual activity, he tapped on the door lightly, then more firmly. If as it seemed Calvin was otherwise unengaged, he wanted his lieutenant at his side, so when Calvin's voice called what sounded like an invitation, he went in. Lee Roy wasn't sure what a whore's apartment would look like, never having seen sin commercially accommodated and not being a moviegoing man. He was relieved and a little bit disappointed to find it adequate but plain, with no evidence of outlandish behavior beyond a scatter of Kleenex on the floor. A very surprised Calvin was lying on the bed alone, his arm in a sling. He hurried to put on his shirt as soon as he rose from the bed, as if it was unseemly to be half clothed before Lee Roy.

Lee Roy waited for no preliminaries. "Come on, Calvin," he said, "they've come back. They're down at the jail."

The streets were filling with cars now as the news spread. Moving slowly they filtered toward the streets around the jail. In the Courthouse square and the park the whispering crowds of Red Branch people grew, frightened, curious, ready to witness what they felt instinctively had to be the last act in what was so far a melodrama. The three boys were not going to be cheated of this moment. They left off following the men when they crossed the canal, turning right and then left, cutting through alleys to reach First Street. Unseen by strikers or anyone else who could bar their way, the boys rode their bikes along the sidewalk of First Street until they got to the far side of the Memorial Hall. They left their bikes there and crept around the back of the building to where the garbage cans were stored. Dickie Hawser stood on one of the cans and gave Richie Thomas a hand-up to his shoulders, from where he could get a leg over the window-sill of the janitor's toilet and worm into the building. No one saw them as Richie pulled back the bolt lock and let the others in the service door, then led the way upstairs to the main assembly room. With their chins resting on the sills of the big windows, they had a perfect view, their eyes on the same level as the balcony that thrust out over the door of the jail. By moving to the far side of the window-pane and pressing a cheek against it, they found they could look down below them and see at least half the crowd of strikers. They got the giggles and, clamping both hands over their mouths, rolled on the floor with suppressed laughter. Ledyard whispered to the others that it was the best adventure he'd ever had.

Jubilee Hubbard had been almost the only person in the crowd at Garfield Park to try to go towards the stage when the police fired the tear gas. He had seen his messiah fall. Against all his instincts, he had tried to go to Cappy's assistance. It was the suddenness of his conversion that made him act that way. Cappy had spoken directly, personally, to Jubilee. He knew and had pinpointed the way that Jubilee was treated; he knew the suffering, the defeats, the poverty of belief in a better world to come that justified the abject spiritual poverty of life in the world as it was. Jubilee had not so much lost his religion in the space of half an hour as gained another Lord. He didn't know much about communism, but he knew his Bible, and except for the hate part of it this man was preaching the word of Jesus as poor people understood it. For the first time in his life Jubilee believed that Jesus could after all have been a white man. Cappy had proved that a white man could see into a black man's soul and read the loneliness and hopelessness that were written there.

He had felt doubly sick after he got himself up off the ground and made his escape through the old zoo, vomiting until he was bringing up bile, and sick at heart that he had been unable to get to his feet when he saw two men carrying Cappy away. He should have gone with them. He should have stayed with Cappy wherever they took him. Not knowing where they had gone, he had staggered home and slept it off. Some time around nine he had walked back into town, to the park, and stood again where he had stood that afternoon. He went up to the band shell and searched it in the descending darkness for any relic of Cappy. Finding none, he sat on one of the concrete benches, straining to memorize the electrifying phrases that had stunned his soul with hope this afternoon, not hope that something would

259

happen to change things for the Jubilees of the world, just hope because someone understood what it felt like to Jubilee. Then he had wandered off in the dark to sit on the steps of the Memorial Hall, up by the door where he was out of the light, and watch the headlights of cars on the highway glance through the trees of the little park the other side of the First Presbyterian Church.

He was still there when men began collecting in front of the jail, and when cars came near but stopped short of the jail. He walked around the back of the Memorial Hall, past the garbage cans that he emptied twice a week, and joined the men at the rear of the group that was gathering. Listening to the hushed talk, he learned with horror that Cappy was in the jail, in a cell that was no better than a tomb, suffering because he knew what was right for the working people, the trodden-down people, for Jubilee. He kept his tongue, remembering that he was a black man mixing in a white man's argument, but inside he writhed with anger until tears streamed down his cheeks. Was Jesus going to have to go on being crucified over and over? Wasn't God someday going to say that's it, no more injustice, no more doing these things to my people?

The steel shutters had all been closed, the lights were out inside, the steel door was closed – the jail was a small gothic castle under siege by the enemy. Occasional movement behind an arrow slit or a battlement indicated there were defenders inside, impossible to say how many. Siege lights blazed out over the front of the building, huge floodlights that were fixed to what were supposed to look like brackets to hold torches. The strikers wore the costume of their trade and might just as well have been medieval peasants. They wore light colored cotton shirts, a few with the sleeves rolled up to the elbow, with cotton trousers, jeans or floppy overalls. A number of them wore straw or felt hats, and those who didn't had white flashes across the forehead where a hat usually protected them from the heat of the sun.

The crowd of strikers swelled to about a hundred, and the two groups of Red Branch men hidden in the dark beside the jail more than equalled that. The strikers, however, had the advantage. Their quiet, angry determination hung over them like a canopy. No smile or half-meant joke broke their intensity. If rage and bare hands, they seemed to promise, could breach the castle, theirs would do it.

At eleven o'clock the door opened just enough for Sheriff Atwater to squeeze himself sideways through the opening to face the strikers, who, blinded by the floodlights, had only the shadowy outline of their nemesis to hate.

The sheriff put on his best ex-preacher voice for the occasion, the cadences and pauses impressive in their patterns, adding nothing to the meaning of his words. His surprisingly strong voice carried over the still crowd: "In case you don't know me, men," he said, "I'm sheriff here, Sheriff Atwater. Now, I don't think many of you could know me, 'cause you don't seem to know how I work or how I think. I'm not known, you see, as a sheriff that likes to work with a lot of people at one time. I like someone to head up a bunch of people and talk for them. I don't try to discuss things like a reasonable man with a crowd. Crowds have a way of turning into mobs, and that's very unfortunate for everybody when that happens. Now inside here, in the jail, is the man who used to be the head of some of you. He did a very silly thing. He played with fire. And that's just about what you're doing right now. We have another man in here in our jail. He did several things, but the one I don't like especially is he incited a riot. That's just another way of playing with fire. Now I reckon you ought to do something for your own good right away. I think you ought to go home and take care of your families – better care of 'em, that is, than when you brought 'em to a riot this afternoon. In order to help things along, I think it might be a good thing if I was to explain the facts and the law to somebody who could be a new head for you folks, a new leader. I think you badly need a new leader. If you can find the right person for that job, just give me a knock on my door and I'll meet with him. I'll tell him what's going on with my two prisoners, and then I'll ask him to advise you boys to break it up and go home so we can all have a good night's sleep. Just knock on my door." He kicked the door with his heel. It opened a crack and then enough to let him slip inside.

The strikers had expected at some time that night to hear "Go away and be good boys" from the Sheriff. They hadn't thought that he would be deliberately insulting, that he would be picking another fight. At first surprised into silence by his badgering, as soon as he had vanished inside they shouted their outrage. The crowd of strikers rolled up the steps to the door, banged it with their futile fists, then rolled back down into the street, where they waved their fists and shouted some more in frustrated ferocity. A small knot of them pulled away to the side to hold a conference. The old man from Las Cruces was at the center of it, with Billy and his friend Vern backing him up. With the steps temporarily empty, a strange figure made his way to the top step. It was Jubilee Hubbard, holding up his hands to ask for the crowd's attention. When there was silence, as much out of curiosity as complicity, he lifted his head and closed his eyes, a shining black mask in the floodlights, and began to pray.

"Oh God, you got two good men in this here jail, and it ain't right. You got two men who do the work of the Lord in here, and it ain't right. You got two men in here in the hands of the ungodly, and it ain't right. These two men, Lord, they come here to fight for us, the poor and the trod-down; they done see the yoke we bears, the hearts that we is bustin', and they come here to help us. And this is what they gets. There ain't no justice in our lives, Lord, we's used to that. There oughta be justice somewheres for the Lord's servants, Lord, that's all we sayin'."

Moved to tears by his own private agony, sobbing for the wickedness that men return in exchange for God's love, Jubilee almost silenced the crowd of men. He continued to pray. Under cover of Jubilee's intervention, Billy and Vern

262

slipped out of the crowd and walked quickly into the dark of Park Street. On the corner of Canal and Park they found a big, solid looking Buick. Vern kicked a tire so that the whole car rocked. When no one shouted at them, they knew it was empty. He took a knife from his pocket and fumbled at it until he found the hole punch blade and opened it, then moved around to the rear of the car, feeling his way until he found the round bulge of the gas tank. Holding the knife in his two hands like a short dagger, he stabbed it up into the tank. When the thrust broke off the tip of the blade to leave a stub about an inch long, he said to Billy, "Got her now." The next stab drove a hole into the tank and the gasoline began to trickle out onto the road. "Gimme your shirt," he said, taking his own off. Billy pulled his off, and between them they soaked the shirts in the gasoline. When these were sopping wet, they ran back to the crowd, holding the shirts behind themselves as they came into the floodlight, and moved behind the crowd until they rejoined the group around the old man.

The strikers were restless, reluctant to break up Jubilee's prayers but increasingly irritated by his message of patient pleading. He himself couldn't have said what the message was. He was moved to pray for the deliverance of the two jailed leaders who knew the suffering in his deepest heart, that was all.

"This here jail," he was saying, "is that same fiery furnace, Lord. The truth is in that book, Lord, the truth that the Lord delivers his own in the time of trial. Like you done delivered them three from that furnace in the olden time, Lord, deliver our brothers into our hands now, out of this furnace of the devil into the hands of the people who loves them, we prays for that now."

Billy said, "Listen to him, he's givin' us away."

"He don't know nothin'," the old man said.

"What's he sayin'?" Vern asked.

"Talkin' about this place bein' a fiery furnace," Billy answered. "Somebody told him."

"Nobody told him nothin'," the old man said. "It's in the Bible. He's talkin' about the Bible."

"You ready?" Vern asked Billy. Billy nodded, fishing out a box of matches from his pocket. Vern turned to two men nearby and ordered them, "Get rid of that nigger. Get him out of there. He's in the way."

The two men did as they were told. They moved around to the right to get to the front of the crowd of strikers. In a rush they pushed to the top of the steps and seized Jubilee. One of them put a hammer lock on Jubilee's arm, twisting it behind his back and pushing up on his elbow until it was between his shoulder blades. The other man pulled Jubilee's legs from under him and bent one of them back hard at the knee. He shouted in pain as the men carried him through the crowd, crossing the road with him and dumping him in the flower bed beside the Memorial Hall. Jubilee scrambled somehow on hands and knees from there to the garbage cans, where he hid in among them, moaning with the pain in his arm and leg.

His shouts of pain produced a reaction from inside the jail. Looking from the big windows, the boys saw four men in tan uniform come out onto the balcony and stand well back in the shadows. The boys hunched themselves onto the window sills, unwilling to miss any of what was happening. From there they could see two shirtless men moving toward the front of the jail, screened from the sight of those inside by a tight line of the strikers. They moved forward carefully, underneath and out of sight of the men on the balcony who were concentrating their attention on the back of the mob where Jubilee still cried out in pain. In a few moments the line of men had moved up the steps to the door of the jail, where the line parted to allow the shirtless men through. They dropped their gasoline-soaked shirts at the bottom of the door and lit matches, which they threw onto the shirts. The blaze leapt up the steel door, then spread out as the soaked shirts released their fuel. There was a roar from the crowd when they saw the flames, then a greater roar as the lights inside the jail went on and voices shouted orders. Up in the windows of the Memorial Hall, Dickie and Ledyard watched the fire in horror. It was no longer fun for them. They inched their way backward off the sills, preparing to get away from the terrible things that were happening. Richie stayed where he was, mesmerized by the sight of the four men on the balcony moving forward out of the shadows into the full floodlight. He could see their tan uniforms, and the light glistened on the leather bills of their caps and the Sam Browne belts across their chests.

Richie sat up to look at the men. "They're the same ones as in the park!" he said. The mob recognized them also, and a roar of fury mixed with screams of savagery ripped the night. That was enough for Dickie and Ledyard, who squirmed the rest of the way off the window sills and ran for the back stairs. "They've got shotguns!" Richie shouted to them, as if the excitement would call the other boys back.

The riot police smelled the fire now. One of them went to the battlements and, crouching down out of sight, surveyed the excited mob below. The strikers, hoping the great steel door was the only way out, waited now for the people trapped inside to make a run for it, milling back and forth as the fire leaked under the door and took hold, shouting for those inside to come out and be torn to pieces. The Red Branch men, directed by Chief Thomas, moved around to the back of the jail where a hidden emergency door was opened from the inside. Forming two protective wings for those making their escape, they watched as Cappy Petrillo and Irish Duffy were hustled away across the Courthouse lawn and into basement cells where drunks were kept until they were sober enough to be sentenced. Through the piercing of the steel shutters of the jail the fire could be seen licking up the walls, and black smoke came out a window at the top of the staircase.

The four riot police, agitated now and pinned down on their balcony by fire and mob, came out into full view, shouting and waving their shotguns, indicating with their

265

hands that they were ordering the strikers to retreat. They raised their guns to their shoulders, but still the mob bayed at them like one immense, amorphous beast that roiled back and forth in front of the door. The nerve of one of the riot policemen snapped. Above the noise of the mob came the bang of a shotgun, clear and deadly, as he fired over the heads of the rioters into the side of the Memorial Hall. The others followed his lead in the instant, their guns slamming above the heads of the floodlighted mob, peppering the side of the hall and shattering one of the big windows opposite their balcony. They reloaded and fired, again and again, gradually lowering their sights, forcing the men to flatten themselves and then get up and run before falling to the ground again. When they stopped firing, at first warily, then in full retreat, the mob fled. At the same time a fire engine turned off the highway into Park Street, siren screeching and lights dazzling. It groaned to a halt as men jumped out unwinding white hoses while another ran to open a port on a fire hydrant. Two firemen ran a ladder up to the balcony, and the riot police scrambled down out of danger. From behind the jail the Red Branch men came half-crouched, cautiously forming a cordon around the building in case the strikers tried to attack the firemen. There were no strikers, however. Every one of them had gone.

The only member of the mob that was left, Jubilee Hubbard, picked himself out of the garbage cans where he had taken shelter and sneaked through the service door of the hall, left open by the two boys when they ran for their bikes. He limped as quickly as his twisted leg would let him up the stairs and into the big assembly room, moving along the wall to the windows, where he had to drop to his knees to avoid the chance of being seen in the fire rig's flashing lights. It was while he was crawling on his knees to where he thought he could lift his head in order to see what was happening outside that he came upon the body of Richie Thomas.

IX

2

Mort Thomas took his wife up to the mountains after the funeral. He rented a house in a part of the mountains that was at an altitude low enough to have live oaks and high enough to have good-sized white pines. The night wind sighed in the pines like something was praying. Lupins bloomed all around the place, their perfume hypnotic with its mixture of honey and spice, and bear clover stung the air. The blue of the sky made him feel he was seeing blue for the first time. When Mort had to go back down to the valley, his wife stayed on at the house, unable yet to bring herself to return. He went back up to the mountains after three weeks, to find the house closed and his wife gone. After searching the mountain towns, and getting the sheriff's men to ask fishermen if they had seen anything suspicious out on Elk Lake, he heard that a woman who sounded like his wife had moved into a cabin near a tuberculosis sanatorium about twenty-five miles along the mountains. There she had found a job as a cleaning woman and night orderly. He found her there, but she said she didn't know him. He talked to her the way you would to a child, asking her to come home with him. The woman said her name was Rosa Allen and she had never had a husband. She told him she hoped he found his wife and that when he found her she was all right, but she asked him never to bother her again.

--

X

1

If there is any value in the phrase "History teaches us that", it is in the conclusion which makes the phrase into the true sentence that reads, "History teaches us that History does not teach us". In a town like Red Branch, with little history and even less History, the teacher is riding a slow horse on a fast track in a fixed race; and gossip, like a spavined, blown nag, is all that remains of History, allowing it as a result to fulfill its function of informing the present and shaping the future without teaching a blind thing. It makes its contribution for better or for worse as nothing much more than a brand on an exposed flank, a provocation to Time the great obliterator.

And still, incident has to have meaning. Even Red Branch, especially Red Branch, requires that. If nothing more than the opportunity to chalk up yet one more experience to coincidence or to God, assuming there is a substantial difference, consideration has to be given either to the nature or the content of the experience itself.

The abstract and brief chronicle of the time is the movie camera. What the good people of Red Branch know of the events of those short, terrifying days is where they were standing or sitting or lying at the time this or that thing happened, what they felt or didn't feel, what they said, what they thought, what raced through their veins or minds. What was that music that they heard just then, what was it like in the light or the absence of it, in those particular surroundings? Their experiences, only hours after the events, are already the script of a movie, and the only history they long for is a shadow play in the dark, flickering on a rectangle of silver at the end of a crowded room. The great virtue of celluloid truth is that it can lie seductively, not the least of its lies being that the action is concluded when the house lights go up; the time that Red Branch receives some benefit from shared experience, which is after all the peculiar gift of history, is during the final reel, not in the silence that comes afterwards. To make sense of the second war of Red Branch, therefore, a final reel in search of something possibly identical to, or equally possibly very different from, truth.

The sour smell of the extinguished fire hung over the center of the town, drawing rather than repelling sightseers. Barrels of cleaning solvent brought from the railroad freight yards blocked off all of Park Street to any vehicles that weren't official. The sightseers' cars came along First Street to the barrels set up there, where they parked just short of the Memorial Hall. People who lived in the houses on First Street moved themselves and their coffee cups out onto their front porches, from where they patiently repeated their experiences, as well as what they had heard about things they hadn't witnessed, to a succession of friends, strangers and reporters. Workmen went in and out of the jail all day, removing damaged furniture and charred woodwork and wet files. Uniformed investigators appeared and disappeared, measured distances, made notes, took photographs, and again and again were drawn back inside the hall, where they could sometimes be seen beyond the blown-in window and its shredded wine velvet curtain. Throughout the day men and women walked, usually in twos, along the sidewalk between the jail and the Courthouse, looking at the hall's empty window, straining to see the white marks made by the shotgun pellets in the pale amber stucco, talking quietly, the women sometimes wiping their eyes on their handkerchiefs. At about eleven o'clock Reverend Ward took the announcement of the topic of Sunday's sermon out of the glass-fronted notice board in front of the Presbyterian Church and replaced it with a black-bordered piece of paper. On it were printed the details of the special service in memory of Richie Thomas, to be held on Sunday in place of the morning service. The business of government ceased altogether as dark-suited men arrived and commandeered offices in the Courthouse, where they argued out the division of responsibilities for the investigation in voices whose perfectly normal pitch and tone seemed to thunder against the hush around them.

Uptown, Red Branch was a painted backcloth. The business of doing business spun itself out in useless arabesques, conversation limping behind inconclusively. The day had the feel of one that would be unable to find a way to end itself. A memory of terror and the dull pull of sadness dogged every passing thought. The reporters who came expecting to write stories about a town racked by violence and people seized by terror saw what they thought was dignified reticence and filed column inches about a town pulling itself together in the face of one family's tragedy. To say they were pulling together was pure fantasy, but to imply they had shared a glimpse of hell was correct.

Louella spent the entire day inside her room with the window shades down and the thin curtains drawn closed. In spite of the sweltering heat, she shivered repeatedly and hugged herself to warm whatever part of her it was that remained chilled. No one from Nick's came to see why she hadn't gone to work, and except for a man who moaned and grunted in the dentist's chair as a bad tooth came out, she paid no heed to anything or anyone all day. Shortly after nine o'clock at night she heard footsteps on the stairs and someone knocked at her door. She sat tense and unforgiving. When the soft tapping continued and she was sure it could not be Calvin, she opened the door to find Old Gomez there with a plate of cold cuts and some fruit salad. She took it from him and thanked him. Finding neither of them had anything to say, he left without speaking at all. She slept the night sitting up in bed wrapped in blankets she pulled out of the cupboard, where she had found them folded in news-papers and rattling with mothballs. In the morning she dressed and packed her few things, waiting for the sound of the dentist arriving. When she heard him, she went down-stairs and knocked on the glass door with "Dr Doddridge Phelps" painted in gold leaf and edged in black.

"Is there any chance of getting the rest of the month's rent back?" she asked without preamble.

It was a measure of the state of the town that the request struck Dr Phelps as perfectly normal. "Of course," he said; "sure, if that's what you want."

"I want to leave this morning," she said.

"Where are you going?" he asked. When she didn't answer he rephrased his question, "What should I say when somebody asks where you are?"

"Tell him I've gone to the moon," she said. "Or better than that, tell him I've gone to Hollywood. Yeah, tell him that."

During the rioting, when the Red Branch men joined up to protect Irish and Cappy as they were spirited away from the jail, the man standing next to Calvin reached to link arms, pulling strongly on Calvin's left arm. The pain sent him staggering out of the line into the darkness, where he collapsed on the grass and passed out. In the excitement no one noticed. The sound of the gunshots made him come to, frightening him in the half-dream he inhabited in his pain, so that he crawled deeper into the darkness like an animal wounded by those guns, trying to get away. The sirens and flashing lights of the police cars and ambulance drove him across the Courthouse lawn and up the street, across the highway, up the avenue and right through the town center until he got to the hospital. There he sat down on the doorstep, its concrete still warm from the day's heat, and waited for someone to find him and take him in hand. It was while he was sitting there that the ambulance returned from the Memorial Hall with the boy's body in it, and in his daze, between the two worlds, the terrible facts came to him through the darkness in pieces and snatches as parts of his nightmare. He was only intermittently conscious for the night and day following, until in the afternoon he was anesthetized so that the doctor could set his shoulder in place. It was another day before he was able to leave for Mrs Rossi's, and another day after that before he found out that Louella had gone to no one knew where.

The following day he went to her room to see for himself that she had gone, then found Dr Phelps and asked for any message.

"She said for me to tell you she wasn't sure if she was going to the moon or to Hollywood, but either way she didn't bother to say goodbye," the dentist said. "She didn't look very good," he added.

Calvin avoided the Rex Hotel and returned to Mrs Rossi's. It was better this way, he thought. In the mental confusion brought on by his injury and the pain that was still with him, he mixed Richie Thomas and Louella in his mind, unable to shake off the conviction that in some way it was Louella who had been the victim. He brooded on his own all that afternoon and evening. When eventually he was able to separate her message from the finality of the boy's death and think more carefully about what she had said, he realized that Louella had not said goodbye for a reason. She was leaving it up to Calvin to decide if he was going to come looking for her, or if he preferred to accept that she was gone. He decided that he would have to think seriously about her challenge.

Lee Roy Stagg let a decent interval elapse before he drove south to get on with the business of farming. In the Imperial

Valley he found an agent who supplied gangs of field hands for the onion and lettuce crops. Between them they worked out a plan for a work gang to replace the Santa Fe workers, and another, less experienced but larger gang to do the picking. They would be Mexicans, and language would be a problem. The agent said he would send with them a small group of overseers who were bilingual. These men would also take care of the workmen's needs, except for housing, which the farmers would have to provide. The overseers would act as middlemen when it came to paying the laborers, also. The agent guaranteed there would be no trouble of any kind; the overseers would take care of that. When Lee Roy, vague memories of Simon Legree flitting through his mind, asked if he could be reassured that at least some of the money would find its way into the pockets of the workmen themselves, the agent drew in his breath, widened his eyes and made a round mouth, then sat back in injured innocence. Lee Roy found the pretense offensive.

"I mean," he said, "in their pockets when you take them back across the border, when you're done with them."

When the agent half rose in his chair in a show that was pitched somewhere between high dudgeon and low farce, Lee Roy added, "I know they're illegal, I'll allow that. But I won't be a party to out-and-out slavery. Understand? We've got our scruples."

The agent smiled and patted the back of Lee Roy's hand. The crops would be picked; the farmers were saved.

Calvin knew if he waited any longer he would not find Louella. A rough chivalry, unbidden, demanded that he look for her if only to let her finish their argument and then say goodbye. On the Sunday following the riots he walked down Greenfield Avenue, turning south before he came to the sanitorium. It took him to a section of humble houses, quiet, respectable, definitely in decline. Porch roofs twisted, window screens bulged out of their frames, pales lay fallen from fences like defenders killed in a lost cause. On the far

278

edge of the area a few last houses, like outposts, guarded against open fields where cows sometimes grazed, dividing the town from Mexican Town. He didn't know exactly why he knew, he supposed from hints and remarks, but somewhere here, he knew, Louella's mother lived, just as he knew Louella had gone home to hide.

Sixth Street reached deepest into the fields. He walked its full length. A graying house with a green roof, its drooping pepper trees shading the sidewalk, was the last one of all. It seemed so obviously from its appearance to be the only house in Red Branch that Louella could conceivably come from that Calvin found it hard to believe it could also be her mother's. The grass was long and weedy and dry, with a concrete walk splitting the yard into two equal parts to get to the front door. Overgrown circles of geraniums bloomed an equal distance on each side of the sidewalk, like patches of rouge on an old woman's crosshatched skin. The two round posts that held up the roof of the small porch were both still decorated with celluloid wreaths from last Christmas, the green and red paint now almost all flaked off. The screen door, designed to keep out insects, had been rendered totally ineffective by the removal of a large, ragged circle near its bottom, apparently so that a cat could come and go without having to wail for admittance. It was a house lived in by someone whose best efforts were undermined by whims and little worries.

Calvin stopped outside the house pretending to adjust his sling, and then lit a cigarette. He caught sight of a hand pulling back the window shade that kept the fierce sunshine out of the house. Elaborately casual now, he stooped to re-tie one of his shoes. This was a mistake; too late he remembered that he had spent a good fifteen minutes getting it tied one-handed in the first place. He tried to disguise his struggles with the lace, feeling his dignity slipping away from him. The initiative he wanted to preserve, assuming this was the right house, was gone. The shade moved again, and this time he saw Louella's face not pulled back quite enough to

279

be hidden. He tried to rise when he saw her, before she could pretend not to be there. As he did, his untied shoe turned under him and he lost his balance. He found himself on the sidewalk on his knees, propped up by his good hand, the shoe now almost lost in the uncut grass, while someone behind the curtain was laughing so hard at him that the window shade shook in her hand.

"God dammit, Louella," he shouted, "meet me halfway. Gimme a hand."

A brown-haired Louella opened the door with one hand while the other was clamped over her mouth to stifle the laughter.

"I never thought I'd laugh again," she said, helping him to his feet. She retrieved his shoe, put it down so he could wiggle his foot into it, and tied the lace. "You better come in," she said.

The cool, dark living room was small and held only two upholstered chairs, a divan that made into a bed, and a square table that was spread with playing cards. Calvin noticed that the game was solitaire.

"Where's your mother?" he asked.

"Gone down south," Louella said. "Sit down. She went to visit her sister in Kern. She wants to get me a job down there. I'd live with my aunt." She shrugged as if it was nothing to do with her.

Calvin sat without speaking, looking at the fingers of his left hand that stretched out from the white sling. He wanted to say something, if only to make a start and break the silence. No words would come, and Louella would not help him. When he looked up after two or three minutes of silence, he saw Louella's hands moving across her face, pulling the flesh down in an act of loathing while her tears rolled silently, unchecked.

"Oh, Jesus, Louella," he said, "how did we get into all this?"

2

Once the funeral was over, life in Red Branch began to return to normal, although it would be more accurate, if confusing, to say that life returned to a new normal. Nothing was changed, but everything was different in a way that was impossible to annotate and equally impossible to miss. Most people in Red Branch would regard that as normal for a town like theirs, a place in which time performs its tricks – sometimes its miracles – without reference to time. The paradox did not strike them as anything of the sort.

Reverend Ward was one of the few people who was unhappy about a return to normality. It was not right, he reasoned, that great events should take place without sound moral lessons being drawn from them. In this he had the support of Lee Roy Stagg. For the first time in their long association, however, he was at odds with Mr Halbkeller. The preacher in him led Reverend Ward to prepare to attack this point several times for his Sunday sermons, only to find each time that when he consulted with his deacon, as he always did, Mr Halbkeller cautioned him on the tone that was being taken, or the sensitivities that might still be lurking, or even on the actual content of his argument. The deacon felt that highlighting the ordeal was not wise, for reasons that were not clear to Reverend Ward. One day he

281

had come upon a sheet of writing paper left on his desk, with one sentence on it in Mr Halbkeller's handwriting. "Let sleeping dogs lie," it said, which as advice was unexceptionable, except that he was disturbed by the implicit warning. Where was there in the events of that summer a doglike, potentially destructive threat?

He recognized the bedfellowship between the police and the men of Red Branch. Since both the sheriff and the police chief had used mobs as a means to accomplish justice, and the police chief had paid such a terrible price for it, that part of any moralizing was unmentionable. Reverend Ward had been asked by one of the special investigators about this and had cautioned against looking too deeply at it. What would be accomplished? There was among the men of Red Branch, especially those on the lower edge of the town's movers and shakers, a need for swagger, a frontier attitude, a desire to be seen as gun-toting vigilantes held in check by their own standards of behavior, not anyone else's. If it had not been for Richie's death, their pride in their mob's defense of their town would have been insufferable. He liked to think in emblems about such things, and he saw the medal the mob might award itself as indelibly bloodstained. Let it stay that way, with no help from him or anyone else.

What other sleeping dog was there, then? What he longed to do was to use the tragic event of Richie's death as proof of the nature of God's providence, its inexplicable core where an understanding of right and wrong is beyond the grasp of man's analysis. Merely thinking about the possibilities made not one but a multitude of sermons rise within him, the sentences and sentiments combining in a flow of Calvinist rhetoric that he felt almost driven to deliver to his congregation. Almost, but not quite. He was prudent, and also patient. He trusted his worthy deacon and accepted his advice. Nevertheless, at some time he would insist on understanding the need for this caution.

*

If he had read more of the big city newspapers, Reverend Ward would have had at least an inkling of what was in Mr Halbkeller's mind. The riots and death had been greeted by headlines, not on the front page but very prominently placed, about the Red menace becoming reality. The whole sequence of events was seen as evidence of the Communist conspiracy which was directed against the very fabric of democracy. (The use of "capitalism" had been quietly dropped in favor of "democracy" as the target of the Communists.)

As with all things journalistic, however, principles tend to give way when a circulation war can be conjured up. The stories were pushing their way deeper and deeper into the unread entrails of the papers, until a report of one of the state investigators strayed off the track to wonder if "the Red Branch pattern" might be likely to be repeated. The editorial writers, quick to please their publishers, flailed away at the Red Menace once again. One particularly ringing, not to say pompous, editorial against Communist infiltration of the unions included warnings about the print-workers, who had it within their power to put a thumb on the jugular vein of the nation any time they or their political masters wished, thanks to their control over the commercial exercise of free speech. In simpler language, a strike by them would silence the newspapers. The printers' union didn't like this one little bit and approached a rival editor who owed the union a favor, who in turn decided the time was right for some investigative journalism. A boxed article on the editorial page announced the assignment of the chief labor correspondent to an independent investigation of the unrest and violence in Red Branch.

The first of several articles by him mused that even the papers crusading against the Red Tide had noticed that the reasons were unclear why the strike had been directed against Red Branch rather than any other area. Another article used the word flimsy to describe as provocation for a major industrial dispute one farmer's bungling of labor relations. It also said that the hunt was on for proof that the union wanted a victory in that place at that time for the purpose of destroying the local economy, rather than simply getting better pay and conditions for the migrant workers. A few days later the correspondent went so far as to suggest that the turning back of the Okie convoy four years before was the real reason for the strike, and that the Communist agitators in the union ranks were dupes of people with old scores to settle, instead of the other way around. Then he uncovered the involvement of the buyers, so that Western Union had to deny publicly that their operator, Al Peart, had revealed to Cappy Petrillo the contents of Karl Whichell's confidential telegram. The buyers had stood to profit from the strike, that much was clear, he said, and a big payoff of the union by the buyers was a rumor that needed to be put to rest. His series of articles ended darkly: He smelled conspiracy, and the only proof needed was a motive strong enough to weave the whole spider's web of conflicts around Red Branch, and someone to manipulate these conflicts to his own ends.

The key to the identification of the spider at the center of the web, when it came, was so unlikely that it was almost missed. It was a piece of evidence presented to the court in the unsuccessful attempt to jail Cappy Petrillo for stirring up trouble while knowing that it would lead to violence. Out of the Babel of legal tongues came reference to the instructions given by Cappy, on paper, to his planted agitator in the Dry Lake Camp. The judge who was hearing the case, Judge Kendrick from Placid City, demanded evidence, the memorandum, which was produced in court by Mr Cook. The migrant worker who had stolen the evidence was long gone, however, and verification of such conveniently damning evidence was gone with him. The judge persisted, until finally the man who received it from the vanished worker was found and brought to the witness stand. He was the same person who was the contact man for the Santa Fe workers, Albert Baines, the domesticated Okie who worked in a garage on the highway three blocks south of Nick's. A few evasive words from him would have preserved many secrets. However, he had a lot to lose if he didn't cooperate on the witness stand; and on the other hand, it was true that an ex-Okie testifying in the way that he did settled an old score or two, as some people were unkind enough to point out.

Whatever his motives, Albert sang like a canary in a mine shaft keeping disaster at bay with his song. Yes, he said, he was the man who had been given the memorandum, and he had taken it to Lee Roy Stagg's house the night before the strike and handed it to Mrs Stagg. Yes, he knew for a fact that Mr Stagg got the memorandum that same night and knew the strike was on. He had no idea why Mr Stagg kept the information secret, they weren't that kind of friends. He was beholden to Mr Stagg for rescuing him and his family back in thirty-five, thirty-six, and he did things for him, that was all. Yes, he had been in close touch with Mr Stagg at other times during all this strike business. For instance, Mr Stagg had also been told by him that the Santa Fe shanty town was evacuated in the afternoon and everyone was gone by the evening, hours before Irish Duffy burned it, so Mr Stagg must have known there would be no workers waiting at the Santa Fe station the following morning. Yes, he supposed this meant that Mr Stagg had known this would give the union people their opportunity to call the strike. No, he had no idea if Mr Stagg and Mr Petrillo had been in touch through Mr Stagg's mailbox in the Red Branch post office. He didn't think they had, somehow. It was news to him if they were, but it was possible. Yes, he agreed that it looked like Mr Stagg had set up Sam Tolin from the beginning. His testimony and cross-examination took all afternoon. At the end of it he sat like a wet doll, unable to get himself out of the witness chair. He asked permission to make a statement in the court: He was glad to be able to testify, because he had been living with the knowledge that Mr Stagg had, for what he had to believe were good reasons, maneuvered Mr Tolin and the other farmers and Red Branch into this strike, and then he had seen it go wrong and he was sorry for his own part in the events that led up to the death of the boy. He didn't have a bad conscience about it exactly; he was sorry, that was all. His son Billy had been a friend of Richie Thomas. Judge Kendrick thanked him and assured him it wasn't his fault.

"But why?" Reverend Ward asked himself this question as much as of the man who sat smugly before him, his deacon, Mr Halbkeller. The deacon opened his hands like an innocent man, examined his fingernail, and sat mute. Reverend Ward went to the door of his study and beckoned Mr Stagg to come in and join them. When he entered, Mr Halbkeller did not rise. Lee Roy took the empty chair, which was in front of the pastor's desk. Mr Halbkeller had placed himself on a plane with Reverend Ward, to that gentleman's right. The battle lines were clear to see.

Lee Roy decided, now that he had to think things out, that the central fact of his adult life had been that he could not explain himself to other men. He wasn't concerned about explaining his conduct to women. What men with families didn't realize was that he had God instead of children. You couldn't tell another man that; even thinking of telling it made him tonguetied. Even worse, he knew that it was not a case of his finding God when he didn't have children to distract him, it was instead God who had found him and sent him to do His service. How could he tell another man that? Well, he couldn't, and that was the long and the short of it. He had read enough about the old church to know that in another age he would have worn a secret hair shirt, something nagging and uncomfortable to remind him that he was not his own person. He couldn't do that without exposing himself to one of Mrs Stagg's smirks, to which he had never found a way of responding, so his badge of office as a servant of God had to be his secret alone. He had been impressed with Mr Halbkeller's fingernail, but he wanted a private token for himself like that hair shirt, not something you waved in other people's faces. One night he made a decision. He locked the bathroom door and then took the scissors out of the first aid kit and cut a nick out of himself. He had thought beforehand about doing it at a place that would ever afterwards make lovemaking painful, but that was too risky. He might have to show a doctor that. He wanted something that could if necessary be passed off as a bizarre but accidental injury. He settled for cutting his left nipple from underneath, almost detaching it. It bled a lot, which made him feel faint and pleased him. As it healed he picked at it nightly so that it now hung like a pale flap over the smeared crab claw scar underneath. It was a duty that he was glad he had done.

The essence of his service, like his secret mutilation, was to do what was needed wherever he found himself called upon. First it had been the Sunday School, which he put back on its feet. When God spoke through Mr Halbkeller, he knew it was time to move on to something else, whatever it was that was needed. It was at this time when he craved enlightenment that he first began to find special messages in what the minister said in his sermons. "The kingdom of God is within you," Reverend Ward said, "the person, the church, the town, all of physical reality. We mime the eternal in our experience of the earthly, we rehearse perfection as God commands us. We imitate the justice of God in our pursuit of His justice here on Earth." He memorized the words and repeated them until he understood completely, and he believed every word of this. Sometimes he thought he believed it stronger than the minister himself. When Tony Rivelli died and the farmers on the west side came looking for a new chairman, he saw his opportunity. Godfearing they may have been, but as practicing sons of God, farmers were definitely the prodigals. He agreed to be their leader, as long as they made him president and attached some salary to the honor. In this position he first became aware of God's work for him. When the Dust Bowl – a phenomenon of

287

God's making, let it never be forgotten – disgorged those rejected people west, it happened to be at the same time as the valley farmers began to see that their future lay in expanding into virgin soil out on the west side. He had seen clearly the dilemma being posed. To take in these people, to give them work and food and shelter, would ruin the farmers. A Red Branch able to serve the will of God would be destroyed. That could not by any stretch of the imagination be God's plan, he concluded. Here in his hands was that hard, cutting edge of God's sword of righteousness. He did not know what God meant to accomplish, and he hadn't the right to guess. He could react only in the way that he knew to be the correct one, and take the consequences. God's elect were not going to be overwhelmed by Pandemonium's castoffs. He had gone into battle and won that war.

Now this war. What was all this union business except more of the same? He had done his reading. He had that mailbox in town so he could get all the papers and books, ones that might make people wonder about him if the rural delivery postman started talking about the titles and where they came from. He had done all his homework, as they say. He knew all about the Communist plan, Satan's plan, and what it would mean for what he had come to regard as his personal responsibility to God. That was why he had recognized the signs before anyone else. The people he wrote to about it, those foundation people as far away as Delaware and Texas, they told him he was right. He had got their help with his plans. You didn't wait to be hit by Communists, you hit them first. First you hit them with knowledge. You got your people, the foundation people, to help you find out about the Reds you were up against. They had ways of knowing that he didn't ask about, and he was grateful, for instance, that he had known all about Irish Duffy before ever setting eyes on him. He wasn't ashamed that he smoked out Cappy Petrillo into the open, that he had trapped him into striking. He had known all about him ahead of time too. He might have been ashamed for taking advantage of

Sam the way he had, except that his sources had told him things about Sam and what he did in the place where he had farmed before that made him realize his friendship with Sam had been misplaced.

No, he felt no shame about what he had done, not even about Richie Thomas. He felt sorrow, genuine sorrow, and it hurt him to see Mrs Thomas at the funeral made so small and helpless by her loss. But he knew what others didn't know, and he wasn't going to tell Reverend Ward or a Grand Jury or anyone what he knew. What Albert Baines didn't tell the judge at that trial – he was scared for his life if he told it, but he needn't have been – was that first Chief Thomas, and then Sheriff Atwater afterwards, both knew that he, Lee Roy, was the manipulator, the person pulling the strings, and for their own purposes they let him go on and do it. They knew all about what had happened at Santa Fe, and they knew about Baines passing all the messages. He'd had his suspicions, and then he knew for sure when the sheriff warned him out at Sam's farm and then backed off and let him go ahead. Chief Thomas let him do it out of his liking for a good fight, out of the instinct of a lowdown cop who knows that violence can solve problems, but who has to restrain himself because he represents the law in the town's eyes. The sheriff let him do it because he was a politician instead of a peacemaker, because he could benefit from the strike, because his religion was half as deep as his ambition. He wanted the strike as much as Chief Thomas did, but he wanted to be sure that someone else caught the blame if it went wrong.

And now with Richie dead, neither of them could admit they had known, and they certainly couldn't admit to giving him a nudge and a helping hand from time to time. They had washed their hands in public, but they had lost their scapegoat. So be it. Amen, as Jubilee Hubbard would have said. Even evil, and this wasn't exactly evil, was the stuff out of which God would perfect his kingdom, if not on Earth then in Heaven to come. Amen. He was satisfied to be as

289

much of a sacrifice as there was going to be. He had done nothing against the law. He probably deserved the scandal which would gather around him, which he was sure the newspapers would provide, but not prison. An innocent had died, true, but not at his hand. He felt clean in the eyes of the Lord.

"But why, Mr Stagg, please tell me, why? Why did you do all this in secret?' Reverend Ward asked.

"I did the Lord's work," Lee Roy answered, closing his mouth firmly as he finished.

"Mr Stagg," Mr Halbkeller said, "you know what the newspapers will say. They will call you a religious fanatic, some kind of a misguided idealist or a zealot. They might even call you a fascist. You went too far."

"Another one might call me a hero, Mr Halbkeller," Lee Roy said. "It's all words. What's your newspaper going to call me? Have you made up your mind yet? Anyhow, none of it will make any difference."

Mr Halbkeller exhaled noisily, winded by the accuracy and casual force of the blow.

"What do you mean, any difference?" Reverend Ward asked.

"It won't change the facts," Lee Roy said. He sat very straight in his chair, physically dominating the other two, setting himself to say only what he willed to say, not what they wanted.

Mr Halbkeller sneered. "The facts?"

"The fact is that we won," Lee Roy said. "God and I won. I fought the Lord's war and won. That's what the newspapers don't like. They don't like it that you can't both take the Lord's side and sell newspapers." He allowed himself some satisfaction in seeing Mr Halbkeller wince again. He paused before adding, "I would have thought you both would like it, though."

His own argument having been used against him, Mr Halbkeller could find nothing further to say. He opened his jaw like a goldfish several times, then gave it up and turned away. Reverend Ward bowed his head in silent prayer. Lee Roy reached inside his shirt as if he was taking care of a minor itch and lifted the secret flap on his left nipple. The sensitive scar tissue sprang to life under the probing of his finger, reassuring him with pain as fresh and sharp as on the day he had maimed himself. He got up then, leaving them in that posture, walking away with the pride of a man who knows his own worth in God's eyes.

3

"Do you want to marry me or not?"

Calvin had asked the same question for six weeks, and he still got evasions. Louella once again turned over her cards without answering.

"Do you want to just sleep with me every once in a while, or do you want to be my wife?" he asked.

She looked up at him without answering, then went back to her cards.

"I'll tell you what," Calvin said. "Here's the way I see it. You don't want to talk to me about it? Okay. If you stick to that brown hair, I'll sleep with you when we feel like it. If you want to marry me, get yourself blonde again. I'll know what you have to say the next time I see you."

He meant it. He got up in exasperation and walked out of Louella's house without another look behind him.

She felt the wave of heat through the door and looked up in time to catch the full flash of the sun. After he closed the door, she sat in clouded darkness unable to continue her card game until her eyes adjusted themselves to the gloom. It was like that every time he left, she thought. She felt only half of herself when he was gone. He took something away with him. He didn't understand what had happened to her, why the death of that boy should have affected her life so much. He didn't know what she was like, how damaged she had been before and how much more damaged she was by Calvin's own part in the tragedy. He didn't really know her, any more than he knew himself. She knew that she was herself; what she was, Louella not Mary, was fixed, like marcelled hair. Calvin – that was different. Someday, when his father died, he would have the chance to be something different, something that he himself could understand. For now, and for as far as she could see ahead into the future, he didn't come together as a grown man. She loved him in bed, and he never threw her good times back at her – he was generous that way. What it came down to was that he could forgive her and maybe everyone else almost anything they had done, but he couldn't forgive either himself or his father because he didn't know what to forgive. And that was where the violence came from that frightened her and made her feel she ought to be ashamed of him. Was loving him the same as knowing him better than he knew himself? Was love really like being hit all over, or was it this knowing that they were only complete together?

All right, he was going to buy Lee Roy Stagg's farm and the house that went with it, now that Lee Roy was going away somewhere to be an evangelist. That meant they would be as poor as the next farmer and his wife. No more Whitmore money when he broke with his father and went to farming on his own. That was all right. She had never known what it was like to have money. It didn't matter much anyway if you were out on a farm where people didn't see the inside of your house very often. Thinking about the house, she admitted to herself how much she didn't like Mrs Stagg. There was something about that woman that was too much like making an effort to hate the world. Maybe she only hated her husband and didn't know it. Louella decided she would have one room painted red, all four walls, and every time she was gloomy at the thought she was living in Mrs Stagg's old house, she would go into that red room and know the old biddy would die at the sight of it.

She would finish her game of solitaire, which would take about fifteen minutes. It would be a little bit cooler then. Even walking slowly, she could be at the drugstore before six o'clock. They had the right kind of peroxide the last time she looked. Life was too damn complicated without Calvin.

Jubilee Hubbard packed all his things together in a shiny brown cardboard suitcase and tied it up with a piece of white clothesline. He took all his garbage man clothes out to the incinerator in the backyard and put a match to a gasoline-soaked newspaper at the bottom. Up went the coveralls that Saralene hated so much, the flannel shirts that in the winter he wore under them, the boots that were so soaked with ooze from the dump that the stink came back into the house even when he left them out on the back porch. He noticed a forgotten toy that one of the children had lost in the long grass and kicked it into full view. Looking at it, he realized it didn't hurt him to miss the children any more. He had got used to it, the way you get used to anything. He went into the house and locked the back door. He picked up his small bundle of clothes and his suitcase from his old easy chair and went out the front door. He locked it carefully and left the key in the lock. Somebody one of these days would get curious and look to see if he was dead. There was no sense in making them break a window to find out he was only gone, not dead.

He walked east from Mexican Town along tractor roads and through a vineyard until he struck the highway, then, enjoying the shade of the eucalyptus trees, south to the corner of the highway with Telegraph Road. Across from the road there was a large, granite rock beside the highway for no reason you could think of. The Greyhound bus stopped here and picked up passengers, if there was a seat and if the driver saw you in time. Jubilee counted again the money he had ready for his ticket and sat down on the rock. When he scrunched down, the shadow from the grapevines behind him gave a bit of relief from the sun's heat. Next stop, Placid City. He would find a room in a cheap boarding house west of the railroad tracks and hang around those Basque sheepherders until he got to know some of them. One day they'd let him follow them to the hills and herd sheep with them. Nobody would ever mistake him for a Basque, that was for sure, and he'd never heard of such a thing as a negro sheepherder. Still, that didn't matter. The sheep wouldn't know the difference, and the girls in the hotel didn't care. Out there on his own except for the sheep, he could practice his favorite gospel songs, and he could amen and hallelujah as loud as the good Lord would allow. No more garbage, no more shoeshining. And no more people, not for a while anyway. Maybe someday, but not for a while. Sheep and grass and sky, and when he came to town every once in a while, a good bath and a nice girl. It sounded like heaven to him.